PAYBACK

GEMMA ROGERS

D1355139

Boldwood

First published in Great Britain in 2020 by Boldwood Books Ltd.

1

A CIP catalogue record for this book is available from the British Library.

Paperback ISBN: 978-1-80048-139-8

Ebook ISBN: 978-1-83889-013-1

Kindle ISBN: 978-1-83889-012-4

Audio CD ISBN: 978-1-83889-009-4

Digital audio download ISBN: 978-1-83889-011-7

Large Print ISBN: 978-1-83889-661-4

Boldwood Books Ltd.

23 Bowerdean Street, London, SW6 3TN

www.boldwoodbooks.com

MIX
Paper from
responsible sources
FSC® C020471

For Dean
The best sidekick a girl could have

1

I didn't see the note when the post was delivered. I was later than usual and in a rush to open the agency. I'd thrown the collection of brightly coloured junk mail, leaflets and envelopes on to my desk to sort later.

Frank arrived as I took off my blazer, the office already impossibly hot, and I hugged him as I did every morning. Enjoying the woody aroma that transferred onto my shoulder. He smelt like home and I squeezed him tight, ignoring the pang in my chest as I was reminded our days together were numbered.

'Morning, poppet,' he said, wrapping his arm around me.

Frank joined the estate agency when my dad started the business in 1989. Around the time I was knee-high and playing with Barbies under the desks, hidden from the customers. Dad had a keen eye for business and when we moved to the small village of Copthorne in West Sussex from South London, there was one estate agency who held the lion's share of the local market. Seizing the opportunity, he built the business from scratch with our family name over the door and learnt the trade. Creating an independent agency to rival theirs and within a year Whites had been established as the premium place to market your home.

Dad was a charmer, but he never cut corners and it was his integrity that became the building blocks of the business, with customer service always his number one priority. Now, I took care of it, since Dad had signed ownership over to me when he retired last year. He and Mum moved out of the two-storey flat above the agency and I'd moved in, as expected. It was strange moving back to the home I'd grown up in, but the memories were ingrained into the plaster. There was comfort, eating dinner in the same kitchen I'd watched Mum bake my birthday cakes in. She and Dad had downsized to a two-bedroom bungalow. At the grand age of sixty-two, she'd already had a hip and knee replacement courtesy of the NHS and Dad wanted to be around more to look after her. They talked about going on a cruise and Mum wanted to buy a beach hut at Lancing for day trips.

I had big plans to expand the business and open another office in a neighbouring village, but even though he no longer technically owned Whites, Dad had never fully let go. It quickly became clear that he still considered himself chairman of the board and even though I'd worked in the family business for almost ten years, I had neither the knowledge nor experience to match his.

My ambitions were put on hold, until Dad took more of a step back or he decided I could be trusted to fully take the reins. So, whilst I owned Whites, Frank managed the day-to-day running of the office. He was in his late fifties and would be retiring soon, leaving a massive hole not only in my heart but also in the Whites empire; which was the reason I had two new starters arriving that morning.

Gary was an experienced estate agent who worked for a

competitor. A career-focused, thirty-year-old, unmarried man who had his sales patter locked down. He fancied himself as a bit of a Cillian Murphy look-a-like, never without his *Peaky Blinders* flat cap. I suspected it was because he was going prematurely bald, but I couldn't be sure. I'd had my eye on him for a while. I'd heard customers liked him, he was smooth and easy to warm to. He modelled sharp suits in bold colours and came across a bit flash, but his sales performance at Osbornes spoke for itself.

There were now three estate agents in the village all vying for a piece of the pie. The initial independent rival was long gone and had been replaced by an established chain. Osbornes followed around five years ago as the small village expanded. Whites managed to hold on to the top position due to our excellent local reputation. Something that Dad constantly reminded me I mustn't let slip.

I'd managed to entice Gary with the pull of an excellent starting salary and the prospect of taking over from Frank in a few months. Often, basic salaries were unimpressive in the property business; if you wanted to earn, you had to sell. However, I learnt that paying peanuts often bought monkeys and with a little extra incentive and a good working environment I was able to retain my staff easily.

My small team were loyal, they worked hard and in return were treated as extended family. There was a small Christmas and summer get-together every year, profit-related bonuses every quarter and the only stipulation was honesty and integrity. All sales were above board and there was no underhand dealing. My dad had run the estate agency the same way and I was carrying on the mantel.

The other addition to the team was Hope, a junior sales assistant. She'd previously worked in telesales fresh out of college and had no property experience. At twenty, she was a blank canvas, ready for training and wowed at interview. Confident and no-nonsense, she seemed much older than her years.

The bell jangled announcing Gary and Hope, who'd arrived together, just before nine. I greeted them with a welcoming smile and firm handshake.

'Welcome officially to Whites Estate Agents.'

'Thanks Sophie.' Hope slipped off her beige mac and hung it next to mine on the coat stand. She was immaculately presented in navy-blue tailored trousers and matching waistcoat over a crisp white shirt. Her almost black hair elegantly tied into a chignon.

I looked away, smoothing down my red shift dress. Hope looked effortless, her make-up was expertly applied, skin flawless with perfectly sculpted eyebrows and a slick of peach-coloured lip gloss. Looking fabulous in your twenties was much easier than in your thirties and she had youth on her side. Gary took off his trademark cap, hanging it beside Hope's coat and flattened down his thinning hair. Oversized garish cufflinks catching the light as he moved.

Frank shook Gary and Hope's hands in turn and showed them to their desks.

'I'll leave you in Frank's capable hands today, but I'll be around to sit with you both later and run through a few personnel details. Pension forms, formal identification, next of kin and that kind of thing.'

'No problem,' Gary replied, already digging his passport out of his satchel.

'Can I get either of you a tea or coffee?' I asked, and once I had their preferences, I headed to the kitchenette at the back. I was always the first one to make the tea in the morning, not believing a hierarchy in the office was conducive to a pleasant working environment. Everyone was treated the same, from the manager to the cleaner.

The bell clanged again, followed by voices, muffled in the kitchenette, but I knew it would be Beth, the office junior, and Lucy, another sales assistant. I chewed on my nail whilst I waited for the kettle to boil, I hoped Gary and Hope would fit in. It was imperative to have a team that gelled, one that would push the business forward.

'Here you go.' I put down the tray and handed out steaming hot mugs of caffeine to fuel the team. Everyone chimed their thanks and I took my cue, retreating to my office to check emails and get the latest property chain updates.

Waiting for Microsoft Office to jolt to life, I fingered through the pile of post. Pizza delivery, window cleaners, a signed contract allowing Whites to market Mr and Mrs Green's bungalow on Tindle Road and, lastly, a plain white envelope addressed to 'The Owner'. Likely a charity letter, asking for direct debit details to support a child in Botswana or sponsor a snow leopard. But what stood out was the handwritten scrawl. Normally those kinds of letters had printed labels, mass-produced with no personal details at all.

Interest piqued, I stuck my index finger into the tiny gap, tearing open the fold. Inside was a sheet of white paper, with a lone sentence in the middle of the page, written in the same hand as the envelope.

Who was your first?

My first what? First sale? First car? First boyfriend?

Without hesitation, I ripped the sheet in half and tossed it into the waste bin, dismissing the note as nothing more than the marketing ploy of a local business to generate intrigue. A second later my email came to life and I turned my attention to everything I needed to action that day.

Frank knocked on the door, even though it was open – one of his many quirks that he still did daily. I waved him in, ready to go through the schedule for the day

'We've got the bungalow on Tindle Road, can you block out some time to see if we can take photos today? Give that one to Gary, and Hope can work alongside him,' I said, holding out the contract for Frank to take.

'Brilliant. Gary is going through what we've got on the books, so he can get himself familiarised. I'm going to get Hope on the phone to everyone registered, see if they are still looking, introduce herself, that kind of thing.'

'Good idea, we can see if she's as good on the phone as her reference implied. Thanks Frank,'

'Oh, do you mind if I turn the air con up, it's stifling today.'

'Sure, go ahead.'

I made a few calls to solicitors, chasing documents which were delaying an exchange of contracts. I spoke to most of the homeowners to give them an update on how much interest they'd had in their property. Keeping in touch with the clients was a high priority. The general public assumed that with websites like Rightmove and PrimeLocation, our job was easy, but securing properties, marketing correctly and fixing breakdowns in the chain was what earnt us our 1.5% fee. Something the team worked hard for.

Later that day, after I'd spent time with both Hope and Gary, the bell clanged announcing the arrival of a lady in her late-sixties, looking hot and bothered in a blue cardigan. Frank and Gary were out at the newly acquired bungalow, Lucy was on the phone and Beth was wrestling with a jam in the printer. Hope got up from her desk to assist, striding towards the lady. My chest swelled, she was a natural and I considered myself a solid eye for spotting talent.

I glanced back to my screen, but the customer's agitated hand gestures caught my eye, although I was unable to hear what she was saying.

'Can I be of assistance?' I smiled politely, poking my head out of my office.

Hope's eyes blazed in my peripheral vision, a tight smile stretched across her face.

'We keep getting leaflets, every day now. We are well aware we've been on the market for a while, but can you please stop. Think of all the trees you're wasting!'

I guided the lady into my office, flashing a grateful smile at Hope, and invited her to take a seat. 'I'm sorry Mrs...?' I spied the gold band on her finger.

'Davidson. Mrs Davidson.'

'Mrs Davidson. I'm very sorry, but I'm unaware of any leaflet dropping we've been doing recently. Could you tell me what road?'

'Park Lane. I'm at 32 Park Lane and I'm on the market with Osbornes.' Mrs Davidson rubbed the side of her temple, sighing.

I let the address sink in, the flash of recognition catching me off guard. My stomach lurched.

'I'm sorry, do you have one of the leaflets?' I stammered, keeping my tone calm so as not to cause Mrs Davidson any further distress.

'No, Gerald has thrown them all away, but they keep coming. I told him I'd come in and see you today, get you to stop.'

'I do apologise, Mrs Davidson, I will speak to the sales manager, but I haven't authorised any leaflet dropping this month.'

The woman unzipped her jacket, her neck flushed. I was worried she was going to have a funny turn.

'Can I get you something to drink? Tea? Some water?'

Mrs Davidson waved me away.

'Let me assure you, Whites don't practise that kind of underhand behaviour with our competitors. I'm sure there's been some kind of mistake. If another is delivered, would you be so kind to keep hold of it, so I can investigate?' I passed Mrs Davidson a business card.

Her eyes darted around the office, her forehead crumpling into a mass of lines. 'But I'm sure they had the Whites logo on them?' she said, more to herself than to me.

'It's fine, Mrs Davidson, it's no problem. If it is anything to do with us, I'll get it rectified immediately. We're always happy to help.' I smiled. Did this lady have all her faculties?

'Okay, thank you, Sophie,' she said, lifting the business card to check my name.

I walked her to the door. Hope was on the phone and looked at me quizzically.

'Sell a lot of houses, do you?' Mrs Davidson asked on the way out.

I stepped onto the street with her as she surveyed the property particulars displayed in the window. Clear plastic cases, filled with houses for sale, hung with gold wires in a four by four pattern. Sixteen properties in the main window suspended beneath the swirly black logo my dad had created when he started the business.

'We don't do too bad,' I replied with a conspiratorial smile. I glanced up at the logo, wishing I could change the curly calligraphy to something more modern.

'Would you come and have a look at ours. Let us know why

we aren't getting much interest?' her voice was small, the stress of selling her home plain to see.

My chest ached and I leant closer. 'Of course. How about tomorrow? Perhaps you can show me one of those leaflets if you get another one through?'

2

After work, I took the team to the local pub, The Boar, to celebrate Gary and Hope's first day. The pub was nothing special, part grimy wood flooring with a carpet that used to be red many years ago, sticky tables and toilets that flushed if you were lucky. It was dingy, stopping short of being uninhabitable. But it was within walking distance and it served alcohol and hot food, if you were brave enough.

Gary regaled us with the antics his old firm would employ to ensure a sale was pushed through. Listening to it made me wince. His former employers were across the road and I eyed the pub's clientele to make sure none of his old colleagues were in earshot. Hope, sat in the corner, clutching her white wine, gazing absent-mindedly out of the window. She hadn't had more than a mouthful.

'How was your first day, Hope? Still want to come back tomorrow?' I asked. Was she still upset about me stepping in with Mrs Davidson?

'It was good. Feels like I've made the right decision.'

I eased back into my seat and drained my vodka and tonic.

That's what I wanted to hear. I must have read too much into Hope's expression earlier.

I didn't stay long, I bought another round but had to get something for dinner. My stomach was rumbling, but my fridge was as barren as my love life. When I left the pub, Frank was telling everyone how I used to leave him presents in his desk when I was little. Books wrapped in brown paper, a tin of buttons, any treasures I thought he might like. His eyes glinted recalling the memories. When I was ten and he was thirty-four I was determined I'd grow up to marry him, but I didn't share that with the team. I'd never told Frank either, he'd blush scarlet I was sure. Now he was a second father to me.

The local Co-Op was busy, lots of singletons carrying baskets filled with dinners for one. I'd read in a newspaper, supermarkets were one of the best places to meet someone, although no one looked attractive under those harsh fluorescent lights. I hadn't had much luck with the opposite sex. A few failed relationships, a string of married men I believed would be uncomplicated but turned out to be anything but. For the time being, I was concentrating on the continued success of Whites. It was the only thing I was good at, plus I had a massive responsibility to ensure we made a profit. Failure wasn't an option. If I was going to flunk at anything, it would be producing an heir to the property empire.

When I got home, I popped back into the office to turn off the lights, except for those above the property details in the window. Those lights were on a timer and didn't go off until ten in the evening, allowing passers-by to see what was for sale. I locked up and headed upstairs to my microwave lasagne and salad. I'd missed a call from my mother, so once I'd eaten and changed into my pyjamas, I dialled the landline.

'Sophie, I'm glad you called.'

'Hi Mum, everything okay?'

'I've had a call from Sue. It's bad news. Gareth died in a car accident almost two weeks ago.'

My blood ran cold and I squeezed the phone, knuckles turning white.

'How?' I asked, the hair on my arms bristling despite the temperature.

'Someone ran him off the road apparently, going around a bend. Sue and Jim are devastated. Losing both your children. It doesn't bear thinking about.' Mum blew her nose down the phone as I tried to take in the news.

I hadn't seen Gareth for years, but there was a time when he meant a great deal to me. The reasons we'd grown apart seemed so silly now, childish even. But that's just what we were, children.

There was a long pause where I could hear Mum snuffling on the other end but couldn't find the words.

'Are you all right, Mum? Is Dad?'

'Yes, we're okay, a bit of a shock that's all. I thought you'd want to know. You two used to be so close.'

'Was he married?' I blurted.

'No, he lived with a woman in St. Albans, but they weren't married. I just can't believe it. Poor Sue, burying both your sons. It's just not right. Your kids are supposed to outlive you.' I could hear the rustle of tissues down the line. Mum and Dad had always been closed to Gareth's parents. They lived a ten-minute walk away from the agency and I'd spent pretty much every Saturday night there as a kid.

'Do you want me to come over?' I asked, chewing the inside of my cheek, but they said they were going to have an early night. I felt bad for feeling relieved. I didn't want to get dressed and drive across town when I was ready for bed myself.

We said our goodbyes and I brushed my teeth, retiring to watch television in bed. I'd promised myself I'd have a tidy tomorrow; the flat was starting to look like a family of four were in residence instead of just me.

I tried to focus on a documentary about adoption, but my mind kept slipping to Gareth. Thirty-six was no age to die.

* * *

Next day, at 11 a.m. sharp, Hope rang the doorbell of 32 Park Lane. I hadn't seen the house for years and it seemed smaller than I remembered. But outside everything looked the same, white metal-framed windows, the mostly glazed front door with its seventies leaf pattern. Even the enormous hydrangea in the sickly pink shade remained in the front garden. Hope had been keen to come along, she wanted, 'to see the property through my eyes'. Learn why it wasn't selling. It would be good experience, although the reason was obvious to be honest: Osbornes had overpriced it.

Mrs Davidson took a while to come to the front door. I could hear muffled voices and her silhouette grew larger through the glass as she approached.

'Hello, please come in,' she said, smiling and moving aside to let us through.

I stepped into the hallway which led to the kitchen.

'Please go through,' she gestured as I hesitated, overwhelmed at the interior, frozen in time and just as I'd remembered.

I walked into the kitchen, unable to stop the memories bouncing around my head. I came to a stop by the larder, taking it all in. The cream cabinets, the checkerboard linoleum flooring, the archway, all untouched by twenty years. It seemed like it had been an eternity, but I could still hear my friends' voices as they were then.

'You okay?' Hope whispered, eyes narrowed.

I nodded, forcing myself back to the present.

'Did you manage to find one of those flyers?' I asked Mrs Davidson as she came in to join us.

'No, Gerald threw them all away and the bin men came early, before I had a chance to dig one out.'

'That's a shame,' Hope said, grimacing.

'Yes, well never mind. We haven't had one yet today, so perhaps that's the end of it. Right, would you like to have a look around. Feel free to have a wander and I'll make some tea.'

'That would be lovely, thank you,' I said, moving straight towards the stairs. Gripping the wooden banister, I inhaled the unique scent of the house. Every home had a different aura, a different aroma, ingrained into the walls and carpets. The occupants would never know it was there, they were blind to it but Park Lane smelt faintly of blossom with a hint of bleach.

I climbed, taking in the green striped wallpaper and beige carpet until I reached the top of the stairs. Every door was open, but I headed instinctively to the master bedroom. It seemed so much smaller, but I was grown now.

I moved between the rooms, Hope hovering a few steps behind, roughly calculating the size and condition of each. Pushing the memories to the back of my mind, I tried to view this house as just another potential listing.

'Well?' Hope said, her voice low so as not to be heard downstairs.

I turned to her on the landing.

'I haven't seen downstairs yet, but basically it's overpriced. It's in need of modernisation, new windows, new bathroom and a new kitchen. The house hasn't changed for twenty years and it's putting prospective buyers off,' I said, gesturing for Hope to go down the stairs. I followed behind and we looked around the ground floor.

Gerald, Mrs Davidson's husband, was in the den, a smaller version of their lounge, watching rugby. He gave an odd salute as I glanced inside. The room felt ominous, not helped by the wood panelling. I couldn't wait to get out, practically thrusting Hope out of the way.

'It's oppressive in here,' I whispered, but Hope didn't answer. The archway remained and so did the ghosts.

We sat down for tea at the dining table, drinking from a teacup and saucer. Pink wafer biscuits had been placed fan-like around the edges of a floral painted plate.

I explained to Mrs Davidson the property had been marketed incorrectly.

'If I may speak plainly, Osbornes are marketing your property as a family home, which it is, of course it is. But the price they are asking for and the modernisation required is what I imagine will be putting families off. You need double glazing, a new bathroom and, although it's well decorated throughout, the amount of money required to bring it to the standard of other properties currently available means any buyer would be spending over the odds.' I pulled some particulars from my bag of similar properties and Mrs Davidson leafed through them.

'Well thank you, Miss White, for being frank,' Mrs Davidson said after a pause through pursed lips.

I knew I wasn't going to be delivering good news, but there was little point in sugarcoating. She didn't strike me as the sort of person who liked having her time wasted. 'I'm sorry, I understand it's not what you want to hear, but that's my honest opinion. I think if you ask Osbornes to lower the price to include the next bracket too, that would increase interest.'

I finished my tea to be polite, even though it was still a touch too hot and burnt my tongue.

After thanking Mrs Davidson for her time and the tea, Hope

and I left, walking around the side of the house to see the back gate I'd used all those years ago.

'Well, that seemed like a waste of time,' Hope said, her hands on her hips, eyebrows raised. Easy to see she was a rookie now.

'Perhaps, but honesty is the way forward. When Mrs Davidson finally loses all confidence in Osbornes, she will call us, and we will take her house on with open arms. This afternoon, I'll get you to make a few calls, there's some people I know who look for refurb projects, quick turnarounds.' I lingered at the gate, casting my eye over the garden before moving on.

'Have you been inside there before?'

My core tensed at the question. Some memories, although partially good, were best left undisturbed.

'No, first time,' I lied.

3

It turned out to be easy in the end. I'd spent all night worrying how I was going to do it. Not to mention totally freaking out about the whole plan. I'd convinced myself I was ready, but as the minutes ticked closer, I wasn't sure. It took forever to fall asleep and when I woke up, Mum was in the lounge, glued to the television, her arms wrapped around herself. I could tell something was wrong. It was Sunday, yet there was no blissful smell of bacon frying and no rustling of tabloids from Dad's chair either. Instead, I found Dad with his arm protectively around Mum as she dabbed away tears with his hankie. Lady Diana had died in a car crash in Paris and the country was in mourning, the BBC News presenter reported gravely.

I was never going to get a better opportunity and it had to be done today. They were so absorbed by the television, I was easily able to take the office keys and slip downstairs unnoticed. I was in and out in two minutes, knowing exactly where I'd find them. Dad had a wooden box locked in his desk. You couldn't be too careful, he'd told me as I watched him hide the box behind a fake panel in his drawer, on Friday after closing. The box housed the keys of all the properties for sale. I found the one I was looking for easily. The address written on the brown tag in my Dad's scrawl. I swallowed down the guilt which threatened to spill and slipped them into my dressing gown pocket underneath a mound of tissues.

Dad didn't open the estate agents on a Sunday, so I knew I'd be able to put it back before he'd notice it was missing. It didn't make me feel any better though. I'd done some things before, pranks mainly, which I'd got into trouble for. Occasionally, I'd been grounded for backchatting or failing to tidy my room. But nothing like this. This was a different league altogether. It couldn't have been more perfect, the planets had aligned, all of us had agreed and everything else had fallen into place. I just had to hold my nerve.

I crept back upstairs, my legs like jelly. I had done it. I'd managed to steal the key and my parents hadn't moved from the sofa. A loud gurgle came from my stomach. I'd have to get my own breakfast this morning.

'Sophie, Diana has died. It's awful. Those poor boys, losing their Mum at such an age. They're so young,' Mum wailed from the lounge as I passed by.

I didn't go in, I needed to hide the key, plus I didn't want to see Mum crying or Dad consoling her. It was terrible, the devastation of the general public leaked out of the television. She was beautiful, and the princes would grow up without a Mum now. But I couldn't understand why *my* Mum was getting so upset? It wasn't like she knew her, was it?

I forced a bowl of Honey Nut Loops down, ignoring the palpitations which fluttered in my chest as I went over the plan for tonight.

We were all meeting at seven, by the postbox towards the end of my road. Then we'd make our way to the house, go through the back garden and in via the kitchen door. That way we'd be hidden from the main road and no one would report a group of kids going into an empty house. Everyone was bringing a sleeping bag and a torch. Elliot had suggested bringing candles, but there was no way. What if someone burnt the carpet? They were all under strict instructions not to smoke or drink anything in the house; I didn't want to leave any evidence we'd been there.

The detached house was devoid of furniture, a shell waiting to be sold, but it was a perfect location for tonight. The owners had emigrated to Spain, so there was no chance we'd be caught by them. Sometimes, if Dad knew the owners wouldn't be there, he'd take me along when he was getting a house on the market. I'd help measure and he'd take the photos, all the time telling me the business would be mine one day. I'd smile and nod, but it wasn't what I wanted to be when I grew up. I wanted to be a journalist like that Kate Sanderson on *Newsround*. At the forefront of the action, reporting from exotic locations. I wanted to travel the world, but first I had to pass my Geography GCSE.

We were going into year eleven in a couple of days, preparing for our GCSEs next summer and the life we wanted beyond secondary school. Robyn, Becca and I had been friends since the first year. We were the middle-of-the-road kids, not nerds or outcasts but not cool enough to be the popular ones either. We left that to the blonde bitches. It was our name for them, although Robyn always took offence; her hair was the perfect shade of gold and the rest of us envied her for it, although of course we didn't tell her. Hayley joined in year nine, her father was an officer or something in the army, so she was always moving around, never settling anywhere. As an only child, she was scarred by years of conveyor-belt friendships that rarely lasted. Woodfield was the first non-army school she'd been to, as her mum didn't want to live in the 'garrison' any more. I had no idea what she meant. Robyn lived around the corner from her and one morning they struck up a conversation as they walked to school and from that day, she was part of the middle-of-the-road gang.

The plan had all started with the blonde bitches, a group of three girls I likened to the witches in *Macbeth*. They were who I pictured when Mrs Purse read Shakespeare's words aloud, hunched over a cauldron, their faces as ugly as their insides. Of course, they weren't unattractive, quite the opposite. They were sickeningly pretty and all of them had boyfriends in the year above. They thought they were, in Becca's words, 'the dog's testicles'. They teased us mercilessly, snide comments before being shoved out of the way in the corridors. The word 'virgin' had started to be thrown around as an insult. It stuck in our throats. It was obvious they'd all copped off with their older boyfriends. You could tell by the way they carried themselves, strolling around with an air of superiority that they'd moved to the next level. Engaging in adult activities: drinking, smoking weed and having sex, whilst the rest of us watched on wishing we could upgrade our boring lives. Worried we were being left behind.

When school broke for summer, it hung over us and we didn't want to leave secondary school with zero sexual experience, which was what we all had. There'd been some snogging, mainly at our classmate Jimmy's birthday roller disco party. We all thought it would be lame, but it ended up being brilliant, with lots of dark corners and distracting flashing lights. The kissing followed on from all the hand-holding we were doing with the boys, who were trying to keep us upright as we skated in circles to 'Free' by Ultra Nate. But that was the sum of our experience.

Us girls had chatted about getting the whole thing over and done with. We had no boyfriends; no boys we even fancied that much. Except for Hayley – it was obvious she had a massive crush on Gareth, a friend of the family who was in our year. I'd known him since we were in nappies apparently. Hayley wouldn't admit it, but her scarlet cheeks whenever his name was mentioned told us all we needed to know.

Because my parents were friends with Gareth's parents, I often got dragged along if they were invited over for dinner on a Saturday night. We'd sit in his room and play Nintendo; disappearing upstairs as soon as we'd finished our meal. Desperate to get away from the 'olds'. Thankfully, there was no awkwardness between us. I thought of him more like a brother than boyfriend material and that suited me fine. I was an only child, so the idea of a brother was something I relished. Gareth had a brother, Craig, who was two years old than us. I rarely saw him; Gareth said he only came home to sleep and eat.

One evening, early in the school holidays, we were hiding out, playing Mario Kart, listening to Gareth's Mum get louder and louder the more wine she drank.

'She's so embarrassing,' he said, gritting his teeth.

I put my controller down, Bowser's kart sped off into a ditch with a loud crash.

'She'll get worse until he takes her to bed, then I'll have to listen to them do it through the wall. It's gross,' Gareth admitted, giggling. I noticed the tips of his ears turning pink.

'Have you ever, you know?' I asked, my face flushing red.

Gareth shook his head and looked at a speck on the carpet, unwilling to meet my eye.

'What about your mates, Elliot, James and Mark. Have they?' I pried.

'I dunno. I don't think so.'

We were both quiet for a while. Gareth picked up my controller and handed it back to me, signalling to carry on with the game.

'What if, your friends and my friends, all, you know, did it?'

Gareth's head spun around like I'd slapped him. 'Together?'

'No not together, you moron. Not like an orgy. I meant, if we all paired up. Get it over and done with. Do you think they would be able to keep something like that quiet? Because it would have to be a secret.' I spoke slowly, concise. Not quite believing what I was suggesting. What I was proposing sounded far too grown-up to be coming out of my fifteen-year-old mouth. Gareth's mouth was still hanging open, until he realised I was waiting for an answer and promptly closed it. His voice when he spoke was measured but I could tell from the blotch of red skin on his neck that he was excited.

'I guess so. I mean, I'm sure they would. Do you want me to speak to them?'

'Yeah, okay. Ask them. Anyone blabs though and it's off,' I said, my voice unwavering but my stomach somersaulting with excitement or nerves, I wasn't sure which.

'All right, shitbag.' A white hacky sack with red stitching bounced off Gareth's head and into my lap. A sneering Craig was stood doubled over in the doorway.

'Piss off,' Gareth hissed, his face turning crimson now.

How long had Craig been standing there? Had he heard?

Craig nodded a greeting in my direction and I nodded back. He was dark like his brother, cropped hair and good-looking. Well-built and already filling out beneath his tight t-shirts, but he had a meanness to his eyes, magnified by his pointed features. He disappeared down the hallway and Gareth got up to close the door.

'He's just got his first car, so he thinks he's the big I am.'

'You'll be like that one day.' I laughed, rolling the hacky sack around in my hands. Craig couldn't have heard; he wouldn't have resisted an opportunity to torment Gareth if he had.

'How would we pick who's with who?' Gareth asked, returning to the conversation.

I considered for a second, chewing the inside of my cheek. 'I don't know. Names out of a hat maybe? It has to be fair; you can't choose.'

Gareth's face sagged and he turned back to the game. Who did he want to pick?

Suddenly there was an awkwardness where it had never been before. We'd been playing in his room since we were tiny, but for the first time the atmosphere was charged. I pretended I needed the toilet to get out of there.

Had I made a terrible mistake, coming up with the idea? Would the whole thing be around school before we even started the new term? The idea of the blonde bitches getting hold of it made me hyperventilate. If this was going to work, we couldn't tell anyone outside of the group.

The next stage was convincing my friends to do it. We'd spent a lot of time talking about it. But talking about doing it and actually doing it were two different things.

4

As we left 32 Park Lane, I tried to shake off the feeling of unease Gareth's death had brought with it. A blanket of foreboding attached itself to my shoulders and I carried it with me, hunched over from the weight. The news seemed to thrust old memories, long forgotten, to the forefront of my mind. We could have walked a different path if I'd changed my mind back then.

When Hope and I returned to the office, I told the team I had to make some calls and retreated behind the comfort of my desk. Closing the door, a sign to be left alone, safe in my sanctuary to gather myself. I typed Gareth Dixon into Google to see what popped up. There were a few hits for a consultant, LinkedIn and Facebook profiles, but there was one from the local paper reporting the accident. The article was brief and gave very little details other than Gareth had died in a car accident and they were appealing for witnesses to come forward.

My shoulders sagged as I bent over the desk, finding the website for Interflora and ordering some flowers to be sent to Sue and Jim. They were like a second set of parents to me as a child, their home as familiar as my own.

My mobile rang, vibrating loudly and skittering across the table. I jumped at the interruption. The number was withheld, but that wasn't unusual. I slid my finger across the screen to answer.

'Hello, Sophie White speaking.'

At first, I didn't hear anything. I strained my ears, just about to end the call, but then I heard a clicking sound and a man's voice spoke.

'Sophie, she was the one. I was crazy about her back then.' There was a cough and the line went dead.

'Hello? Hello?' I dropped the phone and it bounced on the floor.

That voice, weirdly familiar. Who was it? It had to be a joke, not that it made any sense.

I tugged my blazer around me. Was the air con turned up too high, or was it the hint of something that ran through my body, turning my veins frigid? I had to get out, go for a walk and clear my head.

I told Frank I was popping out and took off down the road, striding at a pace to stamp out the thoughts that spiralled. I wandered around the village, on a tour of all my old haunts. Places I hadn't visited for years because I no longer had any reason to. The postbox at the end of the road where we used to meet, the park and then Robyn's house. Afterwards I made my way to Becca's and then to Gareth's, whose parents were the only ones still living in the same place. I almost knocked, but the sight of their closed curtains changed my mind. They were grieving, shut away from the world, and I didn't want to disturb them.

I carried on walking, unable to remember the exact house Hayley had lived in, so many had been painted or had extensions built that it was hard to distinguish which one was hers. Gradually, the sun began to fade and it was time to head back. My head filled with happier times.

Frank was the last one left in the office, and I caught him as he was locking up.

'You all right, poppet?' he asked, eyes narrowed.

'Yeah, one of those days. An old school friend died at the weekend; Mum rang me yesterday. It's weird how it brings back old memories I'd forgotten.'

'Bad ones?' he asked.

'No, not all bad.'

I squeezed his shoulder and sent him home. His wife Diane would be waiting with something warm in the oven.

My mobile rang again, and I fumbled in my pocket to get it, my stomach sinking. I made sure I was inside the office with the door locked and lights off before I answered.

'Hello?'

'Sophie?' A lady's voice this time. Not another prank call.

'Speaking, how can I help?'

'It's Mrs Davidson, Judith. I've taken the house off the market with Osbornes. I tried to speak to them about lowering the price and the salesman told me I didn't know what I was talking about.'

I listened intently. I knew if she gave them enough rope, they'd hang themselves.

'So, I'd like you to take it on. Shall we agree a price of £375,000. How does that sound?'

'Yes. It's more in line with what I was thinking, Mrs Davidson. That way it catches everyone looking up to £400,000. I believe offers in excess of that, what Osbornes were asking, is not realistic in today's market.'

'Perfect, I'll pop in tomorrow to make it official. Shall we say 10 a.m.?'

'Of course, I'll have the paperwork ready for signing,' I agreed.

Mrs Davidson ended the call and I chuckled; she was a force to be reckoned with.

* * *

The week flew by and on Friday morning Gary had arranged five viewings for 32 Park Lane, three of those being property developers looking for a fast turnaround. The only issue with that was, even though they had no chain and were cash buyers, they often wanted the property at a knock-down price. Having a bigger profit at the end of it was what enticed them to buy after all. Mrs Davidson was happy with the progress and a cream 'For Sale' board with Whites' logo took pride of place at the front of her garden. I'd sent Gary and Hope to take the photos and measurements. I had no intention of going back to that house anytime soon.

'Jesus fucking Christ,' Hope crashed through the entrance to the office, hopping from one foot to the other. A take-away coffee cup gripped in one hand.

'Hope!' I hissed, my nostrils flaring at her outburst. Thank goodness it was a little too early for customers.

'Sorry,' she lowered her voice.

I tried to conceal the laugh that was forming in my throat. She looked like a princess who had trodden in faeces.

'What is it?'

'A rat, that's what. A bloody rat. On the doorstep! I just stepped in it! Disgusting.' Hope kicked off her high heels and stomped barefoot to the kitchen.

I shook my head. Rat? What rat? I'd come in the back way from upstairs so hadn't been out front yet. It wasn't until I opened the door to the street, I saw the carcass of a dead rat, mouth hanging open and pointy little teeth on show. It was laid across the concrete below the step up into the agency, bloody and flattened like it had been run over, a gash exposing its entrails. I took a step back, my hand over my mouth, bile rising fast.

'It's okay, I'll deal with it,' said Frank in a calm voice as he came in, stepping past me over the threshold, managing to avoid what Hope had not.

'What the fuck?' I hissed, leaning back on Frank's desk. There was no way that rat had just decided to croak at my door. It had been killed and placed there for my benefit. Who would do such a disgusting thing?

Osbornes, it had to be Osbornes. Revenge for stealing Gary and taking on Park Lane. I was too old for childish bullshit. They wouldn't have dared pull a stunt like that with my father in charge.

Grabbing my blazer from the peg, I thrust my arms in, white-hot flashes blurring my vision.

'Where are you going? Sophie don't do anything rash,' Frank called, clutching a bin bag, as he emerged from the kitchen.

I didn't answer him, leaping over the rodent corpse and storming up the street.

A minute later, I was banging on the door of the estate agents, who were yet to open. When Colin the branch manager answered, I pushed past him. He looked half asleep, clutching a mug of steaming hot coffee. I was tempted to tip it over him.

'Sophie, always a pleasure. Please come in and good morning to you too.' The sarcasm dripping in his voice.

'What the fuck, Colin? Aren't we past this kind of juvenile behaviour? Because, trust me, you don't want to go to war with me. I'm one crazy bitch,' I spat. I must have looked mental. Wild-eyed and ready to blow. The vein in my forehead throbbed.

'I've got no idea what you're on about. Did you forget to take your meds this morning or what?' Smarmy little shit.

I scowled, balling my hands into fists to stop myself lashing out, but I hadn't failed to notice the genuine confusion on his face. 'The rat. Are you telling me that wasn't you?'

'No. I have no idea what you're talking about,' he replied, scratching his receding hairline. Although Colin had previously employed underhand tactics on occasion, he'd never stooped so low before and I didn't think he was lying.

Without another word, I turned and marched out of the office, walking around the block until the rage began to disperse. It if wasn't Osbornes trying to engage in some kind of ridiculous turf war, who was it? Was it someone trying to mess with me? First the weird phone call, now a dead rat at my door. Had someone got a vendetta against me or Whites?

I racked my brain, going around in circles. Who had I upset? No one came to mind. There was a reason why I ran the business the way I did. To avoid all that kind of shit. Had I insulted someone unintentionally? Was someone trying to scare me? I was too angry to feel scared, but the rat hadn't just decided to die on my doorstep. Someone had delivered me roadkill. Who would do such a thing?

I was mystified and still none the wiser when I returned to the office to find Frank had removed it and rinsed away the evidence from the pavement.

I called a quick team meeting to allay any fears that we were being targeted.

'And I apologise for all the swearing. Thank you so much, Frank, for taking care of the rat. How are your shoes, Hope?'

She wrinkled her nose and eyed her stiletto. 'I don't think there are any more rat guts on them.' Which got a laugh from the rest of the team.

'Well, we carry on, business as usual. If someone has an issue with Whites, the best way forward is to push on, sell more and not engage.'

Everyone went back to work, and Frank took me aside in the kitchen as I made tea.

'Was it Osbornes?' he whispered.

'No,' I said, sure it wasn't. Colin's bewildered expression told me he had no idea what I was talking about.

'Is there anything I should know, Sophie?' Frank's brow furrowed.

'No, Frank, and please don't mention it to Dad.'

'Then who was it?'

I knew he was concerned. There had never been anything like this when my father was in charge.

'I don't know, but I'm going to find out.'

5

On Saturday morning I called a security company to install a discreet camera at the front of the agency. Something that would not be obvious to the general public; a small white dome on the edge of the fascia board, connected to my wi-fi so I could view the exterior through an app on my phone wherever I was. No one was going to be able to pull a stunt like that again and not be recorded. I hadn't reported the dead rat to the police; Frank had cleared it quickly and I hadn't thought to take any photos. I was more focused on ensuring it was moved before any customers arrived.

Saturdays were busy, we opened until one o'clock but functioned on a skeleton staff, taking turns who worked from one week to the next. I had Lucy and Hope with me in the office to field customer enquiries and the morning was busy with people coming in off the street who wanted to register. We handed out property particulars like sweets and I had to get Hope to print some more and restock. I received a cheeky offer from a property developer who'd been to see 32 Park Lane. It was twenty thousand under the asking price, so I was reluctant to give Mrs Davidson the news.

Luckily, Hope booked a second viewing. A young family who were keen to visit that day. They weren't put off having to modernise, as they needed a bigger house, but were struggling to find anything within their budget. Hope asked if she could handle the appointment and I was happy for her to go. I was confident Hope could manage it and I was only on the end of the phone if she needed me. Second viewings were often a formality, a time for measuring and deciding what furniture would go where. The decision to buy was made the first time a family entered the house.

'Can you let Mrs Davidson know that she's had an offer, tell her how much it is, but tell her not to rush into agreeing anything. We're aware it's a low offer and hopefully we'll be lucky with this second viewing. We could have another offer for her on Monday.' I didn't want Mrs Davidson to accept anything less than what the house was worth, and I knew the developer was chancing his arm.

At midday, there was a lull in traffic and I retreated to my desk to eat a sandwich I'd grabbed from the supermarket. I hadn't slept well all week; thinking about Gareth and then, last night, every time I closed my eyes, I saw rats. Their dead eyes staring up at me accusingly, as if I'd slaughtered them. It was niggling me as I had no idea who would have done such a horrible thing. Whoever it was must hate me or Whites and that made me feel vulnerable. I was living alone, in a flat above my place of work but I was also the one in charge of the business. Sometimes the enormous sense of responsibility overwhelmed me. When that happened, my dad would have to talk me down from the ledge.

I wasn't sure I wanted the family business and all the history that came with it. The pressure to succeed, to keep turning over money for a family I may never have. Ironically, since I took over, there had been no time for dating anyway. But it was my name above the door, my dad's name and his before him. I owed it to them to try my best and growing up here I'd learnt everything there was to know about selling houses.

I was going to my parents' house tomorrow for Sunday lunch as I usually did. Every week I'd go and check in on them both to see if they needed anything, catch up on what they'd been doing. Mum was cooking roast lamb, my favourite, but I knew the conversation would centre around Gareth's death and for that reason I wasn't looking forward to it.

* * *

On Sunday morning, I woke with the same sense of dread as the day before. I'd tossed and turned all night, imagining I could hear someone scuttling around in the office below. The rat had got me spooked and I considered fitting cameras inside the office as well as outside, to put my mind at rest.

Fuelled by coffee and a hot shower, I trudged downstairs to check everything was normal. The office was empty, as I had left it. There was no sign of any disturbance or that anyone had been inside. I cringed, remembering waking in a daze and being close to calling the police as I was convinced of an intruder. Realising eventually, I was caught up in my own paranoia and no one was in the flat.

Then I saw it. The envelope was handwritten, with only my name on the front, so it caught my attention immediately, sitting on top of the pile of post that had dropped onto the mat. I always picked up the post early every day, even Sunday, in case anything had been hand-delivered. Saturday's post must have been delivered late, after we'd closed, which wasn't unusual.

I bent down to pick up the pile, a flash of recognition that the handwriting looked familiar. Then I remembered the strange sentence written on a blank piece of paper earlier in the week. What I had thought to be a publicity stunt. That was addressed to 'The Owner'; this one was addressed to Sophie White.

I turned the envelope over in my hand as I walked to my desk, discarding the other mail. Dread erupting in the pit of my stomach, causing the hair on my arms to bristle and I shivered involuntarily. Nothing good was going to be inside.

Steeling myself, I ripped open the envelope. It wasn't a letter this time, but a greetings card. A picture of two bright red cherries bound by their stalk and a pastel-green leaf embossed on the front. The slogan 'You are the cherry on my cake' printed in black surrounding the image.

Inside, in the same handwriting as before, was a single sentence:

Who popped yours?

Fear gripped my stomach, wrenching it violently, saliva filling my mouth. All at once, it made sense. Now I understood the connection between the messages: 'Who was my first?' and 'Who popped yours?' What did it matter who my first was? It wasn't anyone's business. Who was playing this silly game?

I tried to tell myself it was a prank, a childish joke, but my jaw tightened. Grinding my teeth as my brain whirled. What if the person sending the notes was the same one who left the rat at my door? But why? It was twenty-odd years ago. Who cared who I lost my virginity to?

I hurried back upstairs and sat at the kitchen table, the card standing to attention like a centrepiece as I scrolled through Facebook. I hardly ever used Facebook, Twitter or Instagram. I didn't have a large group of friends who were dying to know what I did daily or what I had for dinner, but I had to find Elliot and my friends from back then. I believed I was the only one who never left Copthorne.

I typed in Elliot Peters and, as I expected, a long list of people appeared on the screen. I scrolled down and clicked on a few, expanding their tiny profile pictures to see clearer, but none were him. I clicked on Gareth; we'd friended on Facebook a few years ago, exchanged a couple of messages to say hi and catch up.

Gareth's page was still live, his wall full of condolences. Friends sharing their memories and photos of him. I scrolled through them, my stomach flipping. Gareth looked as I remembered him, although he had been seriously hitting the gym. Underneath the muscles, that sweet little boy was still obvious in his chiselled jawline.

I clicked on his list of friends, he had over two hundred, but I found Elliot easily. Men were easy to find as they had one name for life. Finding women who'd married was much harder.

Elliot was living in Australia; his profile picture was him surfing and he looked every bit the same as he did when we were in secondary school. From the cheeky glint in his eye, to the mischievous expression. I sent him a friend request and went back to the list to look for James, before sending him a request too. I'd heard that Becca and Mark had married after being childhood sweethearts at school. Unfortunately, I'd lost touch by then; each of us went on to either college, apprenticeships or straight into work, saying we'd stay in contact but then drifting apart. There was a few calls and emails, but it had tailed off. Just one of those things. The last time I think we were *all* together was the day we collected our GCSE results.

I believed Becca and Mark lived in Brighton, or so my mum said, around half an hour away. Robyn went to university in

Leeds, I think, and Hayley, well, no one heard from Hayley after she left. Unless she got back in touch with one of the others? I couldn't find her on any social media at all.

I sent a message via Facebook to Becca and Robyn, asking how they were and where they were living now. Perhaps I could get everyone together, to raise a glass to Gareth. After all, they were all there that night. Maybe I wasn't the only one who had been contacted?

6

'Oh my god, Sophie, what have you done?' Becca was pacing in circles around my bedroom, her hands wound through her long brown hair, stretching it tight across her knuckles.

'Stop panicking, they won't say anything,' I said, trying to calm the situation.

Hayley had gone as white as a sheet, her orange freckles illuminous against her pallor. She was yet to speak.

Robyn was the only one who looked amused by the whole scenario. 'I think it's a good idea. We get it over and done with. Everyone is sworn to secrecy, so no one knows. It's probably easier doing it with someone you *don't* fancy than someone you do.'

'I think you should do it with someone you love,' Hayley whispered, her expression vague. I was concerned she was going to throw up over my pink shaggy rug. She had eaten a lot of pick and mix from Woolworths on the way back to mine.

'Well, I've thought about that. I'm going to try and pair you with Gareth. I don't know how yet, but I'm going to make it work,' I said.

In seconds, Hayley had turned beetroot at the mere mention of his name. Her eyes were like saucers and she opened her mouth to speak but no words came out.

Robyn fell about laughing and even Becca cracked a smile, although she was still pacing, making me dizzy.

I patted the space on the rug beside me. 'Sit down, Becca.'

She sat, pulling her hair into a loose bun on top of her head.

'What if they tell everyone! Our lives would be over!' Becca dragged her finger across her neck, and I rolled my eyes.

'Stop being so dramatic. No one is forcing you. We've all said it's been hanging over our heads, I thought this might be a good way around it. It's not as if we don't know them,' I said, my own bravado masking the tremble which ran beneath.

'So, Gareth, Elliot, James and who else?' Becca asked.

'I was thinking Mark,' I replied.

Her eyebrows shot skyward. Perhaps Hayley wasn't the only one who had a crush?

'Everyone agreed?' I pushed.

'I need to sleep on it,' Becca said, the idea no longer up for discussion.

Hayley gave a little squeak scooting closer to Becca. Safety in numbers.

'Fuck it, I'm in,' Robyn declared with a grin, popping a cartridge into my Game Boy and switching it on. One down, two to go.

I wondered how Gareth was getting on with the boys. Were they all declaring us too minging to have sex with? None of us were Kate Moss or even as attractive as the blonde bitches, but we were okay. All pretty in our own way, above average at least. We each had our insecurities, which we shared with each other. Becca was carrying a little extra weight around her middle, which she was paranoid about. Gripping an inch of flesh between her fingers to show us in disgust whenever the mood took her. At least she had boobs; I was slow to develop on that front and envied her curves. I resembled a scarecrow in comparison. Hayley hated her braces and her red hair and Robyn suffered with a tiny amount of acne. It wasn't much of a big deal, but when one of the blonde bitches called her 'pizza face', it was the only time I'd seen her cry. Not in front of them; never in front of them. But in the toilets, later, with me as we coughed our way through a cigarette, she'd pinched from her mum's packet that morning.

I had visions of Gareth sat on the floor of his messy room, surrounded by Elliot, James and Mark giving us marks out of ten. Ranking us in order of how hot we were. That's what boys did, right? The idea made me shudder and I pushed the image to the back of my mind. I didn't share it with anyone. Hayley and Becca still needed convincing and I didn't want to give them any reason to say no.

* * *

The following day, we got the bus into Crawley, there were loads of shops there and none in Copthorne. We always wanted to hit the make-up aisle in Boots.

'What do you think of this one?' Robyn pouted into the mirror, slathering a layer of Rimmel's Heather Shimmer across her lips.

'Gross, that's the tester. Do you know how many people have used that?' Becca recoiled, nostrils flared.

Robyn glared at Becca and slipped the tester into her pocket without hesitation.

I flushed pink and turned to leave. I hated it when Robyn stole things, she did it often and we'd all scatter in different directions like someone had let off a stink bomb.

After we'd fled, we gathered down the street, giving Robyn a hard time for pulling another stunt, but she was oblivious. Flopping onto a bench, we looked through our purchases for the day. Make-up, hairbands and CD singles from HMV filled our bags, money earnt from car washing and tidying our rooms. Only Robyn had a job, a paper round after school on a Thursday which make the causal shoplifting all the more ridiculous. She was the only one who could afford to buy the stuff she stole.

Becca pulled out her mobile phone to check if anyone had called her. She did it around fifty times a day as it was new, but she was the first of us to have one, so, the only people that ever called her was her parents. I'd been asking for one for ages, but my parents were immovable. No one saw Mark approach. He crept up and tapped Becca on the shoulder, ducking away behind Hayley when she swung round.

'All right, girls?' he said, standing to his full height, chest puffed out. He towered over all of us.

Mark had a bit of a swagger. He wasn't bad-looking with blond wavy curtains that ended at his chin. The hard man of the group; his dad owned a building business in the village. I'd seen him working on a Saturday, carrying a bag of cement at a house in Bale Street where his dad was building an extension.

Becca twirled her hair around her fingers. I rolled my eyes, not believing I hadn't seen it earlier.

'Hi, Mark,' Becca and I said in unison before collapsing in a giggling heap.

Seconds later, James, Gareth and Elliot joined us and for a few minutes it was awkward. No one wanted to mention the obvious and the conversation stalled until Mark suggested we head to the park to sit in the sun. At the top of the high street, opposite the police station, was the memorial gardens – a large expanse of green space, with a playground and a café too.

When we got there, it was rammed, a typical hot day in the school holidays. James and Gareth were mucking around, play-fighting like children. Mark took off his T-shirt and laid back on the grass. Becca gawped unashamedly. We all did. I couldn't deny it; Mark's top half wouldn't have looked out of place in *More!* magazine's Torso of the Week. Becca looked like she'd be easy to convince, if only I could guarantee Mark would be hers.

We pooled our money and Hayley went with Gareth to get ice creams from the café. Hayley needed a bit of a nudge to go. She was so shy, she had to be pushed in the right direction. I was sure her and Gareth would hit it off. Maybe I was destined to host that programme, *Blind Date*, I was such a good matchmaker.

I watched the kids climbing the colourful frame, wishing I could be eight again. Swinging beside Gareth on the twin set in his garden. Not a care in the world. At fifteen, I felt pulled in so many directions with no idea which way to go. Life wasn't so simple any more and it was partly why I wanted the gathering to go ahead. I wanted to lose my virginity; it would be one less thing to worry about. We could move on and enjoy what the future had to offer. The pressure would be off, and it wouldn't be such a big deal.

I looked from James to Elliot and back again. If Hayley wanted Gareth and Becca was mad for Mark, who would I go with? I didn't know either of them well, not like I knew Gareth. It made me nervous but couldn't be helped. I didn't fancy either of them. Not because they were ugly, they weren't, but there was zero chemistry and I wanted stomach flips and sexual tension. I wanted what I'd seen in the movies. The ones my parents wouldn't let me watch. They both seemed nice enough lads, although total opposites: James was smart, you could tell – when-ever he opened his mouth, he always had something valid to say. Like he only had a certain amount of words and didn't want to waste any spouting rubbish. Elliot was funny, not in a physical goofball way, but he was so quick-witted and able to lighten the atmosphere with a single sentence.

'What are you thinking about?' Gareth appeared in front of me, holding out a dripping ninety-nine, minus the flake which he was eating.

'Oi, that was mine!' I complained.

He sat next to me, so close we were almost touching, and I saw Hayley watching warily out the corner of my eye. He pulled a mobile phone out of his pocket, checking the screen. My eyebrows shot up.

'You've got one too?' I said, feeling put out.

'It's Craig's old one. He's just got a new one.'

'Lucky,' I sulked, taking a lick of my ice cream

We sat in silence for a minute before Gareth spoke.

'It's on. The lads are up for it. Just need to work out when and where,' his voice low, so we wouldn't be overheard.

'I already know where, leave that to me. Next Sunday okay with you?' I asked, aware the holidays were slipping away from us and this wasn't something I wanted to do whilst school was in full swing. I had to hope I could get Hayley and Becca fully onboard by then. A Sunday would be best. You could guarantee my parents never did anything on a Sunday, it was always the same. Roast dinner followed by Dad taking the piss out of *Songs of Praise*, after a few glasses of wine.

'Sure.' Gareth gulped, like he was steeling himself to say something, but I cut him off.

'Great. Remember, no one talks. If any of you lot tell anyone, we'll deny everything, and you'll look like lying losers.'

Gareth shrank back. He looked wounded that I would think so little of him. I didn't, not of him, but I didn't know the others as well. 'Okay, okay. I've told them all right.'

'Oh, and one more thing,' I said, pausing to take a long lick of my ice cream, relishing the crimson colour Gareth's face had turned.

'What?'

'The boys bring the condoms.'

7

'They said it was a blue Volkswagen that ran Gareth off the road, but they haven't caught them yet. No CCTV apparently,' Mum said, impaling a Brussel sprout on her fork.

'God that's awful,' I replied, my appetite ebbing away. 'What did he do for a living?'

'He worked in IT, a software tester I think Sue said.' That made sense, he was good with computers back at school. 'Oooofff,' Mum winced, rubbing her leg. Her knee was sore, the damp air aggravated it and last night there'd been an almighty storm. It had been building for a while and at least had broken the humidity, but I'd been kept awake for three nights in a row for one reason or another. Mum commented, as soon as I arrived, on the dark circles under my eyes. An early night was in order; I was going to drink wine until I passed out, anything to ensure I got some sleep.

I wanted to talk to my dad; there was so much I wanted to get off my chest. I'd always been closer to him, but I couldn't find the right moment. The mood around the dining table sombre as our thoughts were with Gareth and his family. Instead I picked through my lamb, eating as much as I could manage.

'Where's the funeral for Gareth? Are you going to go?' I asked.

'Well, it's being held in St. Albans. I spoke to Sue – they were engaged you see, him and Lisa and she wanted to arrange it there. He'd been living there for over ten years, so lots of friends that way. I don't think Sue is overly happy about it, but there you go.'

'Makes sense,' I conceded.

'The only thing is it's an hour in the car and your mum's knee is playing up a bit. I don't think the journey will be a good one. We were hoping that you'd represent us?'

My heart sank, but I smiled and placed my hand over Dad's. 'Of course, I will.'

'The date's not been set yet. Sue said there's an inquest early this week to record the cause of death, so his body hasn't been released,' Dad continued.

I shuddered; it was alien to speak about someone you knew that way. 'Okay, let me know when you hear. I've sent flowers to Sue and Jim.'

'Thanks, love, we've sent some too,' Mum said.

'How's business with all this Brexit lark?' Dad asked, changing the subject.

'Okay, to be honest, Dad. It doesn't seem to have affected us really, some homeowners have said they are worried about the uncertainty – do they sell now or wait? – but we're still taking on properties.'

'Good, good. Bloody awful business – they just need to get out and stop dragging their heels.' Mum rolled her eyes as Dad continued to get on his soapbox about the Remainers wanting to revoke Article 50. To be honest I switched off, it was the last thing on my mind.

After lunch, Dad assumed his usual position in the front room, falling asleep in the chair, and I washed up.

'Mum, where's the photo box? I want to have a look through old ones from school.'

When we were finished in the kitchen, Mum directed me towards the green plastic box, on top of her wardrobe. It was heavy, and the lid was covered in dust, but I managed to lift it down.

I sat at the dining table going through the photos, the table-cloth almost covered in them. Mum joined me, cooing at my baby pictures, eyes glistening.

'You were such a beautiful baby, Sophie,' she said, her head tilted to one side, staring adoringly at me. Frozen in time, splashing in the bath with bubbles on my head. I flicked through a pile; they weren't in any order. Over forty years of photos from when my parents met. Me as a toddler feeding some goats; me on the swings; then again, country dancing at the school fete. Underneath more baby photos, I glimpsed a school blazer. The crest of an eagle in red and yellow. I slid the photo out – it was me, Becca, and Robyn, pulling faces on the swings in the park. Another, all of us glammed up for the leavers' disco in baby doll dresses, chokers and awful platform trainers. We looked like Spice Girl rejects. I knew there was one somewhere of all of us together and after ten minutes of hunting, I found it.

I closed my eyes, feeling the breeze rippling my hair and the sun on my back from that day. It was the summer holidays, the countdown to the day we became adults. An amazing few days of glorious sunshine. We spent the afternoon in the park, sunning ourselves until our skin glowed pink. Hayley sat in the shade, concerned her freckles were going to merge. Elliot brought his ghetto blaster and we contributed money for the six enormous batteries it held. We laid in the sun, listening to Capital radio and larking around with water pistols. Becca had been gifted a Polaroid and three packs of film from her parents and we spent the day taking pictures. Using all sixty in around four hours. Becca took most of them home; she was making a scrapbook of the summer holidays. A lot of them were of Mark, but she made each one of us take one group shot home as a memento of that perfect summer.

I gazed at the photo now, flipping it over. I'd written on the back 'Summer of 1997'. I rolled my eyes and chuckled. I thought I was so cool. I examined the picture, holding it up to the light. In the shot, I sat in the middle of Elliot and Gareth on the grass; Gareth giving the V for victory sign behind my head. I remember it was taken the second before I turned around to see what he was doing. Mark was tickling Becca, who was giggling but wincing at the same time, her face screwed up. Robyn was making a rude hand gesture and James looked serious, like he hadn't managed to smile in time. Our backdrop was bright blue sky and scorched grass. That summer was hot, and it hardly rained. Everyone's grass had turned brown.

'This was the one I was looking for,' I said to Mum, showing her the photo.

'No Hayley?'

'She was taking it. In fact, I don't think I've got one of Hayley,' I said, pushing the photos around the table as though I could unearth one hidden beneath.

'Such a shame she moved away, nice girl she was.'

'Yep, the last time I saw her was at the Halloween party, the day before they left.'

'She knocked for you the day after that, you know, but you were still in bed, or had you gone out with your father? I can't remember.' Mum stared into the kitchen as if the answer could be found there.

'Really? You never said.'

'I must have forgot. Yes, you'd gone out with your father because the car broke down, remember. We spent all day trying to get it fixed. I think she knocked before they left. Her dad was waiting in the car outside.'

'Did she say anything?'

'Oh, I don't remember, Sophie, it was a long time ago. I don't think so, I think she wanted to say goodbye.'

Strange. She was always more Robyn's friend than mine, but we all hung out together. It was weird that she never kept in touch, never found a way to write or ring any of us. We didn't know where she'd gone.

I slipped the photo of all of us, bar Hayley, into my bag. I was going to try and get in touch with everyone. Perhaps have a kind of reunion, if everyone wanted to. I wanted to find out if anyone else had received any strange messages. Plus, I had to start getting out and about. I wasn't particularly social and had let friendships fizzle out over the years, mostly because I hadn't made the effort. Lucy and I went for a drink every other week or so; she was the closest thing I had to a friend. It was awkward though, hanging out with the boss. Perhaps it was that kind of mentality I needed to shake off? I would invite Lucy, Beth and Hope out for a drink on Friday night. I was sure they would have much more exciting things to do, but if I didn't put myself out there, I'd be relying on my parents for social interaction and at thirty-six that was pitiful.

* * *

Everything was quiet when I got home, no messages, no post on the mat and the office was dark and undisturbed. I changed into my pyjamas and opened a bottle of red wine I'd been saving for a special occasion. There wasn't one, but I was desperate to sleep. I did raise a glass to Gareth as I stuck the photo on the fridge with a magnet. If we could go back, would we have done things differently? Did any of my friends have regrets like I did? I'd wanted to have a child by now, be married and settled.

My phone beeped, a notification from Facebook appeared, first one, then another. I opened the app to see Elliot had accepted my friend request and sent me a message:

Gday Stranger! How are you? Christ it's been years. What are you up to? I'm in Oz, been here seven years now. They wanted recruitment consultants of all things, they let me in that way! How is everyone? Do you still see the old gang? I just heard about Gareth. I can't believe it. Please pass on my condolences to his family. Speak soon. Elliot x

From his photos, it looked like Elliot was living his best life. I was pleased for him. There was no mention of a family or kids on his profile, but a twinge of jealousy struck. Everyone had got out of here except for me.

I spied another notification from earlier. Neither Becca or Robyn had responded to my message yet, but James Miller had accepted my friend request.

I clicked on his photo, which linked to his profile page; surprised to see he only lived in the next village. How odd I'd never seen him around? But would I recognise him? I scrolled through his photos; there were hardly any of him, instead a raft of funny memes he'd posted. There was one shot, an arty one, where he was standing in front of the sun, his face in shadow. I couldn't see how he'd changed.

The information on his profile was limited, only that he lived in Burstow and was a writer. Perhaps he used Facebook as little as I did. I was sure my profile was just as vague.

I penned a message to James, a polite hi, how are you? I commented on the awful news about Gareth and asked if he thought we should all get together? I didn't know if anybody would respond. Perhaps they didn't want me shaking the skeletons out of the closet.

Luckily on Saturday night, my parents didn't go to Gareth's. Sue had a cold and didn't want to spread her germs, so they postponed for a week. I was relieved, I didn't want to face Gareth the night before the event. It would be too weird. Instead, I convinced my mum and dad to let me have the girls over for a pamper evening. Mum drove us to Blockbusters, and we rented *The Craft*, so we could sit like the witches in the film with our lotions and potions. I had a television in my room with a video player built in, so I laid my duvet and pillows on the floor for us to sit on. Mum delivered us pizza and popcorn halfway through. She was always brilliant when I had friends over, getting us whatever we wanted but staying out of the way too. No one liked parents who lingered.

Our faces caked in mud masks and nails painted marshmallow pink, we watched the movie; all wishing we could look like Neve Campbell.

'This is awesome,' Robyn said, pushing a piece of popcorn through the tiny gap her lips would allow.

'I know. God, I'd love to have those powers. Imagine what we could do to the blonde bitches,' Becca agreed, her voice sounding weird because she could barely move her mouth too. The masks had dried so hard. We were all talking like ventriloquists.

'I'd make them all ugly for a day, so they would know how it felt,' Hayley spat.

Becca and Robyn held their faces as they laughed, trying not to split the mask.

'Don't be ridiculous Hay, you're not ugly,' I said, giving her a nudge with my shoulder.

'I know, I know. I'm just saying. Actually, I think making them invisible would hurt them more,' Hayley relented.

'Definitely,' Robyn agreed.

Zero attention would be the best punishment for them. How would they cope being ignored?

No one had mentioned the party and I wasn't sure anyone would if I didn't. But there was an undercurrent of tension in the room which needed dispelling.

'Everyone still okay for tomorrow?' I asked, looking at my friends in turn. Robyn shrugged, Becca nodded and a flush crept up Hayley's neck. They all looked like rabbits caught in headlights. Wide-eyed and searching for an exit. I had to take control otherwise tomorrow they'd be screaming and running for the door. 'It'll be fine. I've figured out how I'm going to make sure you're paired with Gareth and you with Mark,' I said, looking first at Hayley, who was crimson, and then at Becca.

'What? I never said—' Becca began to protest, waving her hands around.

'Oh, whatever. We're not blind,' Robyn countered with a roll of the eyes.

'I'm scared,' Hayley admitted, her voice trailing off. She was the eldest, turning sixteen in November, but by far the most anxious of us all.

'You'll be fine. Gareth is the nicest guy I know,' I said, placing my hand on hers and ignoring the vice tighten around my chest. If he was, why was I letting Hayley have him? *Because*, the voice in the back of my head chipped in, *it's what friends do*. I didn't want him anyway, not really. Plus, it was obvious she was crazy about him; I would deal with the fallout later. I knew deep down that Hayley's feelings weren't reciprocated.

The room fell quiet for a few minutes, and we turned our attention back to the film. Everyone contemplating the events of the next day. I don't know where I'd got the idea from, to me it was a logical step forward where I could be in control of how it happened. Wheels had been set in motion and it was too late to turn back now. Becca had been easy to get onside, after the day in the park with Mark. I only had to remind her of his impressive six-pack, and she was sold. Hayley, however, hadn't been quite so comfortable with the idea. In the end, I think she went along with it to keep me happy, knowing I needed her to make up the numbers. I felt guilty using my powers of persuasion, but there were four of them and there needed to be four of us. I was sure afterwards, she'd see I did her a favour? It would never happen with Gareth any other way. This would be a one-time thing for them. For all of us.

Although wouldn't it be funny if we walked out of Park Lane in couples? Strolling into our final year of secondary school each with a boyfriend. I'd love to see the blonde bitches' faces. I'd convinced myself doing it together would make our friendships stronger in the future, a group experience we'd shared. Our first time, our first sexual experience, simultaneously under one roof. Something we'd remember forever and talk about for years to come.

I'd already told my parents I was going over to Becca's and camping out in the garden whilst we were there, so I had to take a sleeping bag. Dad had dug mine out of the airing cupboard already and handed it over. I'd taken it from him, unable to meet his eye. Would he have handed it over so easily, with a smile on his face, if he knew what it was for? I'd borrowed his torch from under the sink and packed it in my bag. I had a curfew of half nine and hoped the boys would make a swift exit once the deed was done. I knew that part wouldn't take long, in fact I was sure of it. I was eager to exchange details with my friends and giggle over the awkwardness of it, once it was over.

Was I ready to become a woman? Did you change when you got your first period and were able to grow another human inside of you? I hadn't felt a massive change, not in my head anyway. Or did it happen when you lost your virginity? It had to be the latter; when you'd matured enough to start having sex.

Since the day at the park, I'd been struggling to decide who I was going to be paired with. I was leaning towards Elliot. I could imagine if things went wrong or one of us got embarrassed, we'd laugh about it. It wouldn't be a big deal. With James, I wouldn't be surprised if he bought a biology textbook with him. We'd be doing it step by step, using picture references to ensure he got it right. It wasn't the kind of experience I had in mind, not one I'd want to remember. I'd have more fun at home doing it on my own.

When the film finished, we scoured issues of *More!* Magazine, which I kept under my bed – there was always loads of sex tips in there, although not all of them we understood.

'What if we do something wrong and look stupid?' Hayley asked, frowning at the 'Position of the fortnight' drawing that resembled a wrestling move I had seen on tv.

'We're all clueless, Hay. We're all in the same boat. The boys are just as inexperienced as us. That's the beauty of it, there's no pressure,' Robyn replied as she wiped off her mask with her flannel. She seemed the most together out of all of us.

'Easy for you to say,' Hayley mumbled, wrinkling her nose and tossing the magazine onto the floor.

'Take a chill pill! We know the basics right; we know we've got to be safe and use condoms. The most important thing is not to get pregnant! Remember this is just a tick-box exercise,' I said, repeating the term I'd heard my dad say before. Feigning more confidence than I had about tomorrow. I knew when the time came, I'd be shitting myself as much as my friends. But I was the instigator, it was my idea, my plan, and I had to be the leader.

'I don't know that much,' Hayley admitted, her voice low. We'd all had sex education in school, which taught us about reproduction and the importance of protection, but it felt like being given a leaflet on how to drive and then being handed the keys to a car. I'd also sat through an excruciating talk with my mother on how babies were made, but again there was nothing really useful when you were about to do it for the first time.

'Basically, you'll do a bit of kissing, a bit of fondling. He has to be hard and then he'll get on top, normally anyway, and you lay back and open your legs,' Robyn said matter-of-factly.

'Robyn!' Becca screeched and threw her head back, laughing.

'What? That's right, isn't it?' Robyn said.

'Will it hurt?' Hayley asked.

'I don't think so. My sister said it didn't for her,' Becca chimed in. She had an older sister who'd moved out last year to live with her boyfriend.

'Mum got me this book, about getting older, periods and that. There's a chapter in it about sex and how it's done.' I fished around under my bed until I found it and handed it to Hayley, watching her flick to the chapter and start to read.

'I dunno what to wear?' Robyn said, rubbing her forehead.

'I don't know, normal stuff, you know. Jeans, I guess, and nice underwear or something,' I replied and Robyn shrugged. That had been playing on my mind too.

One by one, at around nine, when everyone had taken turns to read the chapter and scoured all the sex tips we could find in *More!* the girls' parents came to collect them. As we each hugged goodbye, I whispered in their ears 'Tomorrow night will be epic,' but only Robyn responded.

'As if,' she said with a laugh.

Once I was alone and had removed all the popcorn and tidied the floor of my room, I ran a bath to shave my legs. Sitting in the hot water was when the anxiety kicked in. What was I going to wear tomorrow? Did I own any underwear that wasn't boring white cotton? Was I supposed to wear something sexy? All the anxiety I had been withholding erupted and I knew I'd be awake late into the night stressing. Would Elliot care what colour my pants were or that my boobs weren't symmetrical? Whether my backside had a dimple on it? Was he worrying about the size of his manhood? What if we got caught? My heart raced. I had to stop; I was overthinking it. Everything would be fine, we'd do the deed and go home. End of story.

When I finally fell asleep, I dreamt Gareth and I were having sex for the first time in my room when Dad walked in. Shame burnt my face and I woke retching, the moon still high in the sky. I lay awake watching the shadows dance on the ceiling until morning. An ominous feeling spreading through my body like poison.

9

SEPTEMBER 2018

Work was uneventful. I scheduled a catch-up meeting with Frank to see if he was happy with how Gary and Hope were doing. Gary had made two sales already and appeared to be up to speed, preferring the transparency of Whites. Although he said working within the rules would take some getting used to.

Hope also seemed to be fitting in fine, she was a hard worker and keen to learn. Her customer service skills were excellent. I'd watched her with the walk-ins, the potential clients – she was funny and warm but still professional. It wouldn't be long before she'd be working on her own properties with ease. I'd moved her from shadowing Gary, who I discovered was fast-paced, to Lucy, who had more patience. Teaching came naturally to her and they were of a similar age so paired well.

We'd made arrangements to go out for a drink on Friday night, the three of us. Beth had plans already with her boyfriend, plus I believed she liked to keep her work separate from her personal life and I respected that.

I asked if we could postpone drinks until Saturday, when I got a call from Mum midweek to say Gareth's funeral was going to be on Friday.

I headed to St. Albans that morning, leaving the office in Frank's capable hands over the weekend. I wasn't intending to come back to work until Monday. A few days off would be the tonic I needed. I booked myself into a travel inn nearby, knowing I would want a stiff drink after the funeral and perhaps even before it too.

Mum had delivered a wreath she'd ordered from all of us for me to take and, without knowing why, I'd slipped the group photo into my bag too.

The Friday-morning traffic was a headache and I sat in tail-backs on the M25 for forty-five minutes, but I'd left myself plenty of time to get there. The funeral wasn't until two and I was looking forward to seeing Jim and Sue, although it would have been nicer under better circumstances. The wake was being held at a pub across the road from the crematorium, so not far to go.

I didn't know if I'd know anyone other than Gareth's parents. Had Gareth kept in touch with anyone from school?

I arrived at midday, having booked an early check-in, enabling me to freshen up and change into my black dress at the hotel, not wanting to arrive all crumpled from the car journey. I called a cab to come at half past one, my stomach churning. While I waited, I dug out the mini vodka bottle I'd packed, travel-size, knocking back the shot in one go to steady my nerves.

Gareth's parents were standing outside the crematorium when I arrived, welcoming guests, and his father enveloped me into his arms. The familiar smell of Old Spice and talc wafted from him and I inhaled deeply, not wanting to let go. Sue hugged me tight, thanking me for coming and for the flowers. They both looked pained, eyes red and sunken, and Sue was almost frail, stricken with grief. I placed our wreath with the others, the word

SON in white carnations pulled on my heartstrings. No parent should have to bury their child, never mind two.

I sat in one of the middle rows, not sure why I was surprised to see the pews packed. I had no idea what Gareth did or how he'd lived his life. A lot of people had turned out to pay their respects and I was pleased for Sue and Jim. In the front row, I could see a blonde lady cuddling a boy, gripping his shoulder so hard her knuckles were white. Next to her, Sue and Jim took their places as music flooded into the crematorium.

Snow Patrol's 'Chasing Cars' echoed around the room and I let my body release the tension I'd been holding. No one liked funerals and even though I didn't know Gareth well as an adult, I mourned for the boy he was. The friend I'd had. My shoulders sagged as the pallbearers carried Gareth down the aisle. It was seeing him brought in which started the influx of tears. Imagining that boy, in the coffin. I knew he wasn't a boy, of course, but that was the only real image I had of Gareth. I saw a photo on the platform at the front, of him laughing, lines around his eyes and stubble I couldn't connect with him, but he'd grown to be so handsome.

I looked around as the priest began to speak, but I didn't recognise any of the faces surrounding me. I lowered my eyes to the order of service on my lap. On the front, a different photo of Gareth, in this one he wore a suit, his smile resonating in his eyes. I recognised some of the hymns and the poem on the rear was the renowned 'Funeral Blues'. We stood and sang, sat to have a moment of prayer and then stood again. I felt as though I held my breath the entire time. My limbs were weak, like Bambi on the ice. As though I was going to dissolve into a puddle and I nearly did when the curtains were drawn as the coffin began to move down the belt.

It wasn't until we were outside in the bright sunshine, the

awkward time spent milling around, waiting to speak to the family, that I breathed again. I wished I hadn't come alone.

A hand touched my shoulder and I turned to see a face I vaguely recognised but couldn't place.

'Sophie White?'

I narrowed my eyes, a smile playing on my lips.

'James Miller?' I guessed and was rewarded with an unexpected hug.

James clutched my shoulders and held me at arm's-length, looking at me from head to toe. I shrank back, self-conscious at being examined.

'You look great, Sophie. I'm so pleased to see you.' He grasped my hand.

'You too, James, you look well,' I replied, my voice hushed.

'I'm going to sneak around the back for cigarette, want to join me?'

A minute later, we stood at the rear of the crematorium, looking out over the graveyard puffing on a cigarette. I hadn't smoked in years, and only ever socially, but if any time was forgivable, it was at a funeral.

James's hair was still light brown with a slight curl but now speckled with grey at the sides. His blue eyes were as intense as ever, framed by long lashes any woman would be envious of.

'I can't believe it about Gareth,' James said. I saw the faintest wobble of his chin, but he bit his lip, looking at me unabashed with watery eyes.

'I know, it's so awful. Were you still friends?'

'Yeah, saw each other every couple of months or so. We'd always make a date to have a boys' night out. Too much beer and a kebab, you know how it is. Not something I do often now,' he admitted.

'Me neither,' I grimaced. I would have liked the chance to get to know Gareth as an adult.

'What about the others? Mark? Elliot?'

'Not seen them really – we met up a few times when we finished school but not since. I bumped into Mark a couple of years back when I was out in Brighton. Him and Becca are still together. He's in the police now.'

'Oh really?' I replied, glad I wasn't the only one who had drifted apart from my friends after school was over.

Stubbing out our cigarettes we headed to the pub across the way to join the other mourners. I bought James, Sue and Jim a drink and was introduced to Gareth's fiancé Lisa and son Ben. She was very petite and pretty, with small elfin features. Her blonde hair was almost white, in sharp contrast to her blotchy pink skin. I tried to picture her with Gareth but I couldn't; I could only see him as a boy and not as a man. Lisa's eyes were blood-shot from crying, but I could see she was trying to hold it together. I bit my lip, eyes straying to Ben, who looked to be around eight, clutching his mother's hand, overwhelmed by all the people surrounding him. Mum never said Gareth had a son.

I passed on my condolences and James found a quiet corner for us.

'Lisa arranged this quickly,' I said, filling the silence that was growing between us.

'Yeah, the crematorium had a window free and I think she wanted it done, not hanging over them.'

'I completely get that. She must have been in limbo since the accident.'

'I think she has been. I can't believe he's gone and Ben's now without a daddy.'

'It's awful,' I agreed, wondering if I'd ever be fortunate enough to be a parent.

I turned the conversation around to happier times and we spent the next couple of hours drinking bourbon straight and reminiscing about our schooldays.

'Do you remember Mark's hair, when it was all spiked like that boy group, I can't remember which one?' James recalled.

'Five!' I blurted out, spluttering with laughter. 'Wait, wait, look at this,' I said, remembering the photo and pulling it from my handbag.

James squashed close to me in a tiny booth, our thighs pressed together.

'Wow. Look at us,' he said wistfully.

James's proximity made my pulse quicken. I could smell his woody aftershave as we leant over the photo. Alcohol had switched on desire that had been dormant for a while. That, coupled with the warmth of James by my side, made me awkward and unsure. Like I was fifteen again.

Looking around the pub, we were the last left that had attended the wake. Lisa and Ben had slipped out earlier and Sue popped over an hour ago to say goodbye and thank us for coming. Businessmen now propped up the bar and there were a gaggle of twenty-somethings in their sequins and heels warming up for a Friday night out. I looked at my watch, my focus blurring. It was almost nine. James and I had chatted away almost five hours. Was it any wonder my legs were like jelly?

'Where are you staying?' James asked, his tone had a serious edge to it. His eyes surveyed me so intently that for a second, I was lost in them.

'Travel inn.'

'Me too.'

'I'll call a cab,' I said, grabbing my phone and calling the same firm that had delivered me earlier.

We were collected within fifteen minutes and James walked

me to my room. I was drunk and maybe he was too, but he seemed more sober than me.

The corridor surprisingly deserted for how early in the evening it was.

'Nightcap?' I asked, knowing full well my room didn't contain a mini-bar.

'Sure.' James's eyes twinkled and I was sure he knew it too.

10

SEPTEMBER 2018

Before I even opened my eyes, a groan escaped my lips. My head throbbed as though someone was playing the bongos inside my skull. I pulled the duvet over me to drown out the banging. My stomach screamed for food and I remembered James and I had barely touched the buffet. We were so deep in conversation in our little corner, by the time we reached the table, there was hardly anything left.

James. Where was James?

I opened my eyes and rolled over, the speed making me wince. Everything hurt. My bed was empty. The room was empty. Memories of drunken sex flashed before me, like a trailer for a particularly rubbish porn film. Why was I wearing James's shirt? If I had his shirt, had he gone back to his room bare-chested? Creeping along the corridor, hoping he wouldn't be seen? I cringed inwardly; was it that bad he had to leave before I woke? I'd have to return his shirt at some point, perhaps apologise, although I wasn't sure for what?

I resumed my position under the duvet, enveloped in the warmth. I didn't have to check out until midday, and I was intending to stay in bed as long as I could get away with. Suddenly, the door clicked and swung open, the room steadily filling with the aroma of meat and grease. A smell like no other and easily recognisable.

James appeared, carrying a brown paper bag.

'Morning,' he said with a smirk, looking annoyingly fresh-faced and unabashed.

I salivated at the smell of bacon and pulled myself to a sitting position. Flattening down my hair and resting my head against the cushioned board.

James unpacked the bags and handed me a bacon sandwich and a steaming-hot coffee. 'I hope you're not a vegetarian. Some-times only a bacon sarnie will do,' he said with a grin, taking a large bite, ketchup dripping out of the edge. The awkwardness I'd felt dissipated.

I couldn't believe he didn't look as annihilated as I felt. I took a bite, chewing slowly, not sure how my stomach would react, but it gurgled gratefully at the incoming solids.

'I feel awful,' I admitted, rubbing my head and smoothing my hair. Clinging on to my dignity. I wished I'd had a chance to look in the mirror before he'd arrived. For all I knew, my face was streaked with mascara.

James wore a white T-shirt – maybe he'd had it on under his shirt last night? I couldn't remember. I wanted to broach the subject of how we'd ended up here, to dispel any awkwardness. But it seemed I was the only one in the room who was self-conscious. James leant on the sideboard tearing through his sandwich without a hint of discomfort.

I pulled the covers to my chest and concentrated on finishing my mouthful. Washed down with the coffee, I began to feel a bit more human, although ready to go back to sleep for a few hours.

'Thank you for breakfast,' I said, dabbing at my mouth with a serviette.

James looked at his watch and I saw his eyebrows lift. 'You're welcome. I've got to head back, there's a deadline on Monday I've got to meet. I'm behind and it's not looking good.' He rubbed the back of his neck.

'Sure, no problem,' I said, a niggle of guilt surfacing as relief flooded in. I wanted to be on my own to process what had happened last night and I couldn't do that with him around.

James stared at me, his lips pressed together. Then it dawned on me.

'Oh, the shirt,' I said quickly. My cheeks flared and I began unbuttoning, my fingers getting muddled.

'No, no, don't worry about that,' he replied, turning away. His ears pink, not wanting to watch me trying to undress myself.

I cleared my throat. Why was I struggling to act normally? It had to be the hangover from hell. 'I'll wash it, or dry clean it?' I offered and he turned back, a smile growing.

'Next time dinner?' he asked, and I agreed. He gave me a kind of half wave, half salute as he left.

I waited until the door closed before allowing a giggle to escape. That was awkward. If I needed a reminder as to why I didn't do one-night stands, that was it. I slumped back on the bed, cringing, not from the alcohol consumption exiting via my pores but from my clumsy interaction.

The drive home, as always, was much quicker than the journey to St. Albans. I waited until midday, giving my mum a quick call and going back to sleep for a few hours. Waking up still as embarrassed as before but no longer intoxicated. I wasn't sure I would see James again, he lived in the next village over and had done for years, but our paths had never crossed. James had not yet married or found the woman of his dreams, if such a thing existed. But his presence had turned an otherwise shitty day into something much more pleasant, if nothing more. I hadn't failed to notice he didn't ask for my number. It was nice to catch up anyway.

He was a writer now, for the local newspaper, and had a column in one of the Sunday tabloids so was doing well for himself. I wished I'd followed in his footsteps, but the media course I looked at didn't appeal to me. I'd opted for a Travel and Tourism GNVQ and spent two years learning about the leisure industry. Even before I gained my qualification, I knew it wasn't for me, I felt at a loss and fell into working full-time for Dad. Moving up the ranks from the Saturday admin girl. While James had rushed home to meet a deadline, I had no plans for the day ahead other than to relax.

Back home the office was closed, and the post picked up and left on my desk. There was nothing there of any immediate importance and Frank had left no messages, so I popped to the shops to get some food in and some hair of the dog for later. I was dreading going out. How stupid of me to arrange a night out the day after a funeral. I was way too old to be drinking two nights in a row. I easily had fifteen years on Lucy and Hope, and I could already see it was going to get messy with a ton of jäeger bombs.

I checked my phone at six. There was a voicemail from Lucy, who sounded horrendous. She'd been sick all last night and most of the day, fearing it was something she'd eaten. There was no way she was going to make it out. I called Hope, intending to postpone, but she sounded so disappointed I relented. She suggested a takeaway and a bottle of wine instead of the pub, which did sound tempting but I told her we'd stick to the plan. The pub was neutral territory.

I got dressed and tried to make myself as presentable as I could with the help of make-up and hair straighteners. We agreed to meet at the Boar at eight. When I arrived, she was waiting at a table, four drinks in front of her.

'Happy hour – two for one, so I got a couple of Mojitos.' She looked pleased with herself and I was glad she couldn't hear my stomach squirming.

'How's your day been?' I asked, and Hope filled me in. She'd been shopping with her Mum and tomorrow they would be visiting showrooms in the search for a new car.

'Well, not new new, but you know, get a feel for what I'd like: Ford, VW, Skoda,' she reeled off.

'Do you live at home with your parents?' I asked.

'No, I moved out, but I'm at Mum's all the time.' She took a sip of her drink and looked at me. 'You weren't in yesterday? Is everything okay?'

'Yeah fine. I was at a funeral.'

Hope's mouth dropped opened mid-slurp. 'Oh god, I'm sorry. No one said anything.' She looked mortified.

'It's fine, it was an old friend. I hadn't seen him for years.' That appeased her, and she went on to talk about what a dive her old job was and how her boss was a sanctimonious knob.

The evening was fun, Hope talked a lot, getting consistently louder with each drink, but we did laugh. At times, I noticed the age gap between us. Some things she said went straight over my head and I was sorry Lucy wasn't here to divert the attention. If James was intense, Hope, one-on-one, was sometimes disconcerting. I wished I'd had a slice of her confidence at the same age.

We stayed in the Boar until chucking-out time and when Hope called the local taxi company, they had a delay of half an hour. I was five minutes down the road and told her to come to mine, so she booked the taxi to pick her up from there.

There were two ways to get up to the flat, either through the agency, via the kitchenette, or through the front door. The front door was around the back of the building and I tried to avoid using that entrance when I could. It wasn't well lit at the best of times and there was nothing but big industrial bins from the shops further down. I hardly ever saw anyone out there, and it had spooked me since I was a kid. Tonight, it was especially dark, and I had to use the torch on my phone to get the key in the door. I didn't want to go through the office and have to tell Hope that the front creeped me out. She would think I was nuts.

'Careful, some bastard has smashed your light,' Hope slurred, crunching on glass underfoot.

'Bloody hell, there's always something,' I moaned, looking around to see if anyone was waiting in the shadows. A feeling of disquiet settled upon my shoulders.

'Probably kids,' I sighed, heaving the front door open and climbing the steps to the second door which led directly into my kitchen.

'Fancy a brew?' I asked, already craving hot buttered toast.

'Nah,' she said, slumping at the kitchen table, her hand propping her head up.

I made a tea anyway, and some toast and we sat at the table to have a slice.

'What's that?' Hope asked, pointing to the fridge.

I saw the photo I'd stuck there when I got home earlier. It looked different, and then I realised someone had drawn on it in thick red pen. A large cross, straight through Gareth's head.

11

AUGUST 1997

I waited at the postbox, my sleeping bag slung over my shoulder and a bottle of Malibu *borrowed* from Mum's cabinet in a Safeway carrier bag. I'd arrived early, a few minutes before seven. Worried no one would come, or even worse, only one person would, and we'd be expected to go and do it on our own. My stomach tossed like tombola that wouldn't stop, and I needed to pee.

A few cars passed, but no one gave me a second glance. I hoped I didn't look like a runaway with all my worldly possessions in a sack. The sun was slowly sinking, bathing the houses in an orange glow and the smell of a distant barbecue hung in the air. My sweaty palm encased the key inside my jean pocket. I wanted to keep hold of it, terrified it would slip out. Dad would go crazy if he discovered I'd stolen it. Suddenly, this didn't seem like such a good idea after all.

'Hi,' Gareth said behind me.

I spun round, I'd been watching for the girls, who would be coming from the opposite direction.

'Hi,' I replied, smiling, glad to see a friendly face. Then I remembered my dream, Gareth naked in my bed and my face burned.

'How are you?' he asked, eyes searching my face, forcing my mask to crumble.

'Terrified,' I replied with a nervous giggle.

Gareth's jaw relaxed.

'Me too,' he admitted.

I pointed down the road as five figures rounded the bend. Robyn, Hayley, Becca, Elliot and James shuffled their way along the pavement towards us. As they got closer, I could see them all laughing and Elliot gesturing, hands flailing.

'Where's Mark?' Becca asked as soon as she reached us, her eyes wide with panic.

'He'll be here,' Gareth said, checking his watch. It was five past seven. My pulse slowed to a normal rate now almost everyone was here, excitement replacing my nerves. Even Hayley appeared calm, her eyes locked on Gareth.

'Did you hear about Diana?' Hayley asked.

'Yeah, it's awful isn't it, my mum was so upset this morning,' I said.

'Mine too,' Elliot added, his eyes downcast. I waited for a punchline, but it never came. Perhaps there was more to Elliot than being the joker?

'So where are we going?' James asked, his brow furrowed. Changing the subject.

'We're going to go to the park first, to have a drink, then there's an empty house that's been refurbished on Park Lane. It's for sale and I have the key.' I watched as mouths dropped open and my chest swelled.

'Oh my god, Sophie, that's amazing!' Robyn said, a wicked glint in her eye.

'What did you all expect? A park bench each?' I replied like it was no big deal.

The boys shrugged, perhaps it was what they were expecting? I wasn't going to lose my virginity out in the open, summer or not. The news of the location seemed to lift the group and we shuffled from foot to foot, making conversation until Mark arrived five minutes later.

'You're late,' Gareth grumbled, shoving Mark's shoulder when he finally arrived.

'Sorry, got stuck washing-up. Do any of you have any idea how many bloody pots and pans there are when your mum cooks a roast. Anyway, it's only ten past!'

'At least your hands will be clean,' Elliot laughed, pushing Mark into the road.

'Ha fucking ha. And, of course, I had to get this.' He pulled a bottle of Strawberry MD 20/20 out of his bag, winking at Becca who beamed as the rest of us whooped.

'Nice one,' I said and we began walking towards a small park on the edge of a housing estate. It was one that we barely used because it's play equipment was too babyish, but at this time it was likely to be empty.

Flopping down on the grass, the only ones in the park, Gareth's hands trembled as he pulled an open packet of twenty cigarettes from his bag and handed one to each of us. Even Hayley took one, and I hadn't seen her smoke for ages. Sometimes we smoked, when Robyn could pinch a couple of cigarettes from her mum or if we could get served at the corner shop, which wasn't often. It wasn't because any of us really enjoyed it, but I sensed we were all relieved to have a delay in proceedings. I hadn't seen Gareth smoke before, but I didn't want to bring it up around his mates. The packet was open, perhaps he'd had one on the way here?

Gareth lit each cigarette in turn with his yellow disposable lighter and Mark opened the 20/20 and began passing it around. Swigging from the bottle and wiping the top with our sleeves before handing it over. It tasted disgusting, sweet and sickly, but we carried on, alternating between that and the Malibu.

'Where did you get a pack of twenty?' Becca asked, gawping.

'My brother bought them for me. Well, for us.'

'You didn't tell him, did you?' I hissed, my legs juddering as I sucked in the smoke.

Gareth took a while to answer.

'No,'

I could tell he was lying but didn't want to push him in front of the others. I knew the girls would cause a scene. Knowing Craig, he probably threatened to beat the shit out of Gareth until he spilt his guts. He was such a dickhead. I just had to hope Craig would keep his mouth shut.

Twenty minutes later, we got to our feet, all slightly unsteady, and made the short walk to Park Lane; easing open the garden gate so it didn't screech and slipping inside the garden one by one. Once inside we were sheltered from view by the surrounding six-foot fence but kept our voices low. I wasn't sure who the neighbours were, and I didn't want to attract any attention, so I told everyone to duck out of sight down the side of the house as I opened the back door.

When we went in, it was eerie, our footsteps echoed on the linoleum floor. We stood, crammed into the kitchen, it was quite dark inside, a massive apple tree blocked out the light from the window.

Gareth pulled out his torch and the rest of us followed suit. Pointing them at the floor so we were stood in a puddle of light.

'How are we going to do this then?' Mark asked.

'Well, first you're going to get your little wiener out,' Elliot began, and everyone laughed.

Mark punched him on the arm, and he winced.

'Shut it four-eyes.'

Boys would be boys.

'Keep your voices down,' Robyn hissed.

I cleared my throat. 'Us girls are going to pick a room. I've numbered them all. I'm going to give you lot a number and you go into the room with the corresponding number. Make sense? No one knows who will be waiting in what room, or who will be coming in. It's completely random. Okay? That way it's fair,' I said.

I was so convincing, I almost believed myself, but it wasn't true. I'd already spoken to Hayley, Becca and Robyn on the phone earlier and told them what room they needed to go into. I was going in room one, the main bedroom upstairs. Becca was going in bedroom number two and Robyn the box room, which would be number three. Hayley was going to stay downstairs in the den, which was going to be number four. I didn't want to use the lounge, I remembered it was huge, but the window looked out onto the road and there was a street lamp which shone straight in. The den was better, off the dining room, at the back of the house. It was smaller, cosy and out of sight.

'No one tells anyone right,' Becca ordered, and we all nodded in agreement.

'Right, go and choose a room,' I said to the girls, 'three upstairs and one down here remember.' I glanced around at Becca, Hayley and Robyn and I could see, even in the shadows, the fear etched on their faces.

They shuffled out of the kitchen, not a word spoken between them. My heart pounded so hard I could hear it hammering in my ears. The boys looked at me expectantly. I fished in my pockets for the bits of paper I'd numbered earlier. My hands quivered, and I coughed, trying to remember what order I had to hand them out in. My mind raced. How I was going to do it without it being obvious the pairs had already been chosen? I looked at the boys, lingering on Elliot's face. Could I go through with it? I froze, rooted to the spot, my hand half out of my pocket.

'It's okay, give me the paper, I'll pass them out.' Gareth reached for my hand, but I snatched it away.

'No, it's fine. I'm just... Never mind,' I said. I looked again at the group before me. Realising I could hand the pieces of paper out backwards, as they were standing in reverse order. Sighing with relief, I gave Gareth the slip marked number four, James the one marked three, Mark number two and Elliot number one.

'Right, I guess I'll go then.' I turned to leave, but James cut in.

'Hang on, we don't know what room is what number,' he said.

I smacked my palm on my forehead. 'Yeah, sorry. You're right. One is the main bedroom upstairs, at the front of the house. Two is the second largest bedroom, at the back of the house, and three is the box room, next to the bathroom. Number four is the den, which is through there,' I waved towards the dark archway leading out of the kitchen.

They started to disperse, and I made to go, but Gareth caught my hand, signalling the lads to go on ahead. We stood, alone in the dark kitchen. I could hear the boys stumbling up the stairs and giggling in the dark.

'What number are you?' Gareth asked.

'I'm in room one,' I whispered, aware Gareth was still holding on to my hand.

He turned the paper towards the light and saw the four scrawled on it in thick black pen.

'I wanted you,' he whispered, his shoulders slumped.

'I'm sorry.'

Gareth leant forward and his lips brushed mine until I eased him away.

'I'm sorry. I have to go,' I said, blinking back tears as I climbed the stairs in the dark.

12

My mind fuzzy with alcohol, it took a second for the realisation to hit. I stared at the photo on the fridge door. Trying to absorb the pen mark across Gareth's face. Before I had a chance to react, Hope's phone beeped.

'Taxi's here.' She jumped up and I started to walk her out, down the stairwell, but she reassured me she'd be fine and would see herself out.

I stayed where I was, rooted to the spot, staring around the kitchen, then back to the photo. The door slammed downstairs. Hope had gone but someone had been in my flat.

My breathing quickened and I scuttled down the stairs to check the door for damage; there was none. Someone had been in here. How had they got in? I double-locked the door. My brain whirled, looping around in circles. I tore through the flat, turning on lights in each room, searching every potential hiding space to ensure I was alone. Once I was satisfied no one was hiding, ready to jump out when I least expected it, I returned to the kitchen and chucked the remaining toast in the bin, my appetite vanished.

The photo was in the same spot I'd put it earlier on the fridge.

I scooted over to look closer, reluctant to touch it. When I'd got back from St. Albans, around three in the afternoon, I'd unpacked my overnight bag and put the photo back in its place. There was no marker pen on it then, I would have noticed. Had Gareth been crossed out because he'd died?

The cards, the phone call, those weren't pranks. Someone was trying to get to me. The photographed proved it. What had I done? What point were they trying to make? If they were trying to unsettle me, they were succeeding. Did someone have a vendetta against me? Surely this couldn't all be centred around the first time I had sex?

Attempts at sleep were futile, my heart spluttered every time I heard the tiniest noise. The flat was old, pipes gurgled, floorboards creaked. Sounds that never bothered me before now grated on my fragile nerves. Even with my alcohol content topped up from the night before coursing around my system, I struggled to relax. I was overtired and overwrought. Sleep didn't come until the sun started to rise and the shadows were chased away.

When I woke late on Sunday, I sent messages via Facebook again to Becca and Robyn. I didn't want to contact James in case I came across too keen. If James had received a card or a note, I was sure he'd have mentioned it. We spent hours talking, reminiscing about our adolescence and what we used to get up to, but the party wasn't mentioned. I had to know if I was the only one being targeted. We were all there after all and if I was the target, I wanted to know why?

After a long shower I checked my phone, Becca had messaged back:

Sorry, Sophie, it's been manic. We're great thanks, living in Hove now. Would love to meet up. Have you got in touch with Hayley and Robyn too? x

I quickly typed a message back:

That would be great, no not heard back from Robyn and have no idea where Hayley lives now. Have you been in touch with her? x

I waited a while for the reply, a stab of jealously when it came. Becca said she would nudge Robyn as they'd kept in touch, but she hadn't heard from Hayley either. We arranged to meet next weekend, place to be confirmed but somewhere central for all of us. I had no idea where Robyn lived.

Had I ignored either of them reaching out over the years? I was sure I hadn't. I couldn't complain, I hadn't made an effort either, until now.

I called my mum to let her know I wouldn't be coming for lunch and gave her a rundown of the funeral. She was a bit short with me because she'd bought a joint of beef from Tesco, but I couldn't face eating. I promised I'd pop in during the week.

As soon as I hung up, my phone rang again, another with-held number and I was reluctant to answer. Curiosity got the better of me, though, and I slid my finger across the screen, selecting the speakerphone option. A crackling sound burst from the phone.

'Hello?' I said, hearing my voice echo.

'Sophie, she was the one. I was crazy about her back then.' A cough like last time and a click, but this time I didn't hear the elongated drone that told me the line had gone dead.

'Who is this? What do you want?' I strained to listen for any clues. I heard faint, muffled breathing. I leant closer to the phone, there was another click.

The man's voice spoke again, so loud I reeled backwards, rocking my chair on two legs. 'It was a laugh, kids' stuff. It didn't mean anything.'

I closed my eyes, filtering the voice in my head, but even though it seemed familiar, I couldn't place it.

The caller hung up. I wished I'd set my phone to record so I could play it back. Next time I would.

What did he mean by kids' stuff? That night at the house? I gritted my teeth. Who was fucking with me? Cowards. Why not come out with it and face me?

After the anger subsided, I decided the best course of action was to carry on as normal. It was the same with bullies – the best way to ward them off was to appear as though you didn't care and, if someone was watching me, that was what they'd see. I tried to ignore the nagging doubt in the back of my mind, though, that things were going to get worse.

* * *

On Monday morning, I opened the office as though nothing was playing on my mind. An offer came in early that morning from the family that viewed 32 Park Lane. It was much more sensible than the one from the property developer, but I asked Gary to try and push for a bit more if we could. It was a gamble, but most buyers expected to negotiate; it was unusual these days for a first offer to be accepted off the bat. However much I wanted rid of that property, I owed it to Mrs Davidson to get the most money for her that I could.

'How were you yesterday?' Hope asked, cornering me in the kitchen when I made the first round of tea.

'Not too bad, what about you?'

She rolled her eyes before answering. 'I felt hideous, didn't get out of my bed all day.'

I handed Hope her tea and carried the tray back into the main office, filling Frank and Hope in on the developments on Park Lane.

'Gary, how's that bungalow going? Any offers there?' As I finished the question, his phone rang, and he raised a finger to indicate one offer before talking into the handset. 'Hopefully it'll be a good week,' I said brightly and retired to my desk where I could remove the mask.

Frank popped in a while later, bringing me another tea and a slice of fruit cake that Diane had made over the weekend. It was delicious and for a while I forgot about the messages, letting them fall to the back of my mind. I was probably overanalysing anyway.

Robyn sent a message mid-morning. My Facebook account had never been so active. I noticed, as I scrolled through my timeline, that Becca and Mark had a joint Facebook account; their profile picture was from their wedding day. Who'd have known all those years ago that those two would get married?

Robyn could meet on Saturday, she suggested Crawley would be a good place, so I booked a table for three at the Hillside pub for lunch. She said she hadn't been able to track Hayley down either.

It wouldn't be all of us together and it was a shame we couldn't get hold of Hayley but I was looking forward to Saturday, to catch up with the girls and see how they'd changed. I was keen to offload to them about what was going on. No one else would understand. Maybe they would have some ideas who was behind it and most importantly why?

* * *

Work was busy, and it was good to keep myself distracted. I carried on working late after the office closed on Monday, and on Tuesday I went to my parents for dinner. Anything to keep out of the flat. I felt uneasy whenever I was there although I couldn't put my finger on why. Mum and Dad wanted to hear more about the funeral, and I told them I'd seen James. I didn't go into detail as to how much of James I saw, of course. Mum was pleased I was meeting with Becca and Robyn at the weekend and asked me to send them her love.

Around lunchtime on Wednesday, I was having a chat with Frank in the main office regarding a property we were finding hard to shift when the bell clanged announcing a customer. I turned, face ready with my most welcoming smile, to see James standing in the doorway.

'Can I help you?' Hope moved swiftly between us as my mouth dropped open.

'Umm, I came to see Sophie,' he said, stepping around her as she looked at me quizzically.

'Hi,' I said, aware the whole office was watching our awkward exchange. A flush began to creep up my neck.

'I was in the area; thought you might fancy a spot of lunch?'

'Sure,' I said after a short pause, trying to rein in the smile that was blossoming on my face. Whisking my coat off the stand and grabbing my handbag, I hurried to the door, eager to leave for somewhere I didn't feel all eyes on me.

'See you in a bit,' Frank said with a knowing smile.

13

James sat across from me, the Formica table reflecting his image as he lifted his toasted sandwich and took a bite. I'd chosen the café over the pub, in case any colleagues popped in. Their faces were a mix of shock and amusement when James had walked in. Frank and Lucy had swapped looks. They'd never known a man to come in to see me specifically before. Not unless he was complaining.

'I wasn't really in the area,' he said, averting his gaze.

'Oh?' I laughed, pulling my sandwich apart and watching the melted cheese drip onto the plate. My appetite waning.

'I didn't take your number,' he admitted, shaking his head at his own stupidity. I beamed; his honesty was refreshing. I wasn't sure whether I would see him again after Gareth's funeral, but I was pleased he'd got in touch. James met my gaze and matched my smile with his own. Any awkwardness between us dispelled.

'I should have asked for yours,' I replied before taking a bite of my sandwich.

I wasn't sure whether to tell him about the notes and phone call now we were sober. It dawned on me the reason I was reluctant was because I didn't want to ruin it. I was fed up with keeping people at arm's-length. James's eyes were kind, he had stubble today which left him looking a little rugged.

I told James I was meeting Robyn and Becca at the weekend and perhaps we should organise a get-together for all of us, Mark and James too. Although Elliot might be a bit of a stretch. James seemed happy to go along with it.

We talked about the deadline he had, the reason why he'd left in such a hurry. Slogging through hours of writing fuelled by coffee when he got back home on Saturday. An hour and a half flew by and there were no awkward silences, even without alcohol.

'It's been good to see you again. Let's go for dinner sometime?' I said, my face glowing like a beacon. Sod it, I was going to be brave.

Thankfully James didn't leave me hanging. He fumbled with his phone and keys, dropping them on the floor as we stood to leave. 'Dinner would be great. One evening next week perhaps?'

I nodded, trying to act cool but failing miserably, my grin stretching across my face like a Cheshire cat.

James paid for lunch at the counter and we swapped numbers before he walked me back to the agency, giving me a brief kiss on the cheek goodbye.

I floated back to my desk, ignoring the smile on Frank's face and the wink he gave me as I passed. He looked like a proud father who had seen his daughter off to prom.

'Sophie, I've got to nip to the post office and send these documents, won't be long,' Hope called before rushing out of the door like a whirlwind.

'Sure,' I called after her, the bell jangling. I was already scrolling through James's photos on Facebook on my phone.

Later on, Gary came to update me on the latest developments.

Mrs Davidson had accepted the Baron's second offer, five thousand pounds higher than the first, and the bungalow offer had also been accepted. It appeared to have been a successful day all round and I insisted we went to the pub after work for celebratory drinks.

The Boar was like our second workplace and Phil the landlord had our drinks on the bar within minutes of us walking in.

Gary bought the first round, ignoring my waving of two twenty-pound notes in his face.

'You get the next one,' he said, handing me a glass of wine.

'So, who's the fella?' asked Hope.

I knew it was going to be a hot topic of conversation.

'Just someone from my schooldays,'

'Wow, did you go out with him at school?' she continued.

'No, not then, but we're going to go out for dinner next week.' I didn't divulge meeting him again at the funeral. Instead, I raised my glass in a toast to my team for their hard work this week. Hoping the subject of my love life would be soon forgotten about. It was, as the conversation turned towards Beth and her pet bulldog that snored louder than her boyfriend.

My mind wandered, thinking about work. We had two chains completing this week, one due on Thursday, one Friday, so that would keep us busy with tying up any loose paperwork and liaising with solicitors. I knew Dad would be pleased; we'd already succeeded our target for this quarter and were expected to surpass the profits projections for this year. What we needed now was more properties to sell. Next week, I would get some flyers printed and drop them into the houses around Park Lane and the street where the bungalow had sold. That usually generated some interest and a couple of valuations. On the whole, business was good, and it was only going to get better.

* * *

On Saturday, I was surprised to find I was nervous about seeing Becca and Robyn and, even though it was ridiculous, I agonised over what to wear. Autumn was well on its way and the Indian summer we'd been hoping for had been ruined by the temperature falling in the past few days. After much deliberation, I chose a mustard top with a navy scarf, dark jeans and heeled boots. I wanted to look successful and confident but also content. I couldn't help but be envious of Becca. She'd married Mark, her childhood sweetheart, and pushed out a couple of kids. Robyn's life was a mystery, but for all I knew she could be in the same club. I wasn't competitive, but I wanted to be okay with the choices I'd made and the life I'd carved out for myself. I didn't want to feel their pity that I was still stuck in Copthorne, single and childless at thirty-six.

I needn't have worried, within five minutes it was as though we were fifteen again. Becca looked great, her dark hair was still long and annoyingly glossy. She looked much more together than I thought she might with two kids running around at home, but what did I know? Robyn was the same, she wore skinny jeans and biker boots and had added nose and eyebrow rings to the collection of piercings since I last saw her. Back then, she already had three hoops in each ear, which in the nineties was quite controversial.

'Christ, Robyn, how many piercings do you have now?' I asked, giving her a wink as she rolled up her sleeves to reveal tattoos on both wrists.

'Nine piercings and seven tattoos. I can't show you all of them though.' She winked back. The punk look suited her, even the pink streak in her hair. She looked great, albeit a bit scary, but that was Robyn; she never gave a toss about what people thought of her. I envied that too.

'Where are you living now?' I asked as our drinks arrived and we perused the menu. I was starving and eyeing the chicken and avocado baguette, my stomach rumbling audibly.

'I'm in Horsham. I live with my girlfriend Chloe,' Robyn said, unabashed.

'A girlfriend? Did James put you off for life?' I giggled.

Becca choked on her drink, her eyes wide. Had I been inappropriate? I wrung my hands under the table, my ears growing hot waiting for someone to speak.

A smile played on Robyn's lips as she hesitated, capitalising on Becca's reaction.

'Only that James and I kind of had a thing last weekend. I wondered if there was something I should know?' I continued at speed, trying to dig myself out of the hole I'd created.

'Oh god, I hope he's more exciting now anyway. If not, then run!' Robyn countered and the atmosphere evaporated.

We glossed over the last ten years. I told them about James and bumping into him at Gareth's funeral. They ribbed me for getting laid at a funeral; did I not have any decorum? Becca told me she was a freelance accountant, looking after clients in and around Brighton. Her and Mark had twin girls, although they weren't so much kids any more. I was surprised when she showed me a photo, they were blonde like their dad, long hair in waves. Tall and pretty too. According to Becca, they were growing up too fast. She and Mark had them when they were twenty so both had turned sixteen this year. Robyn worked in retail, a shop called Base in Horsham, where her and her girlfriend Chloe lived. She said she'd dated men and women over the years but had settled down now as much as she ever would. Robyn had dropped out of university in Leeds where she was doing an Art and Design degree. Couldn't hack the bureaucracy apparently. I didn't pry, it was obvious she didn't want to go into detail, but she seemed happy with her life now.

Neither of them was surprised to learn I was managing Whites. According to them it was always going to happen eventually. Was it tragic that my life had been so planned out? They hadn't heard from Hayley either, although both had looked for her on the internet over the years without success.

'It's like she disappeared off the face of the earth. I remember looking for her when I was twenty-one, and a few more times over the years,' Robyn said.

Our food arrived, and we tore into it, hungry from waiting for so long; the service slow as the pub was so busy. Throwing caution to the wind, I told them about the messages I'd been receiving and the phone calls. I searched their faces in case either were hiding something, but they both looked as shocked and confused as I was. I didn't believe it was them, but it had to be someone who knew about that night.

'Jesus, Sophie, that sounds scary. You have no idea who it is? It's obviously a guy from the phone calls,' Robyn said, midway through chewing a crisp.

'I don't know, it's weird, the stuff he says. It's like he's talking to someone else. It could be a recorded message? I have no idea. I can't place the voice either.' I grimaced.

'Have you told the police?' Becca asked.

'No not yet. I feel a bit silly, to be honest.'

'I'd tell them. You don't know if it's going to escalate. You're living alone, in that flat. I'd be on the bloody phone to them!' Becca said, dabbing her mouth with a serviette.

'Have either of you received anything?' I asked, looking from Becca to Robyn. Becca shook her head.

'No, I haven't. It's weird though. I mean, I don't understand. What's the point of it all and why now?' Robyn frowned.

'I know. It makes no sense,' I replied, frustrated they appeared as clueless as I did. I had to hope the notes and calls stopped, either that or whoever it was confronted me. Whoever had a grudge against me, if they came out into the open, we could work it out, couldn't we?

When I said goodbye to Becca and Robyn a couple of hours later, we agreed to fix a date to bring Mark and James with us. We decided to meet one evening, so we could have a drink and raise a glass in memory of Gareth.

By the time I got home the sun was starting to set, the sky glowing red – shepherds' delight. I couldn't wait to get into my comfy clothes, but as I pulled round the back of the building to park, my pulse raced, making my eyes blur. The car stalled and I staggered out, legs weak, leaning on the bonnet for support. My front door was wide open, blowing back and forth in the wind.

14

As I climbed the dim staircase, I could hear muffled voices and laughter which sounded like Becca. I wiped my eyes, careful not to smudge the mascara I'd applied only an hour before. My attempt at looking older, although I'm not sure who for? No turning back now. Elliot would be waiting. My legs were like lead as I ascended, leaving Gareth alone in the kitchen. Would it be the end of our friendship? It would have been so easy to choose him. It made much more sense. We were easy in each other's company; I didn't have to pretend to be anyone else.

I pushed those thoughts away; I couldn't let myself dwell, not now. I reached the top of the stairs, a muted glow on the carpet from a small window. The sun had almost faded. Every door was shut and, for a second, I was disorientated. Which room was I supposed to be going in?

I stepped forward, a creak erupting from the floorboard beneath my feet, making me jump.

'Hello?' Elliot called out in a low voice. He was waiting for his mystery partner to join him.

I turned to the sound of his voice and saw the door to my left, ajar. When I pushed it open, Elliot was hunched over, laying out his sleeping bag upon the floor.

'Hey,' he said, standing upright. The corners of his mouth twitched, and he put his hands on his hips.

'Hi,' I replied, forcing a smile. He hadn't gone running past me out into the street, so that was a good sign. I wanted to ask who he had hoped it would be, but if I was honest, I didn't want to know the answer.

I unravelled my sleeping bag, zipping it open and laying it on top of Elliot's so it could be our cover. I could feel his eyes penetrating my back as I slipped off my trainers. My skin prickled. Without saying a word, he mirrored me, arranging them by the skirting board. The room was gloomy.

I turned to face him, cloaked in the shadows. My stomach gurgled so loud it made us giggle, dispelling the tension which had been building since the moment I entered the room.

'Do you want more light?' Elliot asked, gesturing to my torch, which lay redundant beside my trainers.

'No.'

'Okay.' After a pause, he took my hand and leant forward to kiss me.

It was different to Gareth. He tasted of smoke and the sweet tang of an energy drink. But it was nice to be kissed and he was gentle, holding me to him. My body shivered, knees knocking together before I could stop them. I held my legs rigid, feet planted on the floor. Elliot's fingers fumbled with the buttons on my checked shirt and I had to stop myself offering to help it took so long. I chewed my lip, my body frozen like a statue. It wasn't until his hands touched my naked skin, I felt any desire at all.

'Should we lay down?' I asked, cold and exposed standing in my bra and jeans, goosebumps littered my skin.

Elliot nodded and pulled his T-shirt over his head. Although his chest wasn't as impressive as Mark's had been in the park, it was hard and smooth to touch. Embarrassment washed over me. I should have done it, I should have undressed him, rather than let him do it all. But as he rolled on top of me, it no longer mattered. I liked the weight of him, but I was a fraud. Surely Hayley was right? To do this, you should love the person and I couldn't pretend I felt like that about Elliot. I tried to push the thought out of my head as his hand strayed lower, beyond the waistband of my jeans and inside my underwear. Blue polka-dot with a hint of lace, I'd chosen that afternoon, the most adult pair of knickers I owed. Wasted, here in the dark.

It seemed like such a rush. Elliot was so eager, and I let myself be carried along.

'Are you okay?' he paused to ask, his breathing laboured. His excitement palpable.

'Yes,' I lied, wishing I was with Gareth. Why had I let Hayley have him?

'Wait, can I... can I use the bathroom?'

Elliot moved off me without hesitation. 'Sure.'

I hurried out of the room and into the bathroom, trying not to listen to the shuffling and groaning from behind the other doors as I passed. Facing the mirror, in the harsh white light, I looked a fright, black streaks down one cheek.

'Get your shit together, Sophie,' I hissed, resting my forehead against the cool glass for a minute before fixing my make-up. This was my idea and I wasn't going to be the one to bottle out.

I washed my hands and pressed my damp palms to my cheeks. Elliot was nice, funny and I was going to hand my virginity to him, gift-wrapped and then the whole thing would be over with.

As I made my way back to the bedroom, I heard a door closing downstairs. Perhaps Gareth had gone to get Hayley a drink or something? But I couldn't dwell on that; I couldn't put it off any longer.

Elliot was sat upright waiting for me when I returned. I took off my jeans as he watched and crawled back under the covers, climbing astride him. I always felt better when in control.

I couldn't say I loved it. But I didn't hate it either. It was fine. It wasn't painful as such. I was a bit sore, but I didn't bleed afterwards, like I'd read I might. We'd managed to navigate the condom and agreed, once it was done, it didn't seem like such a big deal after all. Elliot seemed relieved, I guessed he was pleased he'd lasted more than a few minutes. I hadn't expected him to. I thought it would all be over in seconds, but Elliot took his time, he was really gentle, stopping to ask if I was okay. I saw a completely different side to him that I hadn't seen before. Afterwards, he pulled me in for a cuddle as we wrapped the sleeping bag around us. Neither of us in a rush to get dressed, like we wanted to freeze time. A perfect moment. It felt natural and not forced.

'Shall we go downstairs?' Elliot asked after ten minutes of watching the shadows dance on the ceiling.

We untangled ourselves and got dressed, backs to each other, which seemed silly as neither of us had ever been more naked in front of another person before.

The house was quiet, and we slipped downstairs unnoticed, him first and me behind.

'Found these on the side, Gareth must have left them here?' he said, waving the packet of cigarettes, the lighter tucked neatly inside the box.

'Let's have one.'

As I opened the back door, I heard the creak of the gate ahead. My heart leapt, and I ducked back inside, but Elliot said no one was in the garden. I hurried to the gate and eased it open, looking left, then right, down the street. A figure hurried along the road, it looked from a distance like it was Gareth.

'Who was that? Elliot asked, handing me a cigarette he'd lit for me. We moved down the side of the house, out of view.

'Gareth, I think. I'm not sure though. That's weird.'

'Wow, he was even quicker than me,' Elliot quipped, and I snorted, choking on the smoke. Grateful it had been him with his easy-going nature. At least we could laugh about it.

I couldn't deny, something had changed. I felt more mature, more grown-up. Like I was seeing the world through new eyes.

I checked my watch, it was half past eight, time was running away from me. I wouldn't get to gossip with the girls before I had to leave.

'I'll have to go soon; do you think I should go and interrupt them?' I asked Elliot, unsure what to do. It would be awful to walk in on any of my friends half naked, but at the same time I knew my dad would be pissed if I was late home. Plus, I had to find a way of getting the key back before tomorrow morning. My heart raced as I worried about clearing up, leaving the house as it was when we arrived. My anxiety must have been written all over my face as Elliot put his cigarette out and pushed open the back door.

'Leave it to me,' he said, rolling his shoulders back. 'Guys, come on, we've got to go,' he hissed towards the stairs and again in the direction of the den.

Becca and Mark were the first to come down, both looking dishevelled. Becca's hair was wild, it looked like it had been back-combed, but I was relieved to see she was smiling. Robyn and James appeared a minute later, and everyone moved outside and down the street to wait for us.

I checked the bedrooms with my torch, to make sure no one had left anything behind. The only thing I found was a discarded condom wrapper, which I slipped into my back pocket with a mental note to chuck it on the way home. Otherwise it could be awkward when Mum went through my pockets on wash day. When I returned downstairs, Elliot was waiting for me in the kitchen.

'Have you seen Hayley?' I asked.

He shook his head and I shone my torch towards the archway, the glare reflecting off the closed door to the den.

'Do you think they're still in there?' I whispered, but Elliot shrugged.

'I doubt it.' Maybe they hadn't gone through with it? Maybe it was Gareth I saw leaving. After all, I was expecting someone to chicken out. I hoped he was okay, Hayley too.

I edged towards the door, pushing it open with my hand. Light flooded the room and with it a shiver descended my back, playing notes on my spine.

'It's empty,' I whispered to Elliot. My scalp pricked, hair follicles springing to attention.

'So, where's Hayley?'

15

As I approached, the front door swung towards me as though someone had pushed it. An invisible force. No one stood in the murky hallway, but that did little to still my tremors as I tried the light switch repeatedly. No light came from above and then I saw the bulb had been removed. What the fuck?

I swallowed hard, clicked on the torch function on my phone for light and closed the front door, the wind whistling through the gap as it slid shut. The door was undamaged, no one had kicked it in. Someone had a key. I dragged across the rusty dead-bolt, usually reserved for bedtime, locking the world out and me in. But in with who? I waited, silence overhead, no footsteps or floorboards creaking. No sign anyone was there, but who had left my front door wide open? I knew I'd closed it; I was sure I had.

It was cold inside; the heating was off, and the elements had been allowed in. I crept up the stairs, trying to be as light on my feet as possible. Unsure why I was bothering, the illumination from my torch would give me away, but I didn't have the nerve to climb in the dark. The staircase had no natural light and was always dark even on the brightest of days. If someone was in another part of the flat, they wouldn't see the beam of light, but they might hear my footsteps. Perhaps it was Dad? My parents had a key but, surely, they would have phoned first, left a message and not my door wide open.

My heart thumped so hard I thought it would burst out of my chest to get free. The door separating the kitchen to the stairs was ajar and it was one I always closed, without fail. The front door at the bottom of the stairs, that led out to the street, was wooden and needed replacing; I'd been looking at getting a new PVC one, I was plagued by draughts. It became so bad, I screwed excluders onto the bottom of the inner door to keep the heat in. A new front door was on my list of things to do, another problem I hadn't got around to fixing. The agency always seemed to come first, the flat above lagging.

I could see into the kitchen, through the sliver of the open door, the shadows of the chairs enlarged like giants against the cabinets. At first glance everything looked as it should. I was expecting to find the place turned upside down, my personal effects pulled out of drawers and cupboards, spilling onto the floor. But nothing seemed as though it had been moved. Had I been burgled? Cold sweat pooled at the arch of my back as I crouched at the top of the stairs, listening for any movement. Covering the screen, I waited for my eyes to adjust to the darkness. I should go back downstairs and call the police. Wait outside for them to arrive. But what if they took ages? What if it was me that hadn't shut the door properly?

My hair sparked with electricity, rippling down my neck like dominoes as I continued to look through the crack in the door. I remained crouched for a few minutes, it seemed like an age, but I heard nothing. I had to decide: either I retreated and called the police, or I ventured out into the open. Did I really believe someone was in here with me? I positioned my keys through each of my fingers and clenched them into a fist. If someone did attack me, they'd be getting a fistful of metal in their face.

I uncovered the torch and stepped into the kitchen, trying the light switch, but that too was dead. I started to tremble, imagining a man in a balaclava cutting my wires, but this wasn't a movie. A wave of foreboding washed over me. I had to check the fuse box.

I turned, heading to the next staircase which led to the bedrooms. Beneath was a cupboard which housed the fuse box. I trod on a floorboard that groaned underfoot and paused mid-step, straining my ears. No sounds gave away the hiding place of my intruder. Imaginary or not.

The cupboard door creaked when I pulled it open, every sound amplified. Was the flat giving me up? Shining the light on the fuse box, I saw everything had tripped out, all the switches were in the wrong position. The last time that had happened, the power shower and the washing machine were both running when Mum had used the toaster. Unless someone had broken in to have a wash whilst making toast, I had to assume it had been tripped on purpose.

I pulled the main switch down and light flooded in around me, stinging my eyes. Yellow orbs blinded my vision.

I checked every room, for the second time in so many days, starting to feel stupid. Was it me? Had I left the door open? I couldn't find any evidence that anyone had been inside my home. Nothing apparent was taken, no cards or messages left, or rats thankfully. No additional crosses on any of my photographs.

I talked myself out of calling the police. I could imagine the call.

'*What's your emergency?*'

'*Sorry but I think someone has broken into my flat and tripped my main fuse.*'

'*Has anything been taken?*'

'No but I feel a bit scared and I can't remember if it was me or not.'

They would think I'd lost the plot and I would be inclined to agree with them.

I poured a large glass of wine; it was a bit early for me to be drinking, but I needed one to steady my nerves. The adrenaline coursing through my system took a while to retreat, my muscles continued to twitch, ready to run.

The flat was too quiet, even with the television on. I wanted noise to drown out the silence which was oppressive, but not so much I wouldn't be able to hear someone sneaking around. If indeed someone had been, which I was beginning to question now. But I couldn't be going mad. Someone had been in the flat before; someone had marked the photograph. Maybe they'd left another warning, but I was yet to find it?

My muscles stiffened. I was no longer safe in the place that was supposed to be my sanctuary. I was so preoccupied, I jumped when my phone bleeped. It was a text from James.

Are you up to anything?

Nope.

I couldn't pretend I wasn't hoping he'd come and rescue me from this nightmare.

Can I come over?

Sure

Are you above the estate agents?

I am indeed.

Okay see you soon x

I had a quick five-minute shower and changed my clothes My shoulders already feeling looser knowing I was no longer going to be alone.

When James arrived, I'd managed a brief tidy and lit some candles. When I opened the door he looked grave, like the weight of the world was on his shoulders. He gave me a quick kiss on the cheek before stepping past me and up the stairs two at a time. Once in the kitchen, he didn't pause, taking off his coat and putting it on the back of the chair.

'How are you?' I asked, knowing something was wrong.

'Okay, you?'

'Yeah, I think so, what's up, has something happened?'

James pulled an envelope from his jean pocket, the paper curved where he'd been sitting on it. I knew what it was before he'd even slipped the card out to show me. The handwriting on the front easily recognisable. It was the same card I'd received, right down to the design of blood-red cherries on the front.

James passed me the card and I opened it.

Who did you fuck at the party, James?

My hand flew to my mouth, but it didn't stop the gasp escaping from my lips. This one seemed more venomous than mine. It was personalised for a start, targeted.

James stared at me, his eyes searching mine, reading on my face what I couldn't help but give away. 'You know what this is about?'

'I got one too,' I said, turning to retrieve it from the drawer I had tossed it in the day it arrived.

James took his time, looking at the card, placing mine and

his side by side, examining every inch. Deep lines engraved on his forehead as he frowned down at the table. 'When did it come?'

'Two weeks ago, today, I think. Yes, the weekend before the funeral. It was put through the door of the office, I found it on Sunday morning.' I retrieved my laptop from the sideboard, powering it on. On the fridge, I had stuck the business card of the security company who had installed the camera. 'I've got a camera at the front. I don't know why I didn't think of it at the time,' I said, shaking my head.

James dragged his chair over and we were side by side waiting impatiently for the laptop to stop whirring. He smelt of cigarettes and it made me crave one.

I found the website and logged on with my unique password, able to select past recordings that had been saved into the cloud. I started with two Saturdays ago, after we closed, clicking fast-forward and seeing people whizz past the screen. We watched for a minute and it was around eleven when the figure came. They were only on screen for five or so seconds, pushing the envelope through the door before hurrying away.

'Can you slow it down?' James said, leaning over to take control of the touchpad.

James managed to freeze the image, but all we could see was a person wearing a black hoody, face concealed and dark trousers. Nothing distinguishable about them at all.

'Because of the angle, you can't see how tall or what build they are, everyone looks kind of small.'

I nodded, taking a large mouthful of wine before remembering my manners. 'Do you want a glass?'

'Sure, I'll have one please,' James replied.

I filled a clean glass and sat back down, recounting the events leading up to the card. About the first note, the rat and how I believed someone had been inside my flat. I showed him the photo on the fridge, now with the cross over Gareth's face.

'Why didn't you call me?' he asked, resting his hand on my arm.

'I don't know, I guess I've been hoping it'll just go away.'

'I don't understand what it's all about?' James admitted, rubbing his forehead.

'Me neither, but if it's to do with *that* night, it has to be one of us who was there.'

Saying out loud what had been consuming my thoughts for the past few days weaved a chill down to my toes. Everything felt numb. Why would my friends do this to me? I bounced my leg under the table. My nerves jittery, even with James here I felt ill at ease. For all I knew he could be behind this? It could just as easily be Becca or Robyn, maybe they'd just been playing along when I met them earlier? Perhaps they were all in it together? No, I was being paranoid, but I couldn't deny that I knew nothing now about the friends I was so close to back then. I hadn't seen Mark or Elliot either, could they be behind it? In fact the only one I knew it couldn't possibly be was Gareth, unless he was doing it from beyond the grave. Even I wasn't crazy enough to believe that. As my mind churned over a million possibilities, a deeply unsettling thought came to me. What if Gareth's death wasn't really an accident at all?

16

SEPTEMBER 2018

'What if it's Hayley?' James drained his glass.

'Why would it be Hayley?' I ignored the twinge of guilt for contemplating the same thing.

'Why would it be any of us?' James retorted.

He was right, the whole thing made no sense, but if he'd received a card, had the others too? Was someone playing with all of us, or just me and James?

James helped himself to another glass of wine from the bottle. He'd had too much to drive. Did he assume he'd be staying over? I wouldn't complain, I wanted the company. 'I'm just thinking. Do you remember that night?'

'Of course,' I replied. Surely everyone remembered when they lost their virginity?

'Something happened between Hayley and Gareth, do you remember? We couldn't find them afterwards. Did she ever tell you?'

'No, she didn't. I didn't push her on it and Gareth wouldn't tell me either. But I don't think anything happened, that's the point.

But even if something had, it doesn't explain why she'd wait until now. Plus, why would it be my fault?' It sounded like a whine; I hadn't meant it to come out like that, but why was I being singled out?

'Because I seem to remember it was your idea,' James said, a smile spreading across his face.

I leant into him, craving the safety of his embrace. Sensing how I was feeling he planted his lips on mine, his stubble tickling my skin. What started out as the briefest of touches morphed into a kiss that ignited the desire I'd felt for James after Gareth's funeral. We left everything where it was and slipped upstairs to bed.

* * *

On Sunday morning, a dog barking woke us late and James nipped out to the supermarket when he realised my cupboards were empty. Ten minutes later, he was back, and we snuggled up, eating croissants and watching reruns of *Friends* on my tiny television. Flakes of pastry scattered amongst the sheets; Mum would have had a coronary. Spiteful notes and intruders were forgotten, if only for the moment. I could get used to waking beside someone, a warm body next to mine. Chasing the demons away. It made me feel safer. James seemed more at ease this morning too, the lines ingrained into his forehead had all but disappeared overnight. However, it was clear he'd been mulling things over and I had to refrain from groaning when he raised the subject again.

'I think the next thing to do is find out if Becca, Robyn or Mark have had any cards or letters. If they have, then we need to go to the police.'

I rolled my eyes. 'And say what? We're being tormented

because of a virginity party, which, by the way, officer, was my idea. Oh, and it was over twenty years ago?' I shook my head. Going to the police was a last resort. I couldn't involve the police, not yet. Nothing much had happened other than the rat. It felt like I was making a big deal out of nothing. I could handle a few notes if there were no more uninvited visitors to my home. Perhaps it was time to invest in that new front door?

'What about someone getting inside the flat?' James said, incredulous at my nonchalance.

'Well, I can't say for sure anyone did,' I admitted, although someone had removed my hallway bulb, but I didn't volunteer that.

'Okay, fine, but you said the photo, Gareth being crossed out, happened here?'

Did it? I couldn't be sure of anything any more. Was I going mad?

'Let's see how it goes. We can ask the others when we meet if they've had anything,' I offered.

James grimaced, reluctantly letting it go.

He left before lunch and we arranged to go for dinner midweek. I wasn't sure if this was turning into something permanent, but for the moment I was enjoying spending time with him. James was as smart and intense as I remembered, however now he seemed more comfortable in his own skin. Weren't we all though? At fifteen going on sixteen, it was hard to know who you were or even who you wanted to be. He'd filled out, still tall and lean but now broad-shouldered, his blue eyes haunting like dark lakes. They made my blood rush in all directions and it was strange. An attraction had grown that was never there when we were young. Mum would be thrilled to learn I'd started seeing someone again, especially someone I'd hung out with as a kid.

I arrived at my parents as lunch was being served. Mum was

banging around in the kitchen as I walked in, the sound of plates clanging together.

'I wasn't sure you were coming,' Mum berated, but she warmed up as I helped lay the table and we sang along to Queen on Magic FM.

Over lunch, we swapped stories of what we'd all been up to that week. Mum's knee seemed to be better, the rest had done it good and she was now moving around freely. They'd been to the cinema in Crawley the night before to see *A Simple Favour* and Mum was raving about how good it was. Perhaps I'd ask James to watch it with me.

I told them I'd seen James again. Mum couldn't wipe the smile off her face. I could hear her clock ticking for grandchildren louder than my own. I didn't want to get her hopes up.

Dad wanted help changing their home insurance as it was approaching renewal, so I helped him get a few quotes once we'd washed up. He wasn't a massive fan of computers or the internet and it didn't take long. It was nice to do something easy, mundane even. Taking my mind off of what was going on. I couldn't tell my parents about it; I had no idea where to start and I didn't want to alarm them when it could be nothing.

Back at the flat, it was too quiet. I wished I could forward time to Monday morning. Everyone else would be clinging onto what was left of their weekend but I just wanted to bury my head in work and focus on what I could control. My phone sprung to life around six. I'd taken to jumping around three feet in the air every time it made a sound. It was a Surrey number I recognised. A panting Liz from Graham Jackson Solicitors was at the other end.

'Sophie, I'm so glad I caught you. Sorry to bother you on a Sunday, but that completion for Brampton Road is due tomorrow; I've just realised I'm missing the planning permission from the file. Can you dig it out and send it over?'

I told Liz it would be with her in ten minutes. Gary was dealing with Brampton Road and it was due to complete last Friday, but there was an issue with someone higher in the chain and their ability to release funds.

I headed into the office. We have a filing system; a large set of metal drawers with hanging files, one for each property in alphabetical order. Only the Brampton file wasn't where it was supposed to be.

'Fuck's sake Gary,' I cursed, searching his desk. We also had a clean-desk policy that Gary had obviously forgotten; designed for weekends, so nothing would be left on view from the street. I tried his desk drawers, but they were locked. Sighing, I rummaged through his pencil pot, as that's where I hid my desk key. Bingo. I found the key and got into the drawer. The Brampton file had been chucked on top of a bunch of papers. I pulled it out and flicked through, finding the planning permission certificate easily. Two minutes later, I'd scanned it and sent it to Liz before returning the file back to the cabinet.

As I slid Gary's drawer closed, something caught my eye at the bottom of the pile. A card, with something red and round on the front. I slid it out. It was identical to the one James and I received. I opened it, but the inside was blank.

Was Gary sending the cards? Why would he do that? What did Gary have to gain? Did he even know James? Why would he send a card to him?

I put the card back, a knot forming in my stomach. Debating on what to do next. Should I confront him or wait? Maybe I could catch him in the act?

Was there anything else? I moved the papers around, feeling like a child with my hand in the biscuit tin. It was silly, I owned the place and everything in it, but I would normally always respect someone's privacy. The idea of anyone rummaging through my things made my skin crawl.

Purely by chance, I spotted the flyer, a crude printout on everyday white paper, not glossy weighted stock I used for leaflets. It was a home-made job. *Sell your house with WHITES* in thick red letters. I could have knocked up the same thing in five minutes on Microsoft Word. Was this the leaflet Mrs Davidson was talking about? Gary had taken on 32 Park Lane, had he been dropping flyers? It made little sense as he'd barely started when Mrs Davidson came in to complain and she said she'd been getting them through her door every day. I slipped the flyer into my pocket and got to my feet.

I ran my fingers through my hair. What was Gary up to? He was a great salesman, but if I couldn't trust him, we had a problem. I wasn't sure whether to broach the subject in the morning or watch and wait? Could a customer, or another member of my team have put those things in his drawer? If so, who? And, more importantly, why?

The unanswered questions made my stomach churn. I rubbed my arms to ward off the chill on my skin as I paced the floor. The voice in my head countered: *Whoever it was, if they've been in your flat, they could as easily have been in the office.* There was only one lockable door that separated my home from the business and if someone had stolen my keys, they would have access to both. I hadn't noticed my keys go missing at all. How could someone have got in? Tomorrow I would contact a glazier to fit a new front door. I could balance the books with the extra profits earned this week. My safety was a priority and if anyone did have a key, it would be rendered useless.

I headed out to the kitchenette, locked the door to the office and trudged back upstairs, one thought playing on my mind.

James had been in my home, and the office, albeit briefly. He was there that night; he was a part of it.

After another sleepless night, tossing and turning, imagining every single noise the flat made was someone breaking in, I gave in at dawn and turned the television on. Laying there, dozing, in the warmth of the covers, until I could put off getting up no longer. I felt exhausted, my mind still whirring about the findings in Gary's drawer yesterday. I considered texting James, telling him about the development, but I didn't know whether he'd go in guns blazing and I didn't want to bring my problems to work. Plus I still had that niggling feeling that James knew more than he was letting on. Maybe the cards were nothing to do with Gary after all and they'd been left there for me to find.

I surveyed him as I delivered the tea that morning, trying to detect by some non-existent telepathy whether he was the culprit. He was oblivious and appeared to be acting normal, busying himself gathering paperwork from the four corners of his desk.

'Gary, your desk is a mess. How on earth do you work like that?' My voice reproachful, but Gary didn't bat an eyelid.

'It's organised chaos,' he said with a wink.

Salesmen, I shrugged. They were all the same, using charisma to dig themselves out of a hole. 'I had to get the Brampton file from your drawer last night. Liz needed the planning permission as it wasn't included in what you sent over.'

This time, Gary stopped what he was doing and sat bolt upright, giving me his full attention. He blinked rapidly, caught off guard. A reaction I hadn't seen from him before.

'I'm sorry Sophie, I must have missed it. It won't happen again.' Gone was the charm which seconds ago had oozed from him. Instead, he looked mortified at his mistake and, seeing his reaction, I felt petty for bringing it up.

I took a step back and waved my hand in the air dismissively. 'No problem, but next time can you make sure all the files go back in the cabinet? They're easy to find then,' I said with a smile and Gary nodded.

'Yes, boss, and thanks for the tea,' he replied without a hint of sarcasm.

I retreated to my desk, feeling off-kilter. I was a good judge of character; a trait I'd inherited from my dad. Was Gary the one behind all of this? It didn't sit right. He didn't appear concerned I'd been through his drawer and it didn't seem as though he had anything to hide.

Beth had left some documents on my desk for me to sign, so I started going through them. Hope knocked on the door and opened it wide, allowing Mrs Davidson wielding a large carrier bag to come through.

I stood to greet her. 'Mrs Davidson, how are you?' I grasped her hand and shook it, offering the seat in front of my desk. Out of the corner of my eye, I saw Hope lingering at the door. 'Thanks, Hope,' I said, smiling, hoping she would get the hint. After a few seconds, she turned to leave, and I closed the office door.

'Please call me Judith,' Mrs Davidson began. 'I wanted to

come in and thank you personally. We were on the market with Osbornes for over three months without an offer. A couple of weeks with you and it's sold. I wished we'd come to you first.'

I let the warmth flood through me, I adored this part of my job.

'You're most welcome. I'm pleased; the Barons seem like a lovely family and I'm sure they'll treat your home with the love and respect it deserves. It'll be in safe hands.'

'I agree. I didn't want to sell it to that developer for him to chew up and spit out.' Mrs Davidson wrinkled her nose, then reached into her carrier bag, producing an enormous traybake covered with vanilla icing and sprinkles. She pushed it across the table towards me and I inhaled the sugar fumes from my chair. 'I made this for the office, as a token of my appreciation.'

'That's so kind of you, thank you. It looks delicious. I can see it being devoured today.'

Mrs Davidson stood to leave, and I followed suit, slipping my hand into my pocket for the flyer I'd taken from Gary's drawer yesterday evening.

'Mrs Davidson – Judith, before you go, can you tell me if this is the same flyer you received through your door?'

Mrs Davidson took the paper out of my hand to examine it. 'Yes, we received a good ten or fifteen of them, one came every day!' Mrs Davidson's voice raised an octave as she relived the stress that first brought her into see us.

'Okay, well they certainly weren't sanctioned by me. So, I'll be investigating who took it upon themselves to do a bit of DIY marketing.' I pursed my lips and Mrs Davidson chuckled.

'Well, I'll leave that in your capable hands, dear.'

When Mrs Davidson left, I sat reeling: 32 Park Lane was targeted because of its history. Someone knew that was where the *gathering* had been held and they were keen for Whites to sell it. I had no idea why, but it had to be connected. Everything was pointing to that night, but I was still clueless as to the reason it was being dragged up. Hopefully Becca, Robyn and Mark would be able to shed some light on it at the weekend. I wasn't looking forward to going over ancient history, but at the same time I was keen to get to the bottom of this.

I wanted to get out of the office, so I took the template of the flyer I usually used to the printers and ordered a hundred. The weather was fine, and I used the walk to clear my head which seemed so jumbled. The real flyer boasted: 'Whites has sold a property in your area' and it always helped to bring in some interest. As I posted leaflets through letter boxes in Park Lane, my mind wandered back to 1997. What could have happened to create so much resentment and why now after twenty years?

Returning to the office, my head still a jumble of paranoia and self-doubt, Hope was grinning insanely, practically bouncing in her seat. Lucy stood beside her, a similar expression on her face.

'What?' I asked.

'Go and see what's on your desk?' Lucy said, beaming.

Frank chortled and tutted at the girls.

My face flushed; I knew they had been talking about me while I was out.

'Someone's keen,' Frank said, leaning against the door frame. On my desk was a bouquet of yellow roses that had to be from James. I glowed pink.

'Back to work,' I chided, trying to hide the grin that was spreading its way across my face. I closed the office door and picked up the bouquet, the flowers smelt divine. I pulled the tiny white envelope from the wrapping. It was nice to find one envelope I wasn't afraid to open. But I couldn't be more wrong.

I dropped the card as though it was a burning-hot poker I'd been made to hold. It fluttered to the desk as I stumbled back into my chair. I put my head in my hands. On the card, accusingly written in thick black capitals:

HE NEVER SENT HER FLOWERS!

Who, for fuck's sake? Who never sent who flowers? Whatever sick game I was being dragged into, I wasn't going to play along any more. I launched the flowers into the bin but then changed my mind and picked them out again. It would be too difficult to explain why I was chucking them to the rest of the team.

'Gary, can I borrow you a second,' I said, my voice slightly too high. I waited for him to come through the door before closing it firmly and returning to lean on my desk. I gripped the table, knuckles translucent, the vein on my forehead throbbing.

'What's up?' he asked, waiting patiently as I tried to articulate what I wanted to say.

'Who never sent who flowers?' I snapped, keeping my voice low so the others wouldn't hear.

Gary's bottom lip protruded slightly.

'I'm sorry?' He maintained eye contact, not resembling a man who was trying to evade detection.

'This card – do you know what it means?' I eyeballed him, unable to appease the rage bubbling inside me.

'I have no idea what you're talking about. I'm sorry, Sophie, but I can't help you,' he moved towards the door, a hand on the handle, ready to leave. No doubt thinking I'd lost the plot. Maybe I had? Gary didn't seem to know anything about the flowers.

'Keep this between us please,' I instructed, before he left the room. I was sure now that he had nothing to do with it. You couldn't fake the genuine surprise on his face, but he was surely wondering what on earth was wrong with me.

I was powerless. Unable to stop the victimisation. What did

they want? How could I change what happened twenty years ago? If it was about that, what was I being punished for?

I picked up the phone and dialled the florist from the logo brandished on the card. It was a local number; I'd used them before. I enquired about the order and asked the owner to tell me as much as she could.

'Well, it was an odd one really. Order was put through our door yesterday morning before we opened, handwritten request with cash in the envelope, instructions to be delivered today. We don't normally get them like that which is why I remember.'

'Did you keep the note?'

'Umm, I'm not sure, I'll have to have a look.' I could tell the florist was getting bored of my questions and wanted off the phone.

'Did they leave a name?' I pushed.

'Yes, there was a name on the note, but due to data protection I can't tell you that.'

'Please, I beg you. Someone is stalking me. I'm going to take this to the police, but I need to know.' The florist paused, now I had her full attention. She was considering whether I was worth taking the risk. I kept quiet, not wanting to push my luck.

'It didn't come from me okay? The sign-off on the note was Dixon.'

The phone trembled in my hand as I thanked the florist and disconnected the call. I stared again at the roses, the blood draining from my face. Dixon, that was Gareth's surname. How could Gareth have sent the flowers if he was dead?

18

Walking away from 32 Park Lane was strange. Eight of us arrived together just over an hour before but only six of us left. Hayley and Gareth were nowhere to be seen. I double-checked every room in the house before I locked up, scanning every corner and cupboard with my torch as I didn't want to turn any lights on, not wanting the neighbours to see the house occupied. I was wary in case they were hiding, ready to jump out, but I wasn't really expecting them to. Neither Hayley or Gareth were the practical-joke type. But the house was empty; I made sure it was left in the same state as when we'd arrived. No one would be any the wiser we'd borrowed the property for a couple of hours. I'd be grounded forever if my dad knew I'd taken keys from the office.

We sneaked out onto the street, as quiet as mice, shielded by nightfall as we made our way along the road. Elliot handed out the last of Gareth's cigarettes for us to share and we swapped chewing gum to get rid of the smell. Ready to face our parents when we got home. The mood was weird, the air electric, everyone chipping in with theories as to what might have happened to Gareth and Hayley. Grasping onto the drama to avoid talking about the night's exploits. No one wanted to kiss and tell, at least not tonight.

'Maybe they've eloped,' James said deadpan. It was the first joke I'd heard him crack; ever. If it was a joke?

'Nah, I reckon he bottled it,' Mark sniggered, Becca's hand wrapped in his. Were they going out now?

'Maybe Hayley changed her mind?' Robyn suggested, tucking a blonde strand behind her ear.

'Yes, but, where are they?' I sounded rattled, unable to keep my voice from wavering. Even if I'd changed my mind, I would still have waited around for the others. Pretended I'd gone through with it; for an easy life. To avoid the ribbing from everyone else for chickening out. My stomach felt hollow and I jumped as a car revved its engine driving past.

Elliot eyed me; bemused as to why I was getting so agitated. I hadn't told him about my encounter with Gareth in the kitchen.

'What do you want to do?' he asked, leaning in so the others wouldn't hear. It was funny, we were walking in our designated pairs. Glued together for the night, two by two marching along the road.

'There's nothing we can do. We can't go and knock for them; what if they haven't gone home? I don't want to get anyone in trouble.'

Elliot put his arm around me and squeezed me against him before releasing his grip. I almost asked him to leave it there. It felt nice. I could get used to it, the affection. I looked at Elliot differently now and I wondered if he felt the same about me? Would he ask me out? Now that we'd done it once, would he want to do it again? I knew I did.

'Don't worry, they'll be fine. Gareth's probably walking Hayley home right now.'

I wanted to believe him, but I was positive I'd seen him walk away from the house earlier. And if it was Gareth I saw, he was alone, so where was Hayley?

'I'll call her in the morning,' Robyn offered and I felt myself relax a little.

When we got back to the postbox, we stood for a second before saying goodbye. No one spoke of the transformation; the change we'd all been through in the two hours since we were last there, at the same exact spot. The lads slapped each other on the back, and I hugged Becca and Robyn, promising them we'd talk tomorrow.

Elliot insisted on walking me around the back of the estate agents, to my door, which resulted in a few smirks and raised eyebrows. It was twenty past nine, so I'd made it back on time. There would be no reprimand from my dad to contend with as long as I could get the key back unnoticed. When we reached the back of the estate agents, a few feet from the front door of the flat, I checked I still had the Park Lane key, as well as my own. It was there, cold metal in the depths of my pocket.

'Here, could you get rid of this on your way home?' I said, handing him the condom wrapper, concealed in my fist.

'Sure,' he shoved the evidence into his pocket. 'I guess I'll see you at school yeah?' He shuffled from foot to foot, waiting for me to answer.

'Sure.'

A warm smile spread across his face; it was infectious. My lips tingled, the imprint of our kisses still fresh.

'We're good though, yeah?' his eyes wide and expectant.

'Yes, we're good,' I replied, beaming back at him.

He leant in to give me a quick peck on the cheek, then turned on his heels back towards the direction of the group. Who knew Elliot could be so sweet? We weren't due back at school until

Wednesday and the last two days of the school holidays stretched out in front of me. Two more days of freedom and I intended to do as little as possible.

I called out to my parents, announcing I was home, as I went past the lounge. Making a beeline straight for my room. They were watching an action movie, a car chase with lots of screeching tyres played out on the screen. I shoved the sleeping bag into the airing cupboard on route, weird it would forever be integral to the loss of my innocence. Slipping into comfy pyjamas, relieved to be alone, I laid on my bed staring at the ceiling, replaying the night's events when there was a single knock on the door.

'You okay, love?' Mum poked her head in.

'Yeah, fine,' I replied, hoping she would go away so I could get back to working out what I was going to do about Gareth.

'Oh, okay, you didn't say hello that's all. I just wanted to make sure you were all right,' she said, her face retreating from view as she slid the door shut.

'Sorry, Mum, I did say hello, but I don't think you heard me. I'm fine, just tired, so I'm going to bed,' I answered, guilt niggling at my side.

'Okay, night.'

'Love you.'

Her soft footsteps padded downstairs. I thought about having a shower, my groin ached, but it would be unusual, and my parents would ask why.

I switched my radio on to fill the silence. 'Bitch' by Meredith Brooks boomed out of the speaker, smarting my ears, and I thrust the volume down. Was it a sign? Was I a bitch for leaving Hayley? Should we have tried to find her? Walked to her house, to see if she was inside? My mind ran around in circles, frustrated I wouldn't know anything until tomorrow when I'd be able to ring her. It was too late to make the call now; I was sure her father would tell her off. Sleep wasn't going to be easy. I had visions of my dad bursting in to tell me Hayley hadn't arrived home. Gareth could look after himself, but Hayley, alone at night, wandering the streets? The thought made me shiver and I snuggled into my duvet.

Had I made a mistake, leaving it that way with Gareth? The look on his face when I went upstairs, he seemed wounded. Did he want to be more than friends? What if he never went into the den after I left him? What if Hayley was waiting in the dark for him and he never came? Suddenly I didn't feel grown-up at all. I was a kid, one who wanted to go downstairs, cuddle with her mum and share her fears. It was my fault.

Maybe they got the deed over and done with, then quickly left to go home? But that wasn't the plan. It wasn't what we agreed when we talked it through last night, sitting on my bedroom floor. We'd planned to regroup afterwards. It hadn't happened that way in the end, we'd run out of time, but Hayley didn't know that. She'd just disappeared.

A surge of annoyance stung me like a wasp. I should be revelling in this milestone, reliving the evening in my head and marvelling at how well I handled my first sexual experience. Instead I was worrying about them, but there was nothing I could do now.

I set my alarm for five in the morning. I had to return the key for Park Lane back to my dad's desk and I knew he wouldn't be up for work until seven. It gave me plenty of time to put the key back and get to sleep before the sun rose.

My legs twitched, nerves firing, sending unwanted signals around my system. None of which were compatible with sleep. I rolled onto my side, stretching out. Powerless to do anything tonight, I had to wait until tomorrow, but I couldn't shift the lingering feeling of dread. Something bad had happened and, whatever it was, it was all my fault.

19

OCTOBER 2018

My hands shook and I laid them flat on my desk to keep them still. Someone was impersonating Gareth, using him to get to me. Why? What had I done? Mum said there was another car involved in Gareth's death. Was it on purpose? Have they found that vehicle? So many questions whirled around my head.

I waited impatiently for everyone to leave so I could do some investigating of my own. Before they did, I endured an excruciating conversation with Gary who came to see if I was all right before he went. He must have thought I'd had an episode of sorts or was on the way to a breakdown. I had to explain that someone was leaving me strange messages, but I played it down, so he thought I was more frustrated than scared. He didn't pry but asked if he could help, which was sweet. I gratefully declined, the fewer people knew, the better. I wasn't one to air my dirty laundry in public.

Once everyone had left for the day and I'd locked up, I called my mum. She spent ten minutes telling me about the picturesque pub her and Dad found today, where they'd stopped in for a ploughman's. Retirement sounded like a dream! In the end, I had to interrupt for fear of being there all night.

'Mum, I wanted to talk to you about Gareth. What did Sue tell you about how he died?'

Mum paused to remember. I could almost hear her brain whirring from here. 'She said he'd been run off the road by a Volkswagen going around a bend and they hadn't caught the driver.'

'Do you know if that's still the case?' I asked, hoping there might have been a development.

'No, well, I haven't heard anything, but I haven't spoken to Sue this week. Listen, do you want to bring that nice James to lunch on Sunday?' I rolled my eyes, sure an invite to my parents' for Sunday lunch would frighten him off.

'I'll see what he's doing, Mum.'

I spent another five minutes giving her instructions on how to log on to the email account I'd set up for her a few months ago so she could send some old photos of Gareth to Sue, before I said goodbye.

Outside, it was dark and chilly, since October had arrived the temperature had plummeted and we'd gone from having the air con on to the heating. I disliked sitting in the office when it was dark outside – you were on full display to the street. They could see in, but you couldn't see out. Illuminated like a Christmas tree for your every move to be watched, although there wasn't much footfall past the office after six o'clock. It gave me the shivers. At least in the winter, when the sun set earlier, I wasn't there alone.

I opened a search engine and typed in Gareth Dixon. Numerous hits dotted the screen but not what I was looking for. I typed in Gareth Dixon – death – Volkswagen and got a hit straight away from the *St. Albans Review*, a local paper. The article was reporting the initial crash, that a man had died, and police wanted to speak to the driver of a blue Volkswagen. I'd seen that before. I scrolled down, but there was no further information. Nothing I didn't already know. I switched off my machine and stood to collect my things.

Suddenly there was a loud crash into the glass of the front window, causing it to shake and me to stumble back into my chair. The noise reverberated around the office. How it didn't shatter, I don't know. I stared out into the darkness, unable to see anything. I unlocked the door to go outside and investigate, the bell jangling over the thudding of my heart, which echoed in my ears. The light outside was fading, not yet completely dark, but I couldn't see anyone around. The road was empty. On the pavement lay a water balloon, which I guess someone had thrown at the window hoping it would burst.

'Fucking kids,' I muttered, picking it up. Before realising it was a condom.

I wrinkled my nose and held it at arm's-length as I went back inside, locking the door behind me. I stabbed the condom in the kitchen sink to release the liquid and tossed the disgusting thing in the bin, washing my hands twice. No one had ever thrown anything at the office before and Halloween was three weeks away. Had it been meant for me?

I hurried back to my computer and logged onto the camera out front. Slowing down the footage, you could see the condom crash into the window, but whoever had thrown it had been too far away and out of shot. I had no doubt that I was the intended target and my insides coiled up tight.

I wanted to get out of there, out of view, so I quickly shut down my computer and headed upstairs, locking the back door to the office and checking the flat's front door was locked too. Shit, I'd forgotten to ring the glaziers about getting a replacement. It would have to wait until tomorrow.

As I shoved a prepared pack of hunter's chicken in the oven, I dialled James. He answered straight away.

'Hello, gorgeous.'

I grinned at his greeting. 'Boy, am I glad to hear your voice.'

'Shit day?'

I proceeded to tell James about the delivery of flowers and the water-filled condom thrown at the window whilst I was working late.

'Why would they give Gareth's name when sending the flowers, why not just anonymously?'

'I don't know, probably because they guessed I might ask the florist? Whoever did it wanted me to know. It's made me think Gareth's death might not have been an accident.'

'It was an accident,' James said in a voice so stern it sounded like it wasn't up for discussion.

'What do you mean?' His tone had got my back up. I kicked off my high heels, one of them bouncing off the fridge. What did he know that I didn't?

James sighed down the phone. 'His mum told me the inquest reported that he was twice over the legal alcohol limit. Yes, maybe there was another car involved, but if anything, it sounds like it was more a case of leaving the scene of an accident than attempted murder. Gareth was driving drunk; the other car may have had nothing to do with it at all.'

My gut heaved as though I'd been punched, the wind knocked out of me. How close were Gareth and James?

'I haven't seen that reported in the press?'

'Have you been digging?' he asked. I remained quiet, unsure how to respond, but James continued. 'Jim knows the editor of the local paper, they used to go banger racing or something when they were kids. He asked him to keep it out of the article.' James sounded exasperated.

I rubbed the back of my neck. Now wasn't the time to mention finding the cards and flyer in Gary's desk. I was positive it wasn't him; well, almost positive. Instead, I changed the subject, which James took as a welcome relief, telling me about his meeting in London with an editor to review an idea for a book he wanted to write. I invited him for dinner on Wednesday, I'd cook steak and asked him if he could fix some deadbolts to a couple of doors.

'I'll bring my drill then.' I didn't fail to notice his sarcasm. Had I overstepped the mark?

'You don't have to, I can ask Frank to loan me his drill,' I retorted, a little stung. Frank would have done it for me if I'd asked, without hesitation.

'I was joking, Soph, of course I'll do it. For steak I'd do almost anything.'

* * *

On Wednesday, James arrived, drill in hand, and I couldn't help but giggle when I answered the door.

'What?' he said, pretending to be offended, looking himself up and down.

'You look like you're about to star in a porn film. All you need is a tash!' I doubled over laughing, the glass of wine I'd had already taking effect.

'Maybe I am.' James wiggled his eyebrows and struck a sexy pose which made my side hurt

We had a lovely meal, I'd managed to cook the steaks to perfection, served with chunky chips and onion rings. We sat back, our stomachs full, talking about our terrible tastes in music. He loved classic eighties rock and my guilty pleasure was cheesy pop.

'I'm serious, S Club 7 were my favourite band.'

I snorted. I hadn't laughed so much in ages, my jaw ached. I hadn't realised how stressed I'd been.

'Right, let me get the drilling done before I have another glass, otherwise I'll put a hole in my hand,' James said, covering his glass as I went to refill it. I'd had three already and had forgotten about the deadbolts.

We hadn't talked about Gareth or the messages and it felt nice to have an evening without it being on my mind. James bringing up the deadbolts reminded me why I needed them. A dark cloud drifted overhead, tainting our time together.

James started to descend the steps to the front door.

'You don't have to worry about that one?'

'Why not?' He turned, drill raised like he was 007.

'I'm getting a new UPVC front door tomorrow.'

'Oh okay.' James frowned up from the gloomy stairwell.

'What's wrong with getting a new door?'

'Nothing, just this one is kind of fitting with the period features.' James tapped the stained beam above his head that featured throughout the flat. He traipsed up the stairs, marking where the deadbolt was going on the internal door which led into the kitchen.

'But you're right to get a new one, safety first and all that.' He started to drill, and I felt my shoulders loosen a little. Once the new door was fitted, if someone wanted to get into the flat, they'd have to go through two doors, one with a deadbolt.

Once he'd finished, we got through a second bottle of wine and went to bed. James was happy to stay over as he didn't have a lot on the next day. He'd written most of his column and was waiting on it being signed off.

In the middle of the night, around two a.m., I woke thinking I'd heard a noise somewhere in the flat. Disorientated, I sat up, James oblivious to my movement. Had I heard something or was it James's snoring that had woken me? He sounded like a train; it wasn't something I was used to.

I climbed out of bed, trying not to disturb him, mouth gaping like a fish struggling for air, and slipped down to the kitchen. I switched on the under-cupboard lights, enough to give out a dull glow, and filled a glass with water before sitting at the table.

I could hear James above my head, the rhythmic sound getting louder with each snore. His phone lay on the table, discarded as we'd made our way to bed a few hours earlier. Eyeing it curiously, I felt a pinch of conscience as I reached for it. Feeling its weight in my hand. I bit my lip. Did I want to go down this road? Did I want to pry into James's life? The answer was no, but I had to be sure about him.

I pressed the screen to see if it was on. It came to life, illuminating the room and stinging my eyes. Unable to get past the home screen which requested the passcode or thumbprint, I pushed it away. A twinge of guilt made my stomach clench. I wasn't usually such a snooper. My eyes strayed to his wallet on the side with his keys. I wasn't sure what I was hoping to find, but once the idea took hold, I couldn't stop myself.

I flicked open the wallet, the creased black leather bulging. Comforted by James's snoring upstairs and no longer irritated; the last thing I wanted was to be caught going through his things. What did that make me? It wasn't the most honest way to start a relationship and I didn't really think he was behind any of it, but once I'd looked, I'd be able to put it out of my mind. I liked him, I really liked him, and we got on well. Maybe, in time, things could get serious between us?

There was nothing in the card holder that caused me concern. All the credit and debit cards were in his name. No membership cards to any dodgy fetish clubs or strip bars. There were a few receipts, nothing of any relevance at first, until I found a photo which made my heart lurch. It was of James, his arm wrapped around a beautiful redhead, laughing at whoever was taking the picture. They both looked so happy and my chest twinged.

I turned the photo over and saw H2013 on the back written in blue biro; 2013 was obvious, but who was H? I looked again at the photo. Could it be Hayley? I struggled to remember what colour eyes Hayley had. Were they green or grey? The woman in the photo had green eyes, pale skin and freckles across her nose. It could easily have been Hayley, she was a redhead, but I couldn't be positive. The nose didn't seem right, though. I remembered Hayley's being larger and more roman in shape; but we were fifteen and still growing into our faces back then. Would I ever be able to make James as happy as he looked there?

I bit down on my molars, rocking my jaw from side to side. I knew James had a younger sister. I thought her name was Maria or Marie, but she was blonde and around nine years younger than us. The girl in the photo looked the same age as James, and I didn't see much of a resemblance to convince me they were siblings.

I closed my eyes, trying to picture the last time I saw Hayley. Wearing a nun's costume of all things. The four of us slow dancing to Robbie Williams at the Halloween party, drunk on spiked punch. The more I looked, the more I didn't believe it was Hayley in the photo, although the initial H had me doubting myself. If it was Hayley, it meant James had been lying about not having seen her. I had no idea what he'd done since 1997. We hadn't really talked about it. It was still early days, we were getting to know each other, and I didn't want to seem like I was prying but now I wondered if he had any skeletons he was hiding.

I sat back in the chair, sighing, wafting the photo in front of me. Suddenly the silence seemed to swallow me up. James wasn't snoring any more. The drone in the background had been replaced by a thudding of floorboards overhead. My fingers fumbled as I stuffed the photo back into the wallet and folded it closed, jumping up from the table and banging my ankle on the table leg. Ouch, shit! No idea if I'd put it back into the right compartment, but there was no time to check.

'You okay?' James's voice came from behind me as I rinsed my glass at the sink. He wrapped a warm arm around my waist and planted a kiss on my neck.

'I am now,' I replied as James pressed his groin into my behind and I felt a surge of desire. I turned around to face him, standing in only his boxer shorts. 'I wanted to get a drink and I kept thinking I could hear noises,' I admitted with a nervous giggle.

'Come back to bed,' he said with a grin and led me back upstairs.

* * *

The glaziers fitted the new door in less than an hour. The wooden one was ripped out and replaced by a bright red composite door with a diamond-shaped pane of frosted glass. It was only when I stood by the door, it hit me how badly fitted the old one was. To be fair, it had been our front door for as long as I could remember, over thirty years. I couldn't feel any draughts coming from the outside with the new door closed and I hoped my heating bill would show a difference over the coming months. The most important thing, though, was safety, I had a new key and a five-point locking system. No one was coming into my home without being invited now.

I hadn't asked James about the photograph. How could I without admitting I'd been going through his things? I desperately wanted to trust him. When we were together, he was kind and funny with a caring side to him I hadn't seen in school. But I was keeping more and more from him, unable to be sure whom I could trust. I had no one to talk to, no one to confide in.

Hope picked up on my low mood that afternoon. She insisted we all went for a drink to celebrate her first sale. It was a two-bed flat by the park and she'd got an offer accepted from a first-time buyer who commuted into London. Her excitement was palpable, and she bounced around the office like a puppy. The buzz of a sale made the whole office buoyant. I was happy for the distraction and the excuse to buy the team a few drinks after work.

'So, you and this fella getting serious then?' she asked, her words taking on a slur. Hope had demolished half a bottle of wine in an hour and was motoring her way through her fourth glass. I'd abandoned trying to pace myself, watching the others get rowdier. Phil, the landlord, was used to it.

'Well, not serious as such, but it's going all right. What about you, I never asked, have you got a boyfriend?'

'God no. I can't fucking stand men,' Hope shrieked and burst out laughing.

I was taken aback at her ferocity. She sounded like she truly meant it.

Gary piped up, coming to the defence of the male population and how the world wouldn't exist without them.

Frank took his chance and made his excuses to leave. I rolled my eyes at him, in a 'what the hell am I still doing here' expression.

'Enjoy,' he whispered, kissing me on the head before disappearing out of the door. He'd told me before, he was 'getting too old for this shit'.

'Are you into girls then?' Gary sniggered into his glass.

Without hesitation, Hope threw the remnants of her wine in his lap. Thankfully there wasn't a lot in the glass, but I jumped between them, fearing Gary would blow.

'Right, I think that's enough, time to call it a day,' I said, handing Gary a napkin.

He ignored me, pushing past Hope, knocking the table as he went. Our glasses wobbled and Gary's half-full pint sloshed over the side. He grabbed his jacket and strode out of the pub. I was sure I heard him mutter 'crazy bitch' under his breath as he went.

To be fair, it was a stupid question. It wasn't politically correct to be asking anyone what their sexual orientation was. Hope drained his pint before laughing hysterically. I helped her outside and called a cab. I didn't want to take her back to my flat this time. I didn't want to be cleaning up her sick, which looked like an inevitable end to her evening. I was her boss not her mother.

We sat on the wall outside waiting for the cab to come. I sneaked into the off-licence and bought a packet of cigarettes and a lighter. Hope joined me in having one. She didn't seem so jovial any more, perhaps the air had sobered her up or was making her feel worse.

'Gary's right you know. I am gay,' Hope said, taking a long drag on her cigarette.

'You didn't have to tell me that, you know. It's no one's business but your own. But I'm flattered that you did,' I said, touched that she'd trusted me enough to tell me something so private.

Silence between us stretched out, no one wanting to break it.

'My dad wasn't a good man,' Hope said eventually.

The sentence hung in the air as we continued to smoke. It was awkward, I was unsure what to say. Hope didn't look as though she needed comforting and I didn't want to overstep any boundaries.

'I'm sorry, Hope.'

'What is your dad like?' Hope asked, her eyes wide. I could tell she wanted me to tell her he wasn't that great either. For us to have that in common.

'My dad is lovely.' I said, not wanting to go into detail. Not wanting to rub it in. Hope looked at the ground, flicking her ash on the curb.

'I guess I'm one of the lucky ones.' I said to fill the silence stretching out between us. Hope's head snapped up and she threw her cigarette into the road

'Some people are luckier than others, some people have it all, their whole lives. They get everything they want. They choose, they take, they steal if they have to and the rest of us, well, we have to pick up the pieces, the trash that's left behind.' Hope began to cry, her shoulders shaking.

I put my arm around her unsure what else to do.

Fortunately, the cab arrived then and Hope wiped her eyes on the sleeve of her jacket, smearing black mascara across her cheeks.

'Will you be okay?' I asked, putting my hand on her shoulder. Uneasy after her outburst that she was going home alone.

'I'll be fine.' She shrugged off my hand and got into the cab; it pulled away and she didn't give me a second glance out the window.

21

The alarm catapulted me out of bed and I shuffled downstairs like a zombie. Thankful I didn't have to drag myself far to work. Dad quipped how he was 'never late' or 'his commute had been fine' to anyone who enquired where he lived in reference to the office. I envied my friends who had normal houses with gardens, but my parents countered that there was a park practically at the end of the road that I could use any time.

Whites Estate Agents had always been home from home; the kitchenette at the back with its humming fridge; and plush leather chairs behind walnut-coloured desks. Over the years, they'd been adorned with card rolodex systems and typewriters with carbon copy paper; later evolving to computers, digital data-bases and printers. Sometimes I had to show Dad how to work them. He was great at selling houses but not so great with tech-nology. Luckily, he had Frank for that.

I adored the enormous glass front with what seemed like hundreds of property particulars, hung like decorations to entice passers-by. Every year at Christmas I'd get busy with baubles and tinsel. Dad used to say it looked more like Santa's grotto than an office, but I loved doing it more than our own tree upstairs. The office door even had the original bell which jangled as it opened, something I'd always loved when I was little.

I knew I shouldn't go into the office, not when my parents weren't there. This morning was no different. I'd taken the key from the hook in the kitchen and crept down the staircase in bare feet, trying not to make any noise on the hard wood floor. I knew which stairs creaked and which didn't. The trick was to stay close to the wall. Dad had often talked of getting an alarm fitted as burglaries had been on the rise, but because we didn't have a safe and no money was kept there, it seemed pointless.

Just like when I took the key for Park Lane, it only took a few minutes to put it back. Although I almost had a heart attack when I heard the creak of a floorboard overhead, as I was unlocking the desk. I panicked and dropped the tiny key, which bounced away from me and I had to crawl around on my hands and knees to find it in the shadows. Once I had it, I moved fast, slipping the key back in the box and returning the hidden panel. I climbed the stairs two at a time, my heart hammering in my chest. I paused at the top and strained my ears, reluctant to open the door. Was anyone up? Where had the noise come from?

Suddenly, the door swung open and a harsh yellow light blinded me. My foot slipped away from the top stair, arms flailing as I tried to regain my balance, but a hand caught my wrist and hauled me up.

'Jesus, Sophie, what the hell are you doing down here? We thought we had burglars.' Dad loomed over me and tears pricked my eyes as pain shot up my leg. I'd knocked my shin on the stair as Dad stopped me from falling. I'd had such a fright; I nearly threw up on his slippers as my brain scrambled for a plausible lie.

'I... I thought I heard someone too. I came to get a drink, but I heard a noise.' It wasn't the best excuse, but it was all I could come up with at short notice.

Dad's face was a mass of lines. Frown lines, wrinkles and even the ones imbedded from your pillowcase after laying on it all night. He still looked half asleep.

'Stay there,' he said, softer now and, moving me aside, he descended the stairs, shining the torch. The same one I had put back under the sink last night. I quickly slipped into the kitchen and put the office key back on its hook, returning to wait in the doorway for him to reappear, shivering as the draught wafted from below. I felt like I was going to be found out any second. Dad would read my mind and I'd be done for. He never really went mad; Mum was more of a shouter than he was. But when I'd disappointed him, when he'd look at me with nothing to say, chewing his lip, it felt like an arrow had been shot straight into my heart. I preferred being told off by Mum.

A minute or two later, I heard him thud back up the stairs.

'Are you sure you heard something?'

'Yes, Dad, but it was probably a fox or something.' I didn't know what foxes sounded like, but I'd heard my parents talk about the ones who ran amuck after dark, knocking over bins and screeching.

'Maybe. Get your drink and go on back to bed. I've got to get up for work in a couple of hours,' he yawned, rubbing his eyes. With trembling hands, I filled a beaker with water and took it back to my room. Letting out an enormous sigh once I'd closed my door and heard the latch on my parents' door click shut a second later. Adrenaline coursed through my veins, my body on fire like I'd run a marathon. That was close. Too close. If I'd been caught, I would have been grounded for at least a month with no television and no pocket money. I could see it now, Dad fixing another lock to the door of the office so I wouldn't be able to get in again, shaking his head in disgust. I shuddered, it didn't bear thinking about, especially if he found out why I was there.

I didn't go back to sleep. I was too jumpy and couldn't stop thinking about Hayley, wishing the hours would go by quickly so I could phone her. I distracted myself watching cartoons on the television with the sound low until I heard my parents get up.

'What are you doing today?' my mum asked as she spread peanut butter on my toast. I sat at the table waiting for it to be delivered, my stomach grumbling alongside the dull ache in my groin.

'Not sure, probably just hanging out here. Might go to the park later,' I replied.

'Last couple of days off, make the most of it.' Dad took some paracetamol out of a packet on the table and knocked two back with a gulp of tea.

'Headache, Dad?' I asked.

'Yep, a corker. But no rest for the wicked. Office opens in a bit.' He grinned his best salesman smile at me. It was infectious.

Today was the first of September. A new month, a new week and a new me. I showered and got dressed, staring in the mirror at the now more mature Sophie White looking back. Did Elliot feel the same way? Was he thinking about me as he brushed his teeth? Would he want to do it again? With me? Did I still want to now, the day after? With practice, it would get better, wouldn't it?

I couldn't wait to hear what Robyn and Becca had to say, but before that I needed to get hold of Hayley.

I left it until half nine before I rang. Mum and Dad were in the office and I had the flat to myself. The phone rang around ten times and I was about to hang up when a tiny voice answered.

'Hello?'

'Hayley?' I asked, almost positive it was her, but I didn't want to say too much in case it was her mum.

'Sophie?'

'God, Hayley, I've been so worried. Are you okay?'

'What do you mean?' her voice quivered.

'Well, where did you go last night? Fuck, we were all worried. You and Gareth both disappeared.'

The line went quiet and I heard a sniff. I'd gone too far.

'Hayley, I'm sorry. I was panicking, you know.'

'Why? Because I was with Gareth and you weren't? It's you he wanted, you know, not me.' Another sniff. Hayley was crying now.

My mouth fell, unsure what to say. She filled the silence before I could.

'Nothing happened. I went home okay. Listen I have to go, Mum's waiting.'

I heard a click and the line went dead.

I stared at the phone, a lump in my throat and my legs unsteady. Replacing the receiver, I sat, slumped over the kitchen table, head in my hands.

'Oh Gareth, what did you do?'

Gary apologised to Hope at work the next day. I saw him pull her aside, eyes darting at anything but her, full of remorse. He handed her a box of Quality Street, which she graciously accepted before waving away his apology. A second later, I heard them laugh about how drunk they were. All was forgiven, and I was pleased. A happy working environment was top priority for me. I couldn't have any issues in my team, and I told Gary so when we were alone. He was embarrassed about his behaviour, but I didn't think it would happen again.

Because of the leaflet dropping, we had two new instructions, so I sent Frank and Hope to one and Gary and Lucy to the other. I was happy to stay behind with Beth and manage the office. James called to say he'd booked the Metropole hotel in Brighton and if I checked Facebook, I'd see he'd created an event for Saturday night that everyone had responded to. We were meeting the others in All Bar One at eight. I said I was looking forward to it, but my head was still thumping from last night's overindulgence. We all felt the same so at lunchtime, when Frank returned, I went to the bakery to buy sausage rolls. Hoping the grease would help our hangovers, so we could get through the day.

'It all kicked off last night then?' Frank asked as I retrieved some napkins and plates from the kitchen.

'Not really, just a tiny squabble. Hope was mullered and Gary wasn't too far behind. It was a bit heavy for a school night.'

'Gary said something weird to me the other day, I meant to mention it to you.'

'Oh?' Frank had got my attention and I turned to look at him, putting the plates I was holding onto the counter.

'Yeah, he was asking how long you'd owned the office, how long your parents had been here, that kind of thing.'

I frowned at Frank, that wasn't odd. Maybe he wanted to know more about the history of Whites?

'He said, "Sophie lives upstairs, doesn't she?" so I told him you did. Then he says, if someone broke in, would they be able to get to her by coming through the office?'

I opened my mouth to speak, but Gary swung open the kitchen door.

'I'm starving, can I grab the plates?' he asked with a grin, taking the pile of plates from the counter and disappearing back into the office.

Frank raised his eyebrows at me, and I swallowed the lump that had formed in my throat.

'It might be nothing, but I'm glad you've got that new door.' Frank patted my shoulder as he passed.

I shivered, the hair on my arms bristling. Maybe Gary didn't mean anything by it? Some people come out with all sorts of bizarre things. It didn't necessarily make them dangerous. I'd never felt apprehensive when alone with him, in the office or outside of it. He'd never caused me concern with body language or something he'd said. Although Frank's words, combined with the cards I'd found in his drawer, made me nervous. Maybe I'd been too quick to clear him?

* * *

When Saturday afternoon arrived, James knocked on my new front door, ready to whisk me off to Brighton for the night. Robyn said her girlfriend Chloe worked at the Waggon & Horses and would pick her up after her shift. It was a short taxi ride home for Becca and Mark as they lived in Hove, but we had the furthest to travel. I was looking forward to being away from the flat and the pull of something other than a roast for Sunday lunch. James had suggested fish and chips on the beach and with that I was sold. I loved the seaside and always felt calmer watching the waves crash on the shore. Every time I went, I told myself I would visit more often, but then I never did.

It would be brilliant to see everyone again, but I was also anxious about bringing up the messages I'd received. James told me he'd received another note. He handed it to me as he started the engine, just as I was clicking my seatbelt into place, instantly putting a dampener on our trip. The note was much like the first, but the paper had a pretty border of cherries. Same block hand-writing, in the centre:

YOU DID NOTHING

James shrugged it off, but I couldn't. It was escalating. Whoever was doing it was getting angrier. I could feel the venom in the words.

'You did nothing? What does that mean? Did someone get hurt and none of us helped?'

'I don't know, God it was so long ago, I can't even remember.'

James thrust the car into gear and accelerated hard. I lurched back in my seat. James gripped the steering wheel tightly, his arms straight. I stared out of the window at the grey skyline whizzing past.

'Did Gareth never mention what happened with Hayley that night?' I asked.

'No, he never wanted to talk about it, and we didn't ask again. We all assumed he'd bottled it and gone home. We didn't bring it up; in case he was embarrassed. He was a mate.' James sniffed.

'When you last met him, did you go to St. Albans? Did he seem okay? Had he had any messages?'

'Yeah, I went up there, but no, he didn't say anything about any messages. He seemed fine, happy.'

He didn't want to discuss it any more, although it hung over me like a raincloud. I didn't want to ruin the day or James's mood as I knew he was looking forward to seeing Mark. He wasn't nearly as concerned about the notes as I was. Was it because he was sending them? Did he show me the card to throw me off course? It seemed like a smart thing to do, if he was behind it. Or did I see them as more of a threat than he did, because I was a female living on my own and therefore vulnerable? My mind was happy to play tricks on me. But if I really believed James was behind it, I wouldn't be travelling to Brighton with him. If only I could eradicate the doubt I had, which I seemed to have about everybody.

* * *

We checked in to the Metropole hotel and left our overnight bags, to take a stroll around the Lanes. It was easy to spend hours pottering around Brighton, window shopping. I bought a ceramic trinket box for my mum that was too beautiful to resist. We perused a jeweller full of handmade costume pieces and James picked out a necklace for me to try with an intricate woven pendant. Once I had it on, he insisted he bought it and from there he took my hand as we walked along the cobbled street; as though the act had cemented our relationship. I pushed the earlier thoughts from my mind, determined to enjoy the moment. I had to be wrong about James.

Later, when he came out of the shower and I had dressed for dinner, he secured the necklace back around my neck.

'You look gorgeous.'

'Thank you. You don't scrub up so bad yourself,' I replied. I loved Brighton, you could go out wearing anything and no one would bat an eyelid. The people that lived and partied there were such an eclectic mix, you'd never look out of place. I'd chosen a leather skirt and silk blouse with skyscraper heels, hoping I'd be able to walk in them later after copious amounts of wine. James's eyes bulged when he saw them, but I wasn't sure if he thought they were sexy or whether he was more concerned it might make me taller than him.

We met Robyn, Mark and Becca in Donatella's, an Italian restaurant. They were easing off their coats when we arrived a few minutes after seven. We hugged and kissed in greeting; Mark and James fell into a back-slapping hug and from the outset the banter, that was once created by Elliot, was in full flow.

'This is long overdue isn't it. How long's it been?' asked Mark, beaming at us around the table as the waitress delivered our second round of drinks.

'2016 wasn't it, when I bumped into you in Pitcher and Piano?' James said.

'Ha, yeah. Seems like longer than that. You were pretty wasted if I remember.'

James laughed. My stomach rumbled and I prayed our mains wouldn't be long. I needed some carbs to soak up the alcohol.

'It's a shame we're missing Gareth, Elliot and Hayley,' Robyn said.

'To absent friends.' Mark raised his glass and we all followed suit, taking large mouthfuls of our drinks. The conversation turned to Elliot in Australia and moved naturally on to Gareth and his 'terrible accident'. I kept my opinion to myself; regardless of the amount of alcohol involved, the police wouldn't have named another vehicle if it hadn't been integral to the accident. I wasn't about to push my theory onto anyone else, in fact I'd decided not to mention it at all. Positive if anyone around the table had received cards or anything to do with that night, they would bring it up. But it was taken out of my hands when James mentioned it as everyone was tucking into their mains.

'You know the *party*?'

'The Halloween party?' Becca replied, twirling spaghetti around her fork.

'No, the *other* party, I mean gathering, you know *that* night,' James emphasised the word and to my surprise I saw Robyn pull a face. I'd momentarily forgotten; there were two of us at the table who'd slept with James now.

'What about it? Because I don't think Robyn is up for a trip down memory lane,' Mark said, a smirk forming on his face.

Robyn gave him a whack and I was surprised to see James's cheeks flush a little.

'Went so well I started dating women,' Robyn joked and winked at James.

'Ha ha,' he conceded before continuing, 'well, Sophie's been receiving messages about it.'

'You have too,' I shot back, cross at being thrown under the bus.

'Yes, sorry, I have as well, two actually. We wondered if you'd had anything sent to you recently?' James said, putting his hand over mine and looking at the others in turn. I wanted to brush it off, but I knew it wouldn't go unnoticed.

'When you say cards?' Robyn asked, fishing for more information.

James was about to reply, but I interrupted him. It hadn't got past me that in a stark contrast to everyone's alcohol glow, Becca had gone deathly pale.

'Becca, are you okay?'

'I have,' she replied, 'I got one last week.'

23

From Mark's grave expression, it was obvious he knew nothing of it. He manoeuvred his whole body around to his wife, eyes narrowed.

'What card?'

'It had cherries on it,' Becca whispered.

'What did it say?' James asked.

'I didn't understand it at the time, thought it was for someone else. I didn't think it was what you were talking about over lunch.' Becca glanced at me, her eyes damp.

'What did it say?' Mark interrupted, an urgency in his voice that wasn't there before. He was as in the dark as the rest of us.

'It read "she wasn't as lucky as you", but I had no idea it was about that night. I didn't think about the cherries on the front.'

'I was the same, I didn't get the cherry meaning straight away either,' I said, trying to comfort Becca, who looked like a rabbit caught in the headlights.

'Was the envelope handwritten?' I asked and Becca nodded.

'Hand-delivered?' James added.

Becca's eyes looked watery as she nodded again.

After a minute or so, James picked up his fork and began to move food around his plate. We followed suit, although everyone's appetite appeared to have diminished.

'Has there been more, since what you told us last time?' Robyn asked me, eyes glaring.

I told them about the flowers, my open front door and the condom thrown at the agency window. That I'd recently sold 32 Park Lane, and how someone had been so keen for me to be the one to sell it they'd bombarded the owner with flyers.

'Perhaps they wanted you to go back there? A trip down memory lane,' Robyn suggested.

'Maybe. Someone has an issue with the party, with me, but I have no idea who. I didn't think anyone else knew but us.'

'I didn't tell anyone,' Becca said, affronted.

'Me neither,' Robyn added.

Nods of confirmation around the table followed. It looked as though no one had divulged how we all lost our virginity on the same night, under the same roof.

'Whoever it is knows where we live.' Mark's eyes narrowed and he laid his hand over Becca's on the table. Their gaze met for a second, a comforting exchange.

'It has to be Hayley, who else could it be? Gareth's dead, Elliot's in Oz,' James said.

'Yes, but why and why now?' I asked, my eyes darting around the table.

'Fuck knows, sometimes people do crazy shit, I should know,' Mark replied. He was right, Mark worked for the MET police in London. He'd joined at twenty and worked his way through the ranks.

'I've searched for her online, I think we all have, but no one knows what happened to her or where she moved to,' I said.

'What was her last name again?' Mark asked.

'Keeble,' Robyn supplied.

'Let me take a look when I go back to work. If there's a nutter out there, I want to know who it is. I've got a family to protect.' Mark stopped to take a mouthful of his pint before continuing. 'Listen, Soph, keep a record of everything. Every note through the door, every call. Write it all down. If you receive anything, try not to touch it. Just call the police. Don't engage at all. That's what they want.' Mark closed the conversation down, and we moved on to reminiscing about our schooldays. However, the fun had evaporated, and Becca never fully regained her colour. Something she'd initially thought insignificant could now be a threat to her family.

From Donatella's, we hit a couple of bars, ending the night in a club built under the seafront and designed like a tube tunnel, right down to the white brick tiles. The music was too fast, too techno, and no matter how much we drank, the weight of earlier never left. I didn't remember a lot after Mark ordered shots in an attempt to liven us up. Robyn got collected and Becca had to drag Mark home. James managed to find the hotel when we stumbled out onto the street at two a.m. and I woke on Sunday morning to the grating sound of seagulls. My head feeling like it would explode.

'Owwwwww,' I wailed, rolling over to find my bed empty. Where on earth was James? 'James?' My voice cracking, I heard a grunt from the bathroom.

James appeared on his hands and knees, still fully clothed.

'Christ.' I laughed, although the effort was akin to fireworks going off inside my skull. My phone started buzzing as soon as I switched it on. The memory of a WhatsApp group we'd set up including Elliot came back to me and messages flooded the screen. Photos of James and I kissing. Becca and Robyn dancing, Mark doing shots with a stranger at the bar flashed up. Elliot had just messaged to say it was a shame he'd missed our reunion and we'd have to have the next one in Brisbane.

James got to his feet, so slow he looked in stealth mode, and sat on the bed. His pallor had a green tinge to it.

'I think I better drive home, don't you?'

* * *

I dropped James back and put him to bed before calling a cab to take me home. I'd invited Mum and Dad around for dinner, knowing I wouldn't be back in time for Sunday lunch at theirs. It seemed like a good idea at the time, pre-hangover. Mum would be pleased she wouldn't have to cook, and Dad always enjoyed coming to the flat. I don't believe he ever wanted to move, but Mum wanted a clean break from the business that had been their lives for the past thirty years. If they stayed, she knew he'd be popping his head around the door every day, checking in and it would drive me mad. She was right.

Now, standing in the fridge aisle of the supermarket feeling shivery and nauseous, it didn't seem like such a good idea. The last thing I wanted to do was eat. I grabbed a large lasagne, some pull-apart garlic flatbread and a Caesar salad for the side. That would have to do. Dad was more of a meat and two veg kind of man, hence the reason they'd had a roast every Sunday since they got married. But I couldn't face dealing with any kind of meat preparation, it was going to be hard enough to eat as it was. I knew the hangover was bad when even the offer of a fry-up at the hotel before we'd driven home couldn't tempt me. I'd managed to consume a black coffee and slice of dry toast, which when swallowed felt like sandpaper.

I tidied before my parents arrived at four, it was as much as I could manage, and more hiding things in cupboards than any sort of cleaning. However, I'd forgotten to remove the photograph from the fridge and typically it was the first thing Mum saw.

'Why's Gareth crossed out?'

'I don't know, Mum, I think I did it accidentally,' I lied, changing the subject. 'Do you like the new front door?'

'Very nice, love, bet that keeps the warmth in a treat,' Dad said, wriggling out of his coat. He wrapped me into a hug, and I couldn't resist clinging to him for as long as possible. There was nothing like a hug from your dad when things were rough, no matter how old you were. 'Everything all right?' Noticing my reluctance to let him go.

'Fine, Dad, everything's fine.' I smiled, hoping he wouldn't see straight through me.

'What's with the camera out front then?' he asked. He never bloody missed a trick.

'Just getting a bit more security-conscious, that's all. I've heard there's been a couple of attempted break-ins locally,' I lied.

Dad raised an eyebrow but didn't push for more details.

'There's a new Doctor Who tonight, a woman! I've recorded it.' Mum said as I dished up.

'I know. There'll be a female Bond next,' I said conspiratorially as Dad tutted in our direction.

By the time we ate, I felt better, more human. My appetite returned and the pints of water I'd knocked back since I'd been home had gone some way to rehydrate my system.

Over dinner, I broke the news to Mum that Gareth had been drinking when the accident happened. She wasn't surprised, said that Sue had told her he liked a drink. Craig was the same apparently. I told them about my night out with the old crowd and how Mark was now in the police.

'I thought you might have had that fella here, James isn't it?'

'No, not tonight, Mum.'

'Are you putting off us meeting him, again?'

I coughed and shook my head. My mouth full of garlic bread.

'No why would I do that?' I swallowed down the crust, the jagged edge stinging my throat.

Mum shrugged. It was true, I hadn't introduced a boyfriend to her for a few years. But after Ben, the last serious one, whom I caught actively seeking other women on Tinder, I hadn't wanted to open myself up to that again. That's where the married men came in, until one of them wanted to leave his wife. It turned into a mess and my parents were better off not knowing the destructive rollercoaster I'd been on. I was ashamed of my behaviour and better off single, or so I'd thought until James.

'Is your knee still okay? The stairs weren't a problem, were they?' I changed the subject.

'Yes, it's much better thanks. Back to normal.'

'Here, I bought you this yesterday in Brighton,' I said, fishing the trinket box out of my bag.

Mum looked at it with delight, turning it around in her hands. 'Oh, it's lovely, thank you.'

When we'd finished eating, Mum tried to muscle in on the washing up, but I was having none of it.

'Go sit, Mum. Tell me about your trip to Lancing yesterday, was it cold?

'Bloody freezing, that wind blowing in from the sea was bitter.' She laughed.

I made us all a cup of tea and the conversation turned to Whites, Dad wanted to hear how the business was doing. I beamed as I told them what a successful few weeks we'd had, and how we were well ahead of targeted profits. Dad's eyes twinkled and he relaxed back in his seat, comforted to hear the family business was doing well. When it got to half past seven, they decided to make a move and I walked them out, Dad stopping to admire the new front door.

'Sophie, there's a present left here for you. I almost fell over it,' Mum tutted, handing me a large wrapped box decorated with a yellow bow.

My heart sank, but I plastered on a smile as I took it from her. I knew it wouldn't be from James.

'Goodness, you're a lucky girl,' Mum said, giving me a kiss and thanking me for dinner. Dad did the same, squeezing me tight and I watched as they got into their car and drove away.

I carried the box inside, placing it on the table. It was so light I assumed it was empty, wrapped in blue paper with multicoloured polka dots, its garish yellow oversized bow on the top.

There was a lid, but I didn't want to open it. Nothing good would be inside. It would be another message, another riddle as to what this was all for. My imagination took over, what if it was a dead cat, or a bomb? Or someone's head? I couldn't hear any ticking but the box was so light it unnerved me. It could be a mind game and I could be freaking out over an empty box. If only I had a camera at that door too. I was so sick of this game and wanted to scream into the air: 'What's your fucking problem?' but what would be the point? No one was there to listen.

24

After I spoke to Hayley, I tried to call Gareth. His brother, Craig, answered the phone sounding hungover, and told me Gareth was out. He didn't know where and didn't offer any suggestions either. Helpful wasn't a word I'd use to describe him. He couldn't wait to get off the phone either, cutting me off before I could say good-bye. He was so rude.

Next, I called Becca, who was high-pitched and excitable. She'd already arranged for Robyn to come over this morning and invited me too. I didn't say anything about Hayley on the phone, I wanted to wait until we were all together. I couldn't shake the feeling I was missing something important. Worse than Gareth rejecting Hayley, if there was anything crueller? Hayley must be devastated, but until I spoke to Gareth, I couldn't be sure what had happened.

'Hi.' Becca grinned as she swung open the front door later, standing aside for me to come through.

I saw Robyn's trainers in the hall as I slipped off mine. Becca's parents had a posh detached home on one of the most expensive streets in the village. Well, it's what I'd heard Dad say. Their home was fitted with cream carpets throughout and no one was ever allowed past the doormat with shoes on.

Becca swung her arms around my neck in an unexpected clinch, squashing me against her ample breasts. 'Thank you for last night. It was amazing.' I saw her eyes cloud with tears as she pulled back. Why was she so emotional?

'Are you and Mark going out now?' I asked.

'Yep,' she squealed, bounding up the stairs.

I followed, struggling to match her enthusiasm.

'Hey,' Robyn said as I entered the bedroom. She was sat cross-legged on Becca's bed, clutching one of her cushions. Boyzone, a guilty pleasure of Becca's, played in the background. Her bedroom was a suite, fit for a princess, with her own bathroom. Her white wooden bed had a pink voile canopy and satin bedspread decorated with around ten co-ordinating cushions. It would irritate the hell out of me putting them on and off every day, although I doubted she ever made her own bed. I clenched my jaw as I surveyed her new dressing table and mirror. Unable to stop the jealousy seeping in.

She was spoilt, but I wasn't being fair, Becca was far from a brat. She was super nice and down-to-earth, even though her parents had money. But it was annoying that she always had the best of everything, and all the latest gear before we did. She was the first of us to get a pair of Levi's and she had four pairs of Reebok's classics in a variety of colours, whereas the rest of us had one scuffed pair we wore daily.

So, how did it go with Elliot?' Robyn's eyes glinted.

'Fine. He was sweet actually,' I said and the girls stared at me. Robyn's lip curled into a smirk.

'And?' Becca pushed.

'And what?' I replied.

Robyn threw her cushion at me, which bounced off my arm,

making her laugh so much she flopped onto the carpet. I was so eager for this, for us to meet afterwards and swap the dirty details, but now I was here, it wasn't as fun as I'd envisaged. What had happened between Gareth and Hayley had left a bad taste in my mouth. They had ruined it.

'There's nothing to tell. He was sweet and funny; we had a laugh.'

'But did you do it?' Becca asked.

'Yes, we did it,' I enunciated each word.

Robyn leant forward, wanting more than I was prepared to give.

'What about you two?' It was my turn to ask.

'It was awkward,' Robyn laughed, tucking her hair behind her ear. 'James was so nervous, and we struggled a bit to get going but managed in the end.' It sounded as I'd feared it would be. I was relieved I'd chosen Elliot over James. Robyn had declared, when partners were discussed, that she didn't care either way.

'What about you and Mark?' I asked Becca.

'It was amazing. Magical,' Becca said wistfully, and another cushion flew across the room hitting her square in the chest.

'She's in love!' Robyn sniggered, but Becca didn't protest and she didn't seem to mind the teasing either. She was a ball of energy, unable to keep still, face glowing, but I still felt Hayley and Gareth had put a dampener on last night. I should be in that same bubble, excited about my step into adulthood. I didn't voice that though; the others might think I was a bitch.

At least something good had come out of last night. Seeing Becca's face light up made it worthwhile. I could take credit for being a matchmaker. Maybe I was being too hard on myself, assuming responsibility for what went wrong with Hayley and Gareth. Last night was more like a social experiment than anything else. They'd all agreed, no one had been forced into relinquishing anything. *But*, the tiny voice in the back of my head whispered, *some were coerced*.

'Heard from Hay? I tried to ring her this morning, but her mum said she was in the bath,' Robyn said.

'Kind of. I spoke to her, but she was weird. I don't think they went through with it. I have a horrible feeling Gareth ditched her,' I admitted.

'Fuck!' Becca slumped onto the bed, like a deflated balloon.

'I'll bloody kill him if he did,' Robyn growled.

'Hang on, we don't know what happened yet. Perhaps I'll talk to Gareth and you try to find out more from Hayley?'

Robyn was the closest one of us to Hayley, they still walked to school together every day.

'Maybe they changed their minds?' Becca suggested.

'Whatever happened, I don't think last night worked out for everyone,' I said, staring out of the window, wishing I was elsewhere. I didn't want to spoil the atmosphere, but my head wasn't in the right place for celebration.

'It's not your fault, Soph,' Becca said, her mouth pressed into a hard line.

But what if it was? Should I have seen it coming after what Gareth had said in the kitchen?

I shrugged, not wanting to talk about it. It was a dirty secret, laughable considering the whole of last night was one big dirty secret. Gareth had made our exchange in the kitchen feel like a betrayal to Hayley, to my friends. If I told them what happened, what he said, would they blame me? I didn't want to take the chance.

'How about I go and get some crisps and stuff?' said Becca, already striding towards the door. Maybe all that was needed was a change of subject, a distraction.

'Are you going to see Elliot again?' Robyn asked. But she didn't mean 'see', she meant sleep with.

I managed to raise a smile; it was something I'd been thinking about all morning. 'I don't know. We did have fun, so maybe, who knows. I guess we'll have to see what happens when we go back to school. Right now, I'm just praying none of them talk. You know what boys are like, bragging rights.'

Robyn chewed her lip and cracked her knuckles one by one. I cringed, hating the sound. It turned my insides to jelly. Robyn knew this, but I could tell it was an automatic reaction. 'I don't think so. James wouldn't, I'm sure of it. I'm positive they'll keep quiet.'

Later, after lunch, once Becca had given us a blow-by-blow account of Mark's 'amazing skills' – something I doubted – I told them I was going home. On the way back, I passed the agency and kept going. My parents would still be working and time alone with my mind swirling didn't seem like fun. I had so many unanswered questions, the whole thing was stressing me out. I wanted to know what had happened and, more importantly, how I could fix whatever I'd broken. Perhaps I was overreacting. No one else seemed too concerned.

I knocked on the green door, knowing the bell didn't work. The paint was splintered in various places and long overdue for a fresh coat. It was as familiar to me as my own front door.

Craig answered, his face pale and clammy, eyes red-rimmed. Had he been smoking weed? 'What?' he snapped.

I recoiled, slipping back off the step onto the uneven path.

He turned to leave, and Gareth emerged from the hallway in his place.

'What's his problem?' I said, annoyed that he'd made me jump.

'Nothing. He's fine,' Gareth snapped.

'What's got into you?' I asked, taken aback at the hostility emanating from him.

'What do you want, Sophie?' Gareth looked resigned, like I was here to waste his time. I wasn't sure what sort of reaction I expected, but I didn't think I'd be left standing on the doorstep.

'I want to know what happened last night?' Anger burned in my belly.

'Nothing happened. I went home,' he hissed, closing the door so it was only open wide enough to fit his face through the gap. I didn't know what to say. Gareth's face was twisted, his eyebrows scrunched together. I guessed he felt rejected, pissed off we weren't paired up. Maybe also pissed everyone went through with it. We'd all lost our virginity except for him and Hayley. 'Go home, Sophie. I'll see you at school.' Gareth shook his head as the green door closed in my face.

It was going to be like ripping a plaster off. I was going to lift the lid fast and get it over and done with. I hesitated, chewing my thumbnail which had started to become gnarly. I could throw the box back outside, let the dustmen take it, but I knew that wasn't an option.

I grabbed the top on either side and lifted it in one swift movement. I saw something black and circular move and I jumped halfway across the kitchen. Floating out of the box, to the ceiling, was a black balloon with white string, spinning of its own accord. My heart raced as I peered into the box to check if there was anything else, but it was empty. I sat looking up at the balloon until the message on the front gradually came into view. SLUT in large white capital letters, written in what looked to be Tipp-Ex.

'Nice,' I said, grimacing and pulling on the string to take a closer look. I snapped a photo and sent it to James, with the caption 'You shouldn't have'. Hopefully he would see the funny side. I didn't much like balloons, they seemed to wander around without purpose, moving for no apparent reason. I had to admit they kind of freaked me out, but I wasn't sure if anyone knew that. The message on the front was the point and I guessed it alluded to my being the organiser of *that* night.

It didn't seem like whoever was doing this was going away, but at the same time I wasn't sure it was serious enough to go to the police. I felt threatened and a little scared if I was honest, but I didn't want them to think I was just another neurotic woman, living alone and afraid of her shadow. Other than the rat, there hadn't been anything meant to cause harm to me or the business. Could I be one hundred per cent positive someone had been inside the flat? I mean, I thought they had, with the cross on the photo, and the door being left open, but I couldn't prove it. Mainly, the contact seemed almost childlike, angry yes, malicious even, but I didn't believe I was in any physical danger. It felt like I was the victim of some kind of hate campaign and just had to ride it out.

James pinged back with a 'WTF' followed by a line of exclamation marks before calling to find out what happened. As I told him about my 'gift', I grabbed a small knife from the stand and pricked a hole in the balloon, hearing it wheeze as it deflated. It sat, sad and wrinkled, on the table. It least now it would fit into the bin.

* * *

It was midweek when I heard from Becca. She rang in the evening once she'd put the children to bed. Mark was at work and she was settling down to watch a drama on ITV.

'I thought I'd give you a quick ring. Mark can't find anything on Hayley Keeble, nothing at all. Nothing on the electoral roll, no death or marriage certificates, no driving licence and no criminal record. It's so odd, it's like she's vanished into thin air.'

I sat back in my armchair, scanning the room.

'No missing person report or anything?' I said, thinking aloud.

'Can you remember what her parents were called?' Becca asked. I could hear the television in the background getting louder.

'No, but I'll ask my mum, or maybe Robyn might remember?'

'Yeah I'll try her.'

'Tell Mark thanks for looking. I'll let you go. I'll call you at the weekend for a catch-up. Be safe yeah?'

Becca agreed and rang off.

I stared out of the window looking at the drizzle speckling the glass. How could someone disappear? Unless, she didn't want to be found. If that was the case, then why? *Probably because she's sending you these bloody messages* piped up the voice in my head. The whole thing didn't sit right with me. Had something happened to Hayley all those years ago? We saw her after *that night* at school and then at the Halloween get-together. She seemed normal enough. I remember Robyn saying Hayley didn't want to talk about what had happened with Gareth when they walked to school together on the first day back. She was quiet, but then she always was the quietest of us all. I don't remember her acting strangely.

Gareth too seemed fine as long as no one mentioned losing their virginity. He got a bit stroppy then, but we all collectively assumed he and Hayley hadn't gone through with it. None of us were going to force the issue when they were both clearly embarrassed and unwilling to talk about it.

It wasn't until the next day that all hell broke loose. I got a call from Becca mid-morning when I was out with Frank dealing with a difficult client. He was unhappy with the level of service, even though we'd marketed his terrace house as best we could. He'd had no offers, but he wouldn't reduce the price, even though we'd spoken about his suggestion being too high. He wouldn't have it and wanted to instruct another agent to sell alongside us, believing the competition might motivate us.

I ignored the call from Becca at the time, but when we'd finished with the man and got outside, I listened to the voicemail and it felt like someone had punched me in the gut. My legs disintegrated to mush and Frank, seeing me wobble, held me upright by the elbow.

'What's happened? Is it your dad?' Frank's face etched with concern.

I shook my head quickly, still listening but not wanting Frank to panic. Becca said someone had set fire to her car on the driveway last night whilst Mark was at work. It wasn't long after we'd spoken. The front of the house had been damaged too and she and the kids had to stay in a hotel. The police were involved, and she'd told them about us receiving threatening messages.

I tried to call Becca back, but it kept going to voicemail. Maybe she was on the phone to Robyn? I told Frank not to worry and head back to the office while I called James to fill him in. He sounded nervous and said we should all be more careful as it was one hell of an escalation.

I was on edge all day and jumped at the chance to head to The Boar after work with the others. Anything to put off going home alone. Gary was in a weirdly jovial mood and had the team in stitches, telling us about a speed-dating event he went to at the weekend. I tried to join in but couldn't pretend I was as enthused as the others, although glad for the company.

'Are you all right, Sophie?' Hope leant in to whisper in my ear.

'Yeah fine, just stuff going on, that's all.'

'You might feel better if you talk about it?'

'Someone's dragging up old bullshit from my past. It's ancient history and I've got no idea who is doing it or why it matters now.'

I sighed. It had slipped out, I hadn't meant to say anything at all, but Hope was right. There had been a small shift in weight upon my shoulders.

Hope took a sip of her drink, considering her response. Gary's voice was loud, drowning the two of us out with ease.

'Maybe, you need to work out why it matters?' she suggested, eyes wide as she slurped her straw.

'I have no fucking idea why we're being punished,' I said, more to myself than to Hope.

'We?'

'Some old friends.' I'd said too much already. It wasn't something I wanted to talk about, but maybe Hope was right. I know Mark tried to search for Hayley, but what if there was another way? 'I have to go,' I said, putting two twenty-pound notes on the table and winking at Frank.

He eyed me suspiciously and I saw him make to stand. I waved him away. He didn't look convinced but sat back down, letting me go.

I wanted to drive to Mum and Dad's, but I'd had more than one glass of wine and didn't want to risk it. Instead, I rushed home and rang, getting through the pleasantries as fast as I could.

'Mum, I'm trying to track down Hayley. I remember her dad was some army officer, wasn't he?'

'Yes, I believe so, I didn't know them well though.'

'Do you remember what her mum did?' I needed information to help me find them, but all I knew was the surname and the army connection.

'I think she was a nurse, she worked on the children's ward at St. Mary's.'

'Do you remember her name?'

'Jackie, I think, Jacqueline maybe?'

'That's great, Mum, thanks,' I said, keen to get off the phone and start googling.

'What's this all about, Sophie?' I could hear her voice wavering at the other end.

'I'm trying to find her, that's all, get the old gang back together again,' I said, my voice a touch too high. I hated lying to my mum, but I knew she'd only worry; she was as bad as Frank. I was sure she didn't believe me, but she wished me good luck with the search and said she'd call tomorrow.

I put my pyjamas on and made a cup of tea and some toast, trying to avoid getting butter all over my keyboard, but I was hungry and impatient. I googled Jackie Keeble and Jacqueline Keeble. Nothing came up. I tried adding the word nurse, but that led to nothing relevant. Frustratingly I couldn't find anything on the army side either. It was as though the entire Keeble family had dropped off the grid.

The next day, I asked Frank to man the office as I needed to go out. He still wore the same concerned expression he'd had the night before. As though it had been there all night and the wind had changed, leaving it permanently stuck.

'Don't look so worried,' I said, giving him what I hoped was a reassuring pat on the arm. Frank was so protective. It was like working with my dad.

'But I do worry, love. What's going on? Talk to me.'

'I will, I promise, just not right now.' I knew I'd be heartbroken when he retired. Gary had some big boots to fill.

I jumped in the car and headed to St. Mary's hospital. It was the only avenue I had and I needed to start somewhere. The name Keeble hadn't come up anywhere, on any social media or google searches. There were hundreds of people with the surname, but I couldn't find the Hayley, or Jacqueline I was looking for. On the way, I left a message for Becca to check that her and the girls were okay. I was sure Mark had them hidden away and his search for Hayley would have stepped up a gear too.

On entering the hospital, I wasn't sure how useful the trip

would be, but I had no alternative. The paediatric ward was called Maple and I buzzed the entrance to be allowed in, asking to speak to the ward manager. A stern wiry lady greeted me at the desk, her hair pulled back into a tight bun. Her eyes lingered on my face, trying to ascertain why I was there if I wasn't a visitor.

'I'm sorry to bother you, I'm trying to find a nurse.'

'Do you know her name?' The nurse pursed her lips and I sensed she wasn't going to be forthcoming.

'Her name is Jackie Keeble, full name Jacqueline, but she doesn't work here any more. It was twenty years ago.'

The nurse made a sound like a cushion that had been jumped on. 'Well, there might not be much I can do for you. Hang on, let me ask Valerie.'

Surprised and encouraged by her willingness to help, I thanked her repeatedly. She left the desk and wandered along one of the wards, stopping to ask a doctor on his rounds if he'd seen Valerie.

I waited by the desk, taking in the coloured murals on the walls. It all looked so cheery; it was meant to, but no child should ever have to stay in hospital. The surrounding corridors were far too quiet, which told me they must care for some extremely poorly children.

The nurse returned, bringing with her a stout woman, whose pristine uniform and gleaming white clogs signalled to me that she was old-school. She looked like a matron, her face was lined and weather-beaten, but she peered at me over her glasses with a quizzical smile.

'This lady is looking for Jackie Keeble. You've been here since day dot; do you remember her?'

'Jackie, yes I remember Jackie. Goodness, that was years ago! She was only here for a short while; husband was in the army if I remember rightly?'

I nodded, this was easier than I thought. 'Yes, that's right. I went to school with her daughter. I've been trying to track her down. I believe Jackie left as her husband was stationed somewhere at short notice.'

Are you sure?' she said, staring off into the distance, lines forming on her forehead as she searched the depths of her memory.

'What do you mean?'

'Her daughter got into trouble, that's why they moved. Not because of her husband, although he arranged it all I believe.'

My mouth dropped open and I took a second to regain my composure. She had to be mistaken. 'What sort of trouble?' I didn't remember Hayley getting into any trouble at school. She was always well-behaved and compliant with the teachers. She never gave her parents any cause for alarm.

'There's only one sort of trouble with girls that age, love.' Valerie laughed and gave me a wink.

There was no mistaking what Valerie meant. Could it be true? I felt rooted to the spot, my mind spinning with so many questions. 'You don't remember where they moved to, do you?'

'I believe they went to Oxford, somewhere near there, but it was a long time ago.' I had no doubt that Valerie had the memory of an elephant. She smiled at me for a second before I could see her attention turn to something else and she signalled with a nod of the head to the other nurse. 'Right, come on, Pru, can you give me a hand changing Amy's bed, she's had an accident.' Pru and Valerie turned to leave, bustling down the corridor as I remained frozen, unsure what to do next.

'Can you let yourself out pet?' Pru called over her shoulder and I glided towards the door, pressed the green exit button and wandered out of the hospital in a daze.

I joined the smokers, congregated around a bench and stood a few yards away, lighting a cigarette. I felt unconnected to my body, like I was floating beside it. Hayley was pregnant? How was that possible? My stomach lurched, nausea hitting in waves, struggling to absorb the revelation that shocked my core. I racked my brain, sorting through the memories.

The 'coming of age' gathering was at the end of the school holidays and Hayley left six or seven weeks later, at the end of October half-term. Could Gareth have got her pregnant? I didn't think anything happened between them. That was the impression we'd all been given. Why would they lie? The admission blew me away and I struggled to get my head around that being the reason the Keebles left. But it did make sense. Hayley's father was proud and strict. I could imagine him whisking her away to get the problem sorted. Starting afresh somewhere new, where no one would know their secret. But where exactly?

I headed home to continue the search on my laptop. I went up to the flat using the front door, instead of going through the office so as to avoid bumping into anyone. Luckily, I was able to get upstairs without being seen. I made a sandwich and sat back behind the laptop which I'd left on the kitchen table. This time, I googled army barracks, Oxford, and a list popped up. There was nothing for it, I'd have to get on the phone and ring each one until I found them.

The fifth call was to the barracks in Bicester and a helpful gentleman was able to confirm, after some friendly coaxing, that officer Alan Keeble was a serving resident from 1997. He had retired due to ill health in 2005. As helpful as the man was, he wouldn't tell me where the Keebles lived now, citing data protection and whispering that he'd given me too much information already.

I had to assume they were still in the area, having lived there for eight years before retiring. Especially given that Alan had retired as he was unwell. Next, I tried to look on the electoral register. I couldn't find anything online and kept being pointed to the local council where you could go, in person, and look through the list.

I chanced on a suggested link to 192.com, which found four people with the surname Keeble in Bicester. Once I'd paid a small subscription fee, I could see other residents at the same address. Mr. A Keeble listed a Mrs. J R Keeble residing at the same address. That had to be the one. I wrote the address down and keyed it into my phone. A telephone number was listed against the address too, but for some of the questions I needed to ask it might be better face to face.

I mapped the route using my phone and saw it would take around an hour and a half to get to Bicester. It was nearly midday, so I grabbed my keys and headed out the door. I could leave now and still get back before the office closed. Finding Hayley was becoming more urgent as the days went by. If she could set fire to Becca's car and possibly run Gareth off the road, the father of her child, she was capable of far more than I imagined. Maybe the cards and flowers, even the balloon, were paving the way for things to come? I shuddered, icy tendrils closing around me. Exactly how much danger was I in?

I had a good run to Bicester and was thankful my phone doubled as a satnav; following directions was not one of my strong points. I deliberated whether to call James and tell him what I'd found out, but I had to consider that he might already know. He knew Gareth better than any of us and it was plausible that he knew Hayley had left because she got pregnant. Even if Gareth didn't tell him when we were younger, he could have told him years later. I couldn't shake the feeling there was something James wasn't telling me, and I wanted to give him the news in person, hoping I'd see it in his eyes if he already knew.

Alan and Jackie owned a quaint cottage with a thatched roof on the outskirts of Bicester. I passed a church, a village shop and a pub in the nearby streets on my way. It was a perfect spot for retirement. The whole area was picturesque with lots of greenery and was somewhere I could imagine living happily. Outside the Keebles' cottage was an immaculate garden, complete with hanging baskets and trailing flowers along the stepping stone path. I wanted a cigarette for my nerves but remembered how anti-smoking Hayley always said her dad was. I didn't want to get off on the wrong foot.

I got to the door and tapped gently, waiting a minute before tapping again. I hoped I hadn't come all this way to be disappointed. As I was about to leave, I heard some shuffling and the door opened. Jackie Keeble stood in the doorway, her silver blonde hair piled on top of her head, not a strand out of place. She looked almost identical to when I last saw her. Out of politeness, she smiled, her face impassive, but I struggled to get my words out. The fact she still looked the same, bar a few more lines, had thrown me.

'Can I help you?' she asked.

'Mrs Keeble, it's Sophie. Sophie White, one of Hayley's old friends. My dad owned the estate agents back in Copthorne,' I blabbered.

'Sophie, yes I remember. Gosh you're all grown up. You're a long way from home?'

'I was hoping I could talk to you; do you have five minutes? It's about Hayley.'

Her eyes darkened for a second at the mention of her daughter's name. 'Oh, I see. Well you better come in.'

27

Being back at school was strange at first, all anyone would talk about was Lady Diana's funeral, how sad it was that she had died and all the celebrities that had attended, but by the following week it was old news. That night wasn't mentioned, not openly at school. We'd moved on. However, Hayley seemed more withdrawn than normal, spending most of her time in the library. She told us she was studying as her parents expected her to do well in her GCSEs and she was sinking under the pressure. But even with Robyn, whom she was closest to, she wasn't the same. It was like she was dead behind the eyes, never fully in the present, even when she was with us.

Hayley never did elaborate on what had happened. She didn't tell any of the others more than she'd told me on the phone the day after the party. Her story remained unchanged. Nothing had happened with Gareth. She'd changed her mind and gone home. Eventually we stopped pushing for more details as it was clear she wasn't going to divulge. Although it was strange because Gareth had an almost identical story, word for word in fact. All of us guessed there was more to it, but neither of them would tell.

Becca and Mark were inseparable, and it irked the blonde bitches no end. They all thought Mark was way out of Becca's league and voiced their poisonous opinions at every opportunity. He was one of the best-looking boys in our year, but they hated it more as he only had eyes for her. Even when one of them, Francesca, flaunted her bony arse at him during PE, he didn't bat an eyelid. None of them received any attention from him and we loved him even more for it. With their older boyfriends no longer at school, and their male followers dwindling, they spent their time shooting withering comments and cutting remarks at us.

We hung out a bit more with the lads, minus Hayley. James, as it turned out, was pretty cool. He knew loads of interesting facts and was a massive film buff. Enlisting us in regular trips to the cinema at the weekend. I started seeing Elliot, more casually than Becca and Mark. It was awkward at first as Gareth was still being a bit off, although he swore he didn't care what we did. I still went to his on a Saturday when my parents went for dinner. Occasionally, I'd feign a stomach ache or something and try to get out of it, but when I went, we'd sit and play Nintendo like before. But it didn't feel right, something hung in the air between us. Unspoken. Elliot sensed it when all the boys were together, Gareth didn't want to be around him.

We didn't want to rub his face in it, so most of the time Elliot and I hung out alone. We'd make out and chat about stuff, always finding things to laugh about or people to take the piss out of. I enjoyed being with him, but when we were with the group, we didn't hold hands or kiss. The boys kept their promise and our secret remained untold.

The first term was flying by and we were overloaded with coursework, our A4 folders bulging, some of us taking it seriously for the first time, knowing every piece would now count towards our GCSEs. Teachers were ramping up the pressure and we spent a lot of time studying in small groups. Hayley was always in the school library when she wasn't in class, at lunchtime and sometimes after school too, buried in a textbook. Becca was creating a waistcoat for her textile's coursework. It was magnificent, like something out of *Joseph and his Amazing Technicolour Dreamcoat*, or Willy Wonka. We would often sit with her in the art block at lunchtime as she worked on it. Especially when it was raining. That's where we were when James and Elliot came to find us.

'Whatcha doing?' James asked, and Becca pointed towards the mannequin in front of her, rolling her eyes at the obvious question. 'Wow, that looks amazing,' he said, reaching out to touch the emerald green silk at the back.

'Bogus, you mean.' Elliot bent over laughing. Sometimes he was a dipshit.

'Shut up,' I said, throwing a paintbrush at him I'd been twiddling.

Becca smiled through gritted teeth. 'What do you want, I'm trying to work here?'

'James wants to invite you to his Halloween party,' Elliot smirked, and James blushed.

'My mum and dad are holding a party at the community centre, mainly for my little sister and her school friends, but there's another room we can use, and they said I could invite some mates.'

'Sounds lame,' Elliot interrupted. I glared at him.

'Is it fancy dress?' Robyn asked.

'Yep.'

'Then we're in.'

We spent the rest of the lunch break not so much focused on Becca's waistcoat but more on what we were going to wear. None of us owned costumes. Becca suggested she'd get her mum to order a few and we'd pick from between them. We all readily agreed; I knew my parents would try to make me wear something made from a bin bag.

* * *

The night of the party was the Friday of half-term and a couple of days before Hayley called to ask if she could come with us. James had invited her too, but she didn't want to arrive on her own. Hayley hadn't been out with us for a while, except for a couple of shopping trips into town and a study session at Robyn's. We were excited the gang was going to be back together.

We got ready at Becca's – she'd chosen a witch costume with purple and black striped tights. Robyn had a black onesie with a skeleton on the front, which glowed in the dark. I resorted to a vampire outfit and went way overboard on the fake blood.

'Jesus, you look like Carrie,' Hayley said when I answered the door, bearing my fangs. She wore a nun's habit and I couldn't help but laugh as she stepped over the threshold in her sensible flat shoes and billowing gown. 'I know, right,' she drawled. At least she hadn't lost her sense of humour.

We arrived at the party when it was in full swing. In the main hall, there were loads of toddlers and younger children running around. James's parents had hired a small bouncy castle and the room was dark with glowing pumpkins and orange streamers. James's sister, Marie, was dressed as a devil and kept stabbing anyone who came near her with a rubber pitchfork. We popped in to say hello to his parents before going to what had been designated the teens' party room.

For something which could have been rubbish and a massive disappointment, James had done a great job at turning the little room into a creepy hideout for us to chill in. The walls were covered in long black drapes and green flashing fairy lights. More pumpkins and glow-in-the-dark spiderwebs lined the edges of the room and in the middle was a fake fire. Built with sticks and a brick surround, it had flames of paper which waved magically. Overhead hung a cauldron full of punch. Music blasted out from a boombox on a table covered in ghoulish foods.

'This looks wicked,' Robyn said, diving straight in and eating a breadstick designed to look like a witch's finger. We saw a few other people from our year. There were around twelve of us crammed into the room. Elliot, who was dressed as the hunchback of Notre Dame, joined us, handing out cups of punch.

'It's got vodka in it,' he said in a high-pitched squeak.

I took a sip, coughing.

'It's got a lot of vodka in it,' I warned the girls.

Hayley wrinkled her nose and put her cup on the table. The rest of us took a large gulp, forcing the liquid down.

I spotted Gareth chatting to Alice, a nice girl from my maths' class. He was dressed as a werewolf and waved as I caught his eye. I'd managed to avoid the last couple of Saturday nights at his house, claiming I had too much coursework to do. Mum and Dad were going to guess something was wrong, but I struggled to spend time with Gareth now. Something had fractured between us that night and I wasn't sure it would heal.

'I need to talk to you guys,' Hayley said a couple of hours later. Most of us had indulged in too much punch and were sweating from all the dancing we'd been doing. It had been an awesome night; Becca had been sick, and Elliot and I were caught snogging in the hallway by James's dad. He didn't say much, only 'Come on, guys, there's kids about.' Elliot had retorted, 'Yeah us' under his breath, but thankfully his dad didn't hear.

'What's up?' I shouted over the music.

'I'm moving.'

'What?' Robyn shouted, incredulous.

'I'm not coming back to school. This is my last night here.'

Amplified by alcohol, Robyn burst into tears and threw her arms around Hayley, who looked like she was being choked by her fake crucifix.

'Why?' I asked, shaking my head. And, why wait until the night before to tell us?

'Dad's been stationed up north,' Hayley replied and for the first time I realised how tired she looked. Dark circles beneath her eyes and a milky pallor. She looked beaten and defeated. Her shoulders sagged, all the fight gone out of her. If there was any to begin with. I guessed the move had been the cause of a lot of arguments at home.

Robyn sobbed, snot trickling down her face. Becca joined her, and Hayley's eyes glistened in the disco lights. We danced together as a group, the four of us. Robbie William's 'Angels' played out over the stereo and the boys watched on as we huddled together swaying. When Hayley left the next day, we never saw her after that.

28

Inside the Keeble residence, a musty smell lingered, as though the windows had been shut tight for months. Jackie led me through a narrow hallway into a farmhouse kitchen at the back, directing me towards the pine dining table.

'Take a seat, Sophie. Would you like some tea?'

'Yes please.' I glanced around, absorbing my surroundings. I couldn't see any photos of Hayley in the hallway as I passed, or in the kitchen. Nothing on the pinboard except for hospital appointment letters and reminders. Jackie had her back to me, filling the kettle and putting teabags into mugs. 'You look so well, Mrs Keeble, the same as when I last saw you.'

'Sophie, you're too kind. I wish I felt twenty years younger. Please call me Jackie. Mrs Keeble was my mother-in-law and it's far too formal for me.'

'How's Mr Keeble?'

Jackie looked startled at the mention of his name, like I'd punched her in the gut. She didn't answer straight away, not until she brought the mugs over and sat opposite me. Inwardly I cringed. Had I made a mistake? Maybe Alan had passed away?

'Alan's in the sitting room, watching television. He's got dementia, has had for a few years now, but I look after him as best I can.'

'I'm sorry, that must be tough.' I saw from her watery eyes it was. I couldn't imagine how heart-breaking it must be to watch someone you love slowly slip away from you.

'He thinks I'm his nurse. I have to remind him daily that we've been married for forty-five years.' Jackie sniffed and pulled a tissue out from her cardigan sleeve, blowing her nose. 'You came to ask about Hayley?' she prompted, and her face changed. She became stoic, sitting straighter in her chair and crossing her arms. It put me on edge.

'Yes, I'm trying to track her down.' I didn't want to show my hand.

'Oh, you don't know?' Jackie pursed her lips.

'Know what?'

'I haven't seen Hayley for over twenty years.' Jackie leant back in her chair and sighed as though she was frustrated to be repeating herself.

My mouth fell open and I blinked repeatedly, trying to understand.

Jackie continued, 'We left Copthorne because she'd got herself pregnant, silly girl. At fifteen too! Alan was horrified, he moved us here as soon as he could get a transfer arranged. He didn't want anyone to know. He wanted it dealt with quickly and quietly, but Hayley ran away.'

My brain whirled with questions and I felt my pulse quicken. Feeling lightheaded, I gripped the seat of the chair to anchor myself. So, it was true? But how? She hadn't slept with Gareth that night. They'd both said nothing happened so how could she have got pregnant? And if she was then why on earth did she run away? Where had she gone at fifteen? How could her parents have let this happen? I knew I wasn't being fair, making assumptions knowing very little. Basing them on what Hayley had told us.

'I'm so sorry, Jackie, I had no idea,' I said, shaking my head, unable to match her words with the reality.

'Yes, well, I'm sorry to shock you, pet. I've had a long time to come to terms with it.'

'Do you know who the father was?'

'She would never tell me who the father was. Alan wanted it rid of, he didn't care about the ins and outs.'

I sighed, my heart breaking for Hayley.

'And that's why she ran,' I said softly, a statement not a question, but Jackie nodded anyway, her head bowed. She just went along with it, the dutiful wife, doing what she was told. We were all scared of Hayley's father and tried to avoid knocking for her if we could. He was always so stern and angry looking. 'Was she reported missing?' I asked, waiting for the lie to come, knowing there was no missing person report under the name Hayley Keeble.

'No.'

'Why?' I blurted, unable to hide the outrage I felt.

'Because she made me a promise. She left a note, saying she would ring me every Saturday at three in the afternoon if no one came looking for her, but if we sent the police, we would never hear from her again.'

I was confused, it didn't sound like the Hayley I knew. She wouldn't say boo to a goose. But what people do when they are desperate can be out of character, and she must have been truly desperate. 'Did she ring?' I asked.

'Yes, every week, for two years. She was a few days shy of her sixteenth birthday when she disappeared, but she called every week, as promised, until she turned eighteen.' Jackie's cold exterior crumbled and a fat tear dripped from her cheek. I wanted to comfort her but was unsure how she'd react, so I sat with my hands wrapped around my mug waiting for her to continue. 'I've never heard from her since. We didn't tell the police at the time as I thought I could convince her to come home. I told her I was sorry, begged her to return, hundreds of times. She would be on the phone for five minutes at most. Tell me she was safe and happy and not to worry. Maybe she'd got involved with a cult or something. I searched and searched, but it was like a needle in a haystack.' Jackie broke down and my resolve went with it.

I shuffled my chair closer and wrapped an arm around her shoulders as she sobbed into her tissue. 'I'm sure you did everything you could. If someone doesn't want to be found, they're careful to cover their tracks,' I said, counting the breadcrumbs I had to follow to lead me to this kitchen table. But Hayley was a child, she must have had help from someone. 'So, Hayley ran away pregnant?'

'No, she had the abortion, the clinic confirmed it. I dropped her off and picked her up a couple of hours later. She wouldn't let me stay, didn't want me or Alan anywhere near her. She was so angry with us.' I gasped and my hand flew to my mouth; I couldn't help it. Jackie's tone was flat, resigned. Did Hayley want to get an abortion or was she coerced?

Being made to move and leave her friends, any control Hayley had had been taken away with nowhere to turn. My soul ached for the fifteen-year-old Hayley and I wished I'd been home the day she came to say goodbye. Perhaps I could have helped her? Mum would have helped her; although in truth we would have been no match for Hayley's dad.

Mr Keeble would have hit the roof; I could see it now. He was a typical military man; strict and precise. Hayley was always immaculate, clean and tidy, her bedroom was the same. We used to tease her because her school shoes were so shiny, not like ours, all scuffed and muddy from walking across the field. Hers were polished every night before bed – she told us her father made her do it. He wouldn't have been able to endure the embarrassment of having his only daughter become pregnant before it was even legal to have sex, and whilst she was still at school.

The image of the balloon popped into my head, the word SLUT in bright white capital letters across it. I can imagine he called her one; I bet she had to stand there whilst he tore strips off her.

'I'm afraid I've got no idea where she is, or how she is. I've never stopped looking, but it's as though she never existed. I had a private detective on it for a while. Alan didn't know, he wanted me to wash my hands of her. He found the betrayal too much to bear, but a mother can never abandon her child.'

I clenched my jaw, the irony of her comment ringing in my ears.

'What did the private detective find?' I asked.

'He traced her to a hostel not too far from here, she'd spent four nights there before moving on. No one admitted to knowing where she was going, and the trail went cold.'

I took a mouthful of my tea and Jackie did the same. I was unsure what to say, because nothing I could say would make it better. People didn't usually disappear off the face of the earth and if a private detective couldn't trace Hayley, it was unlikely I'd be able to. As much as I didn't want to admit it, my gut feeling was that Hayley at fifteen, on her own, would have had to make some tough choices. Life on the street wasn't for the faint-hearted. If she was still alive, she'd have turned up in the system by now.

'Nurse,' came a feeble call from the next room.

Jackie closed her eyes and sighed before getting up.

'I'll never forgive myself, you know. For not standing up to him.' Jackie nodded in the direction of the front room. It was a price she would pay until her dying day; I had no doubt about it.

'I know,' was all I could manage.

'I'll be back in a moment.' she wiped her face and went into the sitting room to tend to Alan.

I drank my tea, planning my next move. I balled my hands into fists. I'd hit a dead end, unsure where to go from here. There was no place else other than home.

'How is your mum and dad doing? Is your dad still running Whites?' Jackie asked on her return.

'No, he's retired now, I took it over. They're fine, thanks. I think I'm the only one of our bunch still living in Copthorne.' I picked up my keys and stood, ready to leave.

'What about that nice young man? He came by here a couple of years ago looking for Hayley.'

I froze, a tingling sensation ran down my legs, pooling at my feet and rooting me to the spot like glue.

'Goodness, what was his name, wavy hair, lovely chap.'

'James?' I whispered, fearing the confirmation I knew was coming.

'Yes, that's it, James. He came by, said he'd get in touch if he found her, but we haven't heard from him. Are you two still in touch?'

'Occasionally,' I stammered, my mouth dry, despite the tea. I wasn't sure if my legs would carry me to my car, but I didn't want to alarm Jackie.

I wished her all the best, said I'd give my parents her love and thanked her for the tea. She saw me to the door, and I managed to put one foot in front of the other until I reached my car. Slumping in my seat, I lit a cigarette, blowing the smoke out of the window. Waiting for the nicotine to hit my bloodstream, my stomach spun like a washing machine at high speed. Whatever was going on, James had lied to me. He knew Hayley had disappeared. He knew where her parents lived and he would have known she was pregnant. Why hadn't he told me? Was he protecting Gareth?

Whatever the reason, I knew I couldn't trust him and if he'd lied about Hayley, what else was he hiding from me?

29

Due to the traffic on the M25, I arrived back after Frank had closed and everyone had left for the day. He'd sent me a text to say everything was fine and there was nothing to report. It looked as though I hadn't missed anything important. James had rung twice whilst I was in the car, but I hadn't answered. I wasn't sure what to say to him, or how to play it. I needed time to consider my options. Did I reveal what I'd learnt? Push him to tell me why he'd kept Hayley's secret?

Everything I knew about my old school friends had been turned on its head. Perhaps everyone had secrets they didn't share. My head spun, I wanted to relax and unwind, to shut my mind off. I knew a headache was brewing and once it was in full flow, I wouldn't be able to shift it.

Back home, I ran a bath and had a long soak, trying to undo the tangled mess of thoughts and sort them into order. All I knew was I didn't trust anyone, bar my parents and Frank, and that felt lonely. The water was warm and comforting and I spent so long in there my fingers wrinkled like prunes. The stress melting away, all I needed was a glass of wine.

My eyes were drooping when the phone rang and I jolted upright, sloshing the water over the side of the bath and onto the floor. The caller had rung off by the time I got out of the bath and reached my phone, on top of the washing basket. I'd expected to see James on the display, but it was Becca. I slipped on my dressing gown and called her back.

'Hey, are you okay? Back home?' I asked.

'Yeah, back home now, thank you. Cars a write-off, but it'll get replaced. Insurance will sort that and the front of the house where it was scorched.'

'God, I can't believe it. Who would do this?' Harassing all of us with cards, flowers, balloons and now intensifying to torching cars. Were we all in danger?

'They've arrested Robyn!' Becca said, her voice breaking.

I was too stunned to speak, but Becca continued.

'Her fingerprints were on the petrol can, which was left at the scene. I don't believe it though, there's just no way. She's out on bail, but her conditions are that she can't contact me. That's why I was ringing, if I give you her number, could you ring her. Check she's okay?'

'Of course,' I stammered.

'Have the police been in touch with you?' she asked.

'No, but I've been out all day,' I replied, not wanting to divulge what I'd found out about Hayley. First, I needed to work out who I could trust.

'Well, I doubt they will now. I don't think they are going to look that hard into the cards.' Becca sounded tired and anxious. She was as confused as I was.

I took Robyn's number and said I'd text Becca once I'd been in touch.

I put on my pyjamas and pulled a random box out of the freezer to microwave. It was a leftover Cajun pasta dish from

Mum. I didn't have much of an appetite but knew I needed to eat something. While it was defrosting, I dialled Robyn, who answered after a single ring.

'Yep?'

'Robyn, it's Sophie, Becca asked me to call. Are you okay?'

'Ah fuck, Sophie, it's been a nightmare. I got bail today, had to borrow Mum's savings.'

'What happened?'

'I've got no idea, they came for me, at work yesterday. Carted me off. Christ knows if I've still got a job. Got to go back in and beg tomorrow.'

'Becca said they've got your prints on a petrol can?' I said, hardly able to believe it myself. Robyn wouldn't do that to Becca, I was certain. They were friends.

'Well yeah, the fucking can is mine, but god knows how it got there. I didn't set fire to her car. They'll see when they check my whereabouts. I was with Chloe all night.' Robyn sounded furious, as though she was ready to blow.

I asked her if there was anything I could do, but she only needed me to pass the message back to Becca that it wasn't her.

'Don't worry, Robyn, she knows it wasn't you. But how do the police have your prints?'

'Got picked up shoplifting when I was nineteen, had to do community service. It worked though; I've never stolen anything since.' We both laughed, as I remembered Robyn being light-fingered when we were kids. We'd all leg it, terrified we'd be caught, but she saw it as a bit of fun. I couldn't imagine Robyn being behind it but on the other hand if it wasn't one of us, then who was it?

'Be careful okay, keep in touch,' I said, already penning a text to Becca that Robyn was fine.

I pushed the congealed pasta around my plate. I wasn't

hungry. Not only had Becca's car been torched, but someone had also tried to frame Robyn. Picking us off one by one. Unless it was to divert attention elsewhere? My head started pounding, thudding against my temples. I wanted to go to bed and pull the duvet over my head. Stay cocooned like that until it was all over.

* * *

I woke early in the morning, the consequence of going to bed earlier than normal. Still as unsettled as the day before, I poured boiling water into my jar of coffee instead of my mug. My phone had another missed call and text from James asking if I was okay. I knew I'd have to respond, otherwise there was a chance he'd turn up on the doorstep tonight, or worse whilst I was at work.

I sent a quick message to say I was fine but had a long day at work and sorry to text back so late. Hopefully it would bide me some time. I still didn't know what to do or who it was targeting us. If it was Hayley, why had she appeared out of the blue twenty years later with a vendetta we knew nothing about? It made no sense.

Work was busy and it was what I needed. I had plenty of emails to get through, two new instructions and a review with Gary and Hope on their initial six weeks at Whites. The day flew by and Frank brought tea and lunch to my desk to keep me going. He stopped to ask how I was, and we caught up briefly.

'I've put a bulb back in your hallway, I noticed there wasn't one in there the other day when the kitchen door was open.'

'Ah thanks, Frank. I've been meaning to do that. Actually, do you know what circuit it's on? Is it the office one?'

'Yes, think so. Why?'

'No reason,' I said lightly, although now I knew why the bulb had been removed in the first place. It must have been the one light that still worked after the fuses were tripped.

'What am I going to do without you?' I continued.

Frank shrugged, his eyes twinkling. 'Diane keeps hassling me about you coming over for dinner.'

'Sure, just let me know when.'

Frank began to cough and left my office to get some water.

Hope came in for her one-to-one and we had a quick chat about her progress. Was there anything she required more training on? How was she finding the sales role? Frank and I were thrilled with her progress and the fact that she'd made a sale so soon was fantastic.

'I'd like to stay if you'll have me,' she said, her hands clasped together tightly.

'Of course! I think you're perfect for the role. I'll organise some more training on the sales system and how you can view each sale through from offer to completion. It helps if you can see the whole process and what you'll need to provide. You're doing an amazing job, Hope.' She beamed at me, eager to please.

Hope bounded out of the room when my phone rang. I spent ten minutes talking to a solicitor because the purchaser of Highlands Drive was certain it was listed for sale with the jacuzzi included, however it had mysteriously disappeared from the fixtures and fittings list. Once I'd finished, I called Gary in, he delivered another cup of tea, which put him in my good books.

'Nice move, bringing me tea.'

'I can't pretend I made it,' he admitted with a smile. Gary was charming, but I was unable to relax completely in his company. What with the flyer and card found in his drawer, as well as what he said to Frank about me living upstairs. I'd be lying if I said it didn't freak me out a little, but he had been nothing but polite and professional to me. Plus, he was excellent at his job. I gave him a glowing review and he was modest, telling me he believed he could do better, sell more.

'Gary, it's important that you sell obviously, that's your job, but you've exceeded your monthly target already. I'm not telling you to slow down, but I want you to be happy and healthy with no burn-out. I want to retain my staff, and as long as you keep doing what you're doing, I'm thrilled to have you onboard.'

Gary shook his head. 'This place is so different to where I was before. I'm still trying to get my head around it.'

'I don't believe estate agents have to operate like that, flogging their sales team and encouraging underhand behaviour where they only care about their money. Our industry has such a bad reputation already. I'm trying to break free of that preconception.'

Gary looked at me in awe and I felt my underarms start to dampen.

'One other thing, we need to make sure the office is a harmonious place, so be mindful of what you say once you have a few drinks. I can't have any discord between the staff. Are you and Hope okay now?'

'Yes, we're fine. I apologised and, absolutely, I'll think before I speak in future.' Gary swallowed, his Adam's apple bobbing in his throat.

'Anyway, that's enough from me. Have you got any concerns or comments you wish to add?' I said, shuffling my papers like a newsreader.

'No, I think we're done. I'll carry on as is boss.' Gary shook my hand before leaving the office.

I disappeared upstairs a little while later, my stomach somersaulting and the unpleasant tang of salt in my mouth. I just managed to reach the bathroom before being violently sick in the toilet. Two hours later, I was still there, wrapped in a blanket, my throat burning and stomach sore from all the heaving. I must have picked up a bug from somewhere.

30

OCTOBER 2018

A noise from outside woke me around three, I heard some shuffling, a grunt, followed by a loud smash. Then all hell broke loose. I'd never heard the alarm before, only the tiniest beep when Dad had pressed the button to test it. I covered my ears, it was so shrill. It screamed through the flat and out into the street, so loud my head throbbed. I stumbled out of bed in a blind panic, still weak from the lack of food or drink as I'd tried to flush out the bug.

Pulling on my dressing gown, I ran down the first set of stairs, then the second. Almost crashing through the door into the kitchenette and again into the office. As I thrust open the door, expecting to find looters, filling their bags with whatever they could find, a gust of wind shoved me back.

It was freezing and dark except for the blue flashing beacon that resembled police lights spinning around, illuminating houses nearby. I wasn't going to be popular with my neighbours. I switched on the lights and looked around, an icy breeze crawling up my bare legs. Why was it so cold? Then I saw why; a complete pane of glass had been smashed. The sheet that stretched across my office, allowing me to look out onto the street. Property particulars and shards of broken glass littered the floor. I looked down at my feet, exposed skin ready for slicing. My heartbeat thudded like the speaker at a club. I couldn't hear anything, only the wailing siren, but my heart was pounding against my ribcage as if afraid it wouldn't be heard.

'Where's the panel?' I muttered, confused by my panic. The alarm had been going for a good three minutes now. The sound so ear-piercingly loud, I was disorientated. I had to turn it off.

Stepping gingerly across the floor, I trod on some glass and stubbed my toe on something hard.

'Fuck!' I shouted, fear turning to anger. I clutched my foot, blood dripping through my fingers. Limping on, I found the panel by the door to the kitchen and keyed in the same code I'd used every morning since I took over. It was the same code Dad had keyed in for the last thirty years. The screaming stopped, although my ears didn't adjust, the wailing continued like a ghostly echo. Had I damaged my eardrums?

A dog barked nearby, angry at being woken, no doubt like its owners. I stumbled back to the object I'd stubbed my toe on, slipping on the blood and landing hard on my behind. Hoping the dressing gown had prevented me embedding glass into my buttocks.

I picked up a brick that had a note tied to it. The obvious choice for throwing through a window. I slid the elastic band off and pulled the paper away from the brick.

SHE SUFFERED, NOW YOU WILL TOO

Who was she? It couldn't be Hayley; she wouldn't refer to herself in the third person. Unless this whole mess wasn't about Hayley at all?

'Excuse me, mam, are you all right?' A flash of light waved

across my face and I looked up to see a police uniform coming towards me.

'Yes, I think so. I mean, I've cut my foot, but otherwise I'm okay,' I said, trying to stand. The female officer slipped a hand under my arm and helped me to my feet. She led me a few steps to Frank's desk and I sat on the edge.

'I'm Constable Morris. Are you the owner?' she asked, moving around the office, using her torch for the darker corners. I realised that one of the lights had been smashed too. What a mess.

'Yes, Sophie White.' My voice was weak, unrecognisable.

'I was just clocking off when I heard the alarm as I was driving past.'

'Sophie?' A shout from the street carried on the wind before Frank stepped over the threshold into the office. He was wearing pyjama bottoms with a thrown-on jumper, and slippers. His hair standing on end, fresh from his pillow. He only lived in the next street and must have heard the alarm. I'd never been so pleased to see him.

'Frank,' I wailed and burst into tears as soon as his arms wrapped around me.

Half an hour later, I was drinking a cup of hot, sweet, tea in my kitchen upstairs whilst having my foot bandaged by a paramedic.

'I'm so sorry, I can't believe they called you,' I said, mortified.

'Don't be silly, it's no trouble. To be honest, you may need stitches, so make sure you go to the walk-in tomorrow and let them take a look.' He stood to pack his medical kit.

I bid the paramedic a goodnight and he left, passing Frank, panting as he emerged from the stairs.

'Right, I've swept up and washed the floor with a mop. I think all the glass has gone. The insurers are on their way to board the window, but it'll be a couple of days before a new pane is sorted.'

I sighed and rested my head in my hands. I was so tired I wanted to go back to bed and forget this night ever happened. The nausea from the bug had never left, my mouth felt like it was swimming in saliva. I swallowed it down.

'What's going on, Sophie?' Frank asked, rubbing his whiskers. In all the years I'd known him, I don't think I'd ever seen him with stubble. He was clean-shaven every day, but tonight he looked like an old man.

'Ms White, we've secured the premises. Would I be able to take a statement from you now?' The constable arrived and drew back a chair next to Frank.

I could feel all eyes on me, waiting for me to speak. I shifted in my seat, my bandaged foot propped on a chair opposite; acutely aware I was wearing a flimsy nightdress in front of a stranger and my surrogate father. I pulled my robe together tighter and the officer retrieved a black notepad from her pocket. I could have pleaded ignorance and said I had no idea what the note was about, but I was exhausted by the relentless threats which were now being put into action. Was I even safe in my own home any more? All I wanted was for it all to go away, but I had no idea how to make that happen.

So, I told Frank and the constable everything, from the first note, to the card, the calls, the flowers, the rat, all of it. I gave them a brief overview of the night at Park Lane and why we were there at the house. I felt my cheeks flush and could barely look at Frank as he sighed and shook his head. I told them I had no idea why we were being targeted after so much time had passed.

The constable listened intently, scribbling page upon page in her notebook. Her eyes growing larger as I went on. I could see she was trying not to convey how far-fetched it sounded as I weaved the tail of how we were connected. How Gareth's death, Becca's arson and now the damage to Whites could all be down to the same culprit. Frank's frown deepened the longer I spoke and when I'd finished, the constable asked me to hand over all the evidence I'd accumulated. I wrote down the number that had been calling too, but I doubted that it would be traced. It would likely be a pay-as-you-go, what do they call them? A burner phone.

'Who do you think is targeting you?' the constable asked.

'I thought it was Hayley Keeble, as she was known back then, but now, I really don't know.' I drank the remnants of my cold tea, the taste making me gag. Once the statement had been taken, we viewed the CCTV, but whoever it was knew it was there. Dressed in black again and in view for seconds, launching the brick through the window before making their escape.

By the time the constable left, citing a detective would be in contact with me later that day, it was almost four and dawn didn't seem so far away. My foot throbbed and it hurt to put pressure on it. Frank gave me some painkillers and helped me upstairs to bed.

'Shall I call your dad or that fella you've been seeing?'

'No, thanks, Frank. I'm fine, and don't you dare tell Dad okay. I'll tell him about the office tomorrow.'

'Why didn't you tell me all this was going on?' he asked wearily.

'I didn't want to worry you.'

'Well I am worried! You're like one of my own, Sophie. I can't look after you if I don't know what's going on.'

'It's not your job to look after me, Frank,' I managed, although I was grateful he was.

'I'm glad I didn't have to worry about my Tommy getting up to antics like that when he was your age.' Frank shook his head, a smile playing on his lips.

'Rubbish! You just never knew what he got up to,' I teased.

'I'll go out through the office and lock you in. I'll pop by later. Shall I ring the guys and tell them we're not opening today?'

'Would you? I think it was Lucy and Beth on with me for the Saturday shift. Tell them to enjoy their weekend and I'll see them bright and early on Monday. Ask Beth to cancel any bookings we had. She'll have access to the database from home.'

Frank nodded and leant to kiss the top of my head before disappearing out the door. I listened to the stairs creak as he made his way down.

The wound on my foot pulsated as I lay awake, waiting for the painkillers to kick in. I was exhausted but at the same time too wired to sleep. Having told the police everything, a weight had been lifted. Although I wasn't sure why? What could they do? Were they going to find the culprit? I doubted it. They'd already thought they'd solved the case of Becca's car, which I told the constable had to be a set-up.

I wasn't sure how much more I could take. Was I going to end up like Becca, or Robyn, or worse, like Gareth? How far was this person willing to go to get their message across? What did they want? To punish us? To get their pound of flesh? It was like a jigsaw puzzle, but I didn't have all the pieces to make it fit together. How could I make it stop?

31

The painkillers Frank had given me, which I had in the cupboard, pilfered from Mum's stash when she had her knee operation, knocked me out until midday. I hobbled downstairs and found him in my kitchen, making tea and toast as though it was the most normal thing in the world.

'Have you not been home?' I joked. Trying to ignore the uncomfortable niggling in the pit of my stomach, that he was in the flat without my knowledge.

'Can't you tell?' He rubbed his smooth face.

I sat at the table and he delivered my brunch. I was surprised to find that I was hungry, the bug finally eradicated. 'Thank you.'

'I didn't mean to startle you. Only you haven't been answering your phone and I was getting worried. The electrician came to install another light, he rang when he arrived and I had to let him in, so I thought I'd pop up and check on you.'

'Frank it's Saturday, I could have done that! Crikey, go home to Diane, would you.'

'He's almost finished, I'll lock up and see you Monday, or do you need me to run you to the walk-in centre?'

'I'll be fine,' I said, raising my eyebrows and enunciating each word. He was as bad as a mother hen.

'I've just fitted another outside light, this one's a sensor. I had one tucked away in the garage as a spare at home. Saw yours was smashed. You're not having much luck with lights, are you? When did that happen?'

'God, about three weeks ago. I kept meaning to get it replaced.'

'Well, it's all done now, love.' Frank winked, his eyes twinkling.

'Honestly, I just don't know what I'm going to do when you retire.' I felt my bottom lip quiver and Frank's ears tinged pink as he turned to leave. Stomach tightening, I found my toast hard to swallow. 'Thanks, Frank, for everything. I really appreciate it.' Choking the words out as my throat constricted.

'Take it easy pet.' Hot tears pricked my eyes, but I was grateful Frank had descended the stairs before he'd noticed. I pushed my palms to my eyes and muttered.

'Hold it together Sophie.'

'Who are you talking to?' A cheery-looking James popped his head around the door. Frank must have let him in. The expression changed as soon as he saw the state of my foot and the tears in my eyes. I must have looked a mess, but I didn't care. 'Holy shit, what happened to you?

'Have you not seen the office?' I retorted.

'No, I came around the back?'

I told James about the brick but left out the note. He immediately dived into conspiracy theories based around Hayley and I listened half-heartedly whilst I ate. Any other day, I would have offered to make him tea or something to eat, but I was tired, irritable and not in the mood to play hostess to his lies. My foot throbbed like it had its own pulse.

As James spoke, my mind drifted, consumed. He'd been to see Hayley's mum. He knew everything I knew, maybe more as he was friends with Gareth. How much hadn't he told me? What kind of game was he playing?

'Well, it's in the hands of the police now, I've told them everything,' I interrupted.

James's eyes widened at that. 'What did they say?'

'They're going to look into it. Becca's car and now the agency window, whoever it is, it's not just cards any more. They're escalating into acts of violence.'

James frowned, tilting his head to the side. He didn't know about Becca's car, or was pretending he didn't. I explained about the arson attack and Robyn's subsequent arrest. He puffed air out of his cheeks and put his hands behind his head. 'Jesus Christ.'

'Look, James, I'm sorry but I'm tired, I'm in a shitty mood and I've got to go to the walk-in centre. Can we do this another time?' I said, concentrating on my toast, not bothering to see if my words had caused any offence. As far as I was concerned, he was a liar, for whatever the reason. What had started between us was not going any further.

'Well, I'll take you, go get dressed and I'll run you there now,' he replied, unfazed.

I hesitated, not wanting to spend any more time with him than I had to, but now I'd relieved Frank, I'd have to call a cab. The cut on my foot twinged on cue; something told me I'd be getting stitches today.

'Make yourself a tea, I might be a while,' I sulked, biting into my toast and throwing the remnants back onto the plate.

James filled the kettle and I hobbled upstairs to have a quick wash at the sink and get dressed. The only footwear I could get over my bandage were soft, UGG-style boots. I knew I looked a mess with unwashed hair and jogging bottoms, but it would have to do. I'd fit in at the walk-in centre – it was usually full of pissheads and reprobates looking to get some shelter from the weather. It was another reason I came round to the idea of James accompanying me.

Before we left, I wanted to see the damage in daylight. Hopping through into the agency from the kitchenette, it looked the same, although I could see my office was in total darkness due to an enormous board where the glass should have been. Frank had done a fantastic job clearing up and I made a mental note to buy him something nice to say thank you.

James enquired about the CCTV, but I told him it was with the police. It wasn't a lie exactly, but I didn't tell him there was nothing useable on there. I was intrigued in case he gave anything away. Whether he would be nervous now the police were on the case. What was it my mum used to say? 'Keep your friends close and your enemies closer'.

* * *

The walk-in centre was full, as it always was. We managed to find two seats next to each other at the far end. However we had to sit next to someone who smelt like he'd washed his clothes in ammonia. It did nothing for my stomach, which felt like it was hanging in the balance.

I was seen by the triage nurse within twenty minutes, who confirmed I would need either stitches or glue. I had to go back to the waiting room until a doctor could see me to confirm and close the wound properly. In the space of time between seeing the triage and the doctor, James and I witnessed one fight, a couple having a drunken lovers' tiff and had listened to a baby screaming on loop for over an hour.

'God, it's like *EastEnders* in here,' James whispered. I couldn't help but giggle, he was right.

'A cross-section of society, shall we say.' I laughed, trying to sound as pompous as I could.

'Sophie White,' called a nurse from the door.

James helped me stand and I hobbled down the corridor and into a side room.

The doctor was a kindly West Indian gentleman, who assessed my foot and thankfully said glue should do it. While he typed up notes, the nurse who had called me in cleaned the wound again and glued it closed, placing surgical strips over the top. I was given a prescription for antibiotics and painkillers as well as some crutches. My initial excitement at being handed them soon faded when I realised they were difficult to manoeuvre.

'I think you need a licence for those,' James said as I nearly tripped him over.

'They've got a mind of their own,' I giggled, surprised to find my terrible mood had been lifted by a two-hour wait, some glue and a spot of people watching.

James stopped at the chemist on the way home and left me in the car to get my prescription filled. I sat, checking emails on my phone and flicking through Facebook, but there was nothing new, until I came to Gareth's page. Someone, with the name Anonymous Amy, had a post on Gareth's wall, which was provoking his friends and mourners. It read: *Are you sure you knew him at all?* It had caused a tirade of angry faces.

My phone buzzed. A text came through from a number I didn't recognise:

WHAT IS HE HIDING?

My mouth dried up and I found it hard to swallow. Who's 'he'? Did the text mean James? I spun around, but the parade of shops was empty. Someone must be watching me, but only a mother and daughter had come past since we parked. The car park was empty apart from one other car. I whipped my head around, trying to look out of each window, my view clouded by steam. If I didn't have a bandaged foot, I would have jumped out of the car and searched, but that wasn't an option. I was a sitting duck.

A loud tap on the window made me scream, but it was James clutching a paper bag from the pharmacy, signalling to me to unlock the door. I must have done it by accident.

I thrust my phone into my pocket and unlocked the car. James climbed in, wiping the window with his sleeve.

'What you been doing in here? Party for one?' he said, passing me the bag and strapping himself in.

'You know I'm full of hot air,' I quipped, unable to stop my eyes from darting around, still searching for the mystery texter.

James started the engine and lowered the windows to clear the steam. I pulled on my seatbelt and sat, ready to go, but we didn't move. James was staring straight ahead, looking at nothing in particular out of the windscreen.

'James, what is it?'

'I've got something to tell you,' he said, turning the engine off and swivelling his whole body to face me.

'What?' I tried to keep the tremor out of my voice.

James stared at me, eyes piercing as he decided whether to impart the information. I wrapped my arms around myself, trying to keep the warmth in. Acutely aware I was unable to run even if I wanted to.

'I don't think it is Hayley behind this. I've searched, but I can't find any record or trace of her after 1997. If I'm honest, I think there's a chance she may not be alive.' He lowered his eyes as he delivered the news, a poor attempt at a mark of respect. I didn't admit I'd been thinking the same thing. People don't disappear off the face of the earth. A flash of annoyance struck, and I tried to bite my tongue, but I couldn't.

'You went to see her parents,' I snapped, releasing the anger that had been building.

'I did, that's what I was going to tell you, but I'm guessing now that you visited too?' James's face crumpled, resigned now he knew it was game over. His secret was out, but I still didn't know why he'd visited?

The car was beginning to steam up again. We sat in silence for a minute, the vein in my head and foot throbbing simultaneously.

I broke the silence first, the words escaping from my lips with no control. 'Who's the photo of, in your wallet?'

He bit his lip and stared out of the window so I couldn't see his face. 'You've been going through my wallet?'

'It fell out when I moved it,' I lied unapologetically.

'Helen was my girlfriend in college. I didn't realise that photo was still in there.'

'She looks like Hayley. I mean, how Hayley did when we were young.'

His face turned back, a flash of anger in his eyes. 'No, she doesn't.' He was so abrupt, I was about to argue, but a text message came through on James's phone, the annoying chime interrupting us. He glanced at it and scowled, letting the phone drop into his lap.

My phone beeped on cue and I unlocked the screen to view the message:

DON'T TRUST HIM

'Are you getting texts now too?' He leant over to peer at my screen.

I snatched it away, like a child refusing to share a toy.

James rolled his eyes and held out his phone, showing me the screen:

STOP LYING TO HER

My voice caught in my throat. Whoever it was, they were reading my mind. It's like they could hear inside the car. But how?

I rubbed the condensation from the window, straining my eyes to see through the streaks.

James spoke first. 'I'm not lying to you, Sophie, I promise.'

'What happened to Helen?' I asked.

'Helen? What's she got to do with this. You sound a little crazy, Sophie.' He stared out of the window, away from me.

'You sound like you're avoiding the question,' I persisted.

'Helen and I were engaged in college, we were young, only nineteen. She was my first love and I guess you could say she broke my heart. She fucked my best mate.' He snapped back around, venom in his voice. I recoiled and the silence stretched out between us.

'Why did you visit Hayley's parents?' I asked, my voice lower, calmer.

'I was looking for Hayley.'

'Why?'

'Because Gareth was looking for her and I was helping. Do we have to talk about this now?'

I sighed; it was useless trying to get a straight answer out of him. Perhaps the texter was right.

'James, please take me home. I don't know what's going on, but I know there's stuff you're not telling me.' I shifted my body away from him and stared out of the window.

A minute later, the engine started, the car reversing out of the parking space. We drove home in silence, neither wanting to be the first to speak. The atmosphere was frosty and all the way back I was second-guessing myself. I didn't believe James meant me any harm, but how did I know for sure that he was a victim in all this too? There was so much he wasn't telling me about Gareth and Hayley. I knew he knew more than he was letting on. Was he simply protecting Gareth's memory? Or was there more to it?

James drove around the back of the agency, right to my front door, jumping out to rush round and help me out of the car. The atmosphere had dispelled a little, my anger fading. I was too tired to continue the argument. What was the point?

'Thanks for taking me to the walk-in centre,' I said.

James stared at me, his eyes boring into mine so intensely I had to force myself not to look away. 'No problem. I'm going to nip to the shop to get some bits. Can I get you anything? Microwave meals?'

I smiled at that but shook my head. 'No thank you.'

'They're trying to break us. You know that, don't you? We're stronger together.'

I wanted to believe him, but so many things didn't add up. With everything that had happened, I didn't know who to believe any more.

'I need some time,' I replied as I tried to manoeuvre my crutches into position.

James took my keys from me. 'I'm just going to open your door for you.' He held his hands, palms outwards in a placating gesture.

'Thanks,' I said, limping through the door as he held it open. 'I'll call you,' I added.

James let me go, although he looked deflated. The fight had gone out of him too.

Once I'd locked myself in, I cranked the heating to high, flopped onto the sofa and pulled the throw over me. My foot ached where it had been poked and prodded and I wanted to sit and feel sorry for myself. I knew I'd have to ring Dad, get to him before he spoke to Frank. I didn't want Frank to have to lie on my behalf, but I was dreading the call. Whenever anything happened with the business, Dad flew into panic mode. He couldn't let it go, couldn't let me run things by myself.

Just as I closed my eyes for a few minutes, the tiredness

sweeping in, there was a loud knock on the door below. I wished I had one of those high-tech security entrance buzzers as I hobbled down the stairs. Before I could open it, a knock came again, raising my hackles. I was slow, but I was in pain. I unlocked and heaved open the door, hopping on one foot.

'Ms White?' A stubby man wearing a beige mac with round glasses on the end of his nose held up a warrant card for me to examine. His fingers tremored as they closed the black wallet before I'd had a chance to see more than just his photo.

'Yes?'

'I'm Detective Constable Wren and this is Constable Morris. I believe you have already met. May we come in?' I manoeuvred around the tight hallway, pulling open the door wide and seeing Constable Morris, who came out to the alarm last night, appear behind him. I directed them both inside, up the stairs, hobbling after them.

'May I help you?' Detective Wren turned, halfway up, holding out a hand.

'No, I'm fine, thank you though. Please take a seat in the kitchen.'

'Shall I stick the kettle on?' Constable Morris asked once we were all in the kitchen and I nodded, feeling a flush rise up my chest as Detective Wren looked around the room and surveyed me as he sat down.

'Constable Morris has given me an overview of the events leading up to the criminal damage, but can you tell me in your own words what has been going on?' He withdrew a notebook from his pocket, flipped it open and sat, pen poised.

As I spoke, reiterating what I'd told the constable the night before, he remained quiet, listening intently, his body language passive. I repeated the story chronologically, beginning with the night when we were kids, to receiving the first note, the flowers and calls. Before moving onto Gareth's death in St. Albans and Becca's car fire in Hove. Everything up until the brick thrown through my window last night. I told Detective Wren how we were all connected, pulling the photo down from the fridge to show him the cross over Gareth's face.

He rubbed his chin more than once, his face a constant frown, occasionally taking a mouthful of tea that had been delivered by Constable Morris. I wrapped my fingers around mine, to absorb the warmth.

'You believe this is a vendetta, against all of you for something that happened twenty years ago?' he confirmed.

I didn't think he looked overly convinced and I had to admit it sounded far-fetched. 'I know how it sounds, but someone is doing this to us. I'm sure it's connected.'

'I agree. I don't believe in coincidences. So, Hayley Keeble is the lady's name?' Eyes wide, I nodded, and Detective Wren underlined Hayley's name on his pad. He rubbed his chin again, scraping the stubble with his fingers. He didn't seem particularly dynamic, but I felt my shoulders ease down, just hearing him say he believed they were connected too. I wasn't going mad. 'Whoever it is, it's certainly escalating from harassment. I would advise you and your friends to be cautious, Ms White, is there somewhere else you can stay for the time being?'

'Yes, there is, but the estate agency is my business, it makes sense for me to be here.'

'Understood. You must take precautions; lock up as soon as you get in, leave lights on and be extra vigilant.' I nodded although I was pretty much doing all of those things already. Detective Wren stood to leave.

'I believe you've given everything you've received to Constable Morris already?'

'Yes, I think so,' I replied. He fumbled in the pocket of his coat and drew out his wallet, holding a white card out to me. 'My contact number is on there if you need anything.'

I took the card, nodding.

'Let me look into this, I'll contact Hertfordshire police and do a bit of digging on Ms Keeble.' I eased myself up from the chair, my tea untouched. 'No, stay there, we'll see ourselves out.' Detective Wren frowned at my bandaged foot.

'I have to double-lock the door anyway.' I smiled tightly, feeling a wave of tiredness wash over me. The relief of getting everything off my chest and onto someone else's plate. I believed Detective Wren would be thorough in his investigation and he stood a far better chance of finding Hayley than any of us.

Once they were gone, I locked myself in, drawing the dead-bolt across and feeling instantly safer. I padded through to the lounge, ignoring my rumbling stomach to lay down for a nap on the sofa, knowing I was putting off the inevitable. I pulled the throw over me and snuggled down. Calling Dad could wait until later.

* * *

When I woke, it was dark and I banged my foot on the coffee table sitting up, disorientated and confused as to why I wasn't in my bed. Howling into the air like a beast of the night, I clutched my foot and attempted to switch on the lamp beside the sofa. The tall stem wobbled precariously. I was clumsy at the best of times and a bandaged foot seemed to exacerbate things. My phone lay on the coffee table, almost out of charge. I pressed the screen, gasping as I'd slept until half eleven. I'd be awake all night.

There was nothing for it, I needed food. I limped to the kitchen, forgoing the crutches as I was quicker without them, and created a feast. I cooked an omelette with Micro Chips on the side, followed by a half-full tub of ice cream hidden at the back of the freezer. I munched away, enjoying a David Attenborough documentary on insects. Intrigued by how cut-throat they were, females executing the males, seconds after they'd mated. I wasn't overly interested in nature, but his voice soothed even the worst of days. When I'd finished and let my food go down, I fashioned a waterproof dressing with tape, cling film and a carrier bag. Managing to have a bath with my bad foot hanging over the side. It wasn't comfortable, but it was nice to be clean and in fresh pyjamas.

I checked my emails and messages. Called the mysterious texter a few times, hoping if anything, I'd piss them off by calling in the middle of the night. The phone rang but wasn't answered and there was no voicemail to leave a message. I googled Hayley Keeble as I did most days, to see if anything new came up. I knew it wouldn't, but it had become a force of habit. It was the same today: Hayley couldn't be found on Facebook, Twitter, Instagram or LinkedIn. If she was alive, which deep down I doubted, what kind of life might she be living now? At school she'd been great at science and wanted to go into forensics. Maybe she was managing a lab in New Zealand? Maybe she'd married and had a new name? I hoped that wherever she was, she was alive, happy and not mixed up in any of this.

I moved onto Facebook, but nothing new had been posted from Becca or Robyn, not for a while anyway. I'm sure they had more important things to think about. Other random acquaintances had posted pictures of their cats and gym sessions, but I wasn't interested in those. I had a look at Gareth's page, the mournful messages remained, with some added I hadn't seen. I clicked through his photos. There were a few from our school-days and it made my stomach lurch to see him as I remembered him. The boy with the floppy brown hair and cheesy grin.

As I scrolled through, I saw a video for the ice bucket challenge that was popular a few years ago. Frozen in time at the perfect spot; Gareth with an avalanche of water about to hit. It was a charity craze; you had to pledge a tenner and douse yourself with a bucket of ice-cold water, then nominate your friends. Gareth's video looked like it had been filmed in a caravan park. There was lots of giggling in the background and the image shook for a second before focusing on Gareth:

'I'm doing the water bucket challenge for ALS and I've pledged ten pounds. I nominate Barry, Mick, Louis and Jade.' Without hesitation, he lifted the bucket over his head, dousing himself in the freezing water. Lots of swearing and laughter followed.

My heart leapt into my throat. I struggled to swallow, as though I was the one under a torrent of glacial liquid, chilled to the bone. Gaping at the screen, shuddering, I replayed the video twice. Positive the voice I'd heard down the phone, from those anonymous calls, was Gareth's.

I dropped the phone onto the sofa, Gareth's words, his deep gravelly voice on loop inside my head. I was right. It was a recording being played down the phone. I remembered the clicking of the tape recorder going on and a cough in the background. I didn't recognise the voice, but why would I? I didn't know Gareth as an adult. We'd never spoken and as far as I knew he was dead. It wouldn't cross my mind the voice was his.

What had he said again? I closed my eyes, replaying it in my head, trying to remember. For the second time, I wished I'd recorded the phone call, but it seemed so insignificant. He was talking about someone; Gareth had said he was "crazy about her back then". I didn't realise at the time but it seemed he was talking about him and me. I didn't know who 'he' was.

Stupid I hadn't made the connection sooner. I knew he was disappointed not to be paired with me that night. I wasn't sure I'd made the right decision at the time. We were such good friends, it made sense for our first time to be with each other. But what was I supposed to do? Hayley was mad for him. If I was honest, I

didn't want him, not like that. I only started having feelings for
Elliot afterwards.

We dated for around a year. I guess you could say he was my
first love. He went on to college in Horsham to do a Social Studies
course and left me behind. We didn't break up as such, we were
both busy and just kind of parted company. It was all very
amicable and when I did bump into him a couple of years later
on a night out in Crawley, he bought me a drink and we had a
giggle over old times.

Back then, I was more interested in trying to play cupid for
my friend. My plan was, if I made it happen, Gareth would see
how great Hayley was, and they'd start going out. It was stupid
and childish, but I didn't see it at the time. Love needs to work
both ways. I'd made a mess of things, thinking I was so clever.
Something must have happened between them that night, even
though they didn't admit it. All this time, had I been missing the
obvious? Had they had unprotected sex and Hayley got pregnant?
As a result, her parents had made her move almost a hundred
miles away and pushed her into having an abortion.

Did she even want to get rid of her baby? She was a child
herself, but how would I have reacted if it was me? I imagined
Hayley telling her mother, being terrified to admit the truth to
her military father. It was strange though, she seemed fine at the
Halloween party. Perhaps it was the relief it was out in the open,
at least with her parents, and she was moving away? Or maybe
she was resigned to her fate? It was such a long time ago I struggled to remember. The secret must have eaten her up. It was such
a stigma to get pregnant as a teenager. Had her dad punished her
or made her feel dirty? It made me wince and I hobbled up,
attempting to pace the room so I could think clearly, but I only
lasted a few steps before collapsing back onto the sofa. It was
such a mess and guilt weighed on me, like an elephant sitting on

my chest, for being a part of it. For being the organiser, the instigator.

I'd ruined her life without even realising it and been blissfully unaware for the past twenty years. What could I do to make amends? How could I say I was sorry when I had no idea where she was? Hot tears splashed onto my fleece pyjamas and I curled my knees to my chest. Were we all going to end up like Gareth? My gut told me his death wasn't an accident; I didn't care how much alcohol was in his system.

Who had recorded him? Surely not James? Yet he was the only one still friendly with Gareth. He said himself they met up regularly. James must have got him talking about the schooldays, about that night? Was he picking us off one by one in revenge for Hayley? If so, why? They barely knew each other. Both were shy and quiet; I don't believe I ever saw them exchange more than a few sentences outside of school. But I felt James held the key to this puzzle. Going to see Mrs Keeble, still being friends with Gareth before his death. What and who was he protecting? The longer he withheld information, the more dangerous it was becoming for all of us involved. I had to challenge him.

I had even more questions than before and still no answers. I was going around in circles. I took some of the painkillers the doctor had prescribed and went upstairs to bed, hoping they would knock me out. I had never been more alone and vulnerable in the place that had always been my home. Even with a new front door, CCTV outside and extra deadbolts, I didn't feel safe.

* * *

I got a taxi to my parents' house mid-morning on Sunday, having been too cowardly to ring my dad beforehand. After the initial shock when I came through the front door, I was ushered in and stationed in the kitchen with my foot elevated while Mum fussed around me.

'Goodness, love, what have you done?'

'It's not as bad as it looks, Mum.'

Dad fetched me a cushion and made tea while Mum carried on cooking. She had numerous pans on the stove bubbling away that she was juggling. She was an amazing cook and baker; the kitchen really was the heart of the home when we all lived at the flat. Mum would bake bread sometimes or scones, banana loaf, all sorts. The smell of roast chicken made me salivate as I filled my parents in on what had happened.

I tried my best to play it down, I didn't want to worry them unnecessarily. I didn't tell them I was targeted, or that a note had been tied to the brick that came through the window. Instead, I said the police believed it was most likely drunks coming back from The Boar on Friday night. Dad seemed appeased once I'd told him everything was going to be replaced on Monday or Tuesday, all covered by insurance, and Frank had rushed from home to help.

'Frank was amazing, my knight in shining armour.' I grinned, taking a sip of my scorching tea. He'd called my mobile whilst I was in the taxi on the way over. Checking I was okay and making sure I'd gone to the walk-in centre to have my foot seen to.

'I wish you'd rung me Sophie,' Dad grumbled.

'I didn't want to worry you, Dad.'

Everything seemed better once we'd eaten. Dad had made his famous trifle, which he'd been making since I was a child. It was real comfort food and at times I wished I still lived with them so I could be looked after. It wouldn't be long before the roles were reversed, and it would be me looking after them.

'How did you get on with the search for Hayley?' Mum asked, putting the dessert bowls to one side.

'Not bad actually. I went to Bicester last week, I found Hayley's parents.'

Mum gawped at me. 'Really? How are they?'

'Jackie's fine, looks as glamourous as ever, but Alan's got dementia.'

'Oh dear. And what about Hayley? How's she?'

'They haven't seen her since 1997. They left because Hayley got pregnant. Moved her out of the area, so she could start afresh, but she ran away.'

Mum's hands flew to her mouth and she pulled her chair in tighter to the table. 'That's awful, the poor girl.'

'I know, it's so sad. We've all been looking for her, but it's like she never existed.' Mum shook her head, saying it was every parent's worst nightmare.

'We had Sue and Jim over for dinner last night. I cooked a shepherd's pie, it was nice. They're very low, bless them, obviously. We've convinced them to come away with us. Your dad's always wanted to do Christmas in a log cabin. It'll be hard for them this year, no children left to visit, no grandchildren. Of course, you're welcome too, love'

I nodded, my smile stretched tightly across my face. It didn't sound like the most inviting Christmas invitation. 'Maybe, we'll see what happens.'

'I guess you'll be spending it with that fella. You need to bring him round, I'd like to meet him,' Dad said as I got up to clear the plates.

I shrugged and with that he took his cue and disappeared into the front room, eyes heavy and belly full.

It wasn't until later, when I was helping Mum put the plates away, that she spoke of when I was young.

'It was so nice when you were fourteen, fifteen. Finally, a group of friends that you got on with. That Robyn was a bit rough around the edges, but the rest were nice kids from nice families.'

I snorted. Mum was such a snob and if Robyn could hear her, she'd be spouting obscenities. 'Yeah, they were a nice bunch.'

'Gareth was smitten with you; we could all see it. Sue and I always hoped you'd get together one day.'

'I think he was the one that got Hayley pregnant.' I felt a sharp twist in my chest saying it aloud.

'I don't see how, love.'

I frowned, surely, I didn't have to explain to Mum how babies were made. 'What do you mean?'

'Well, Sue told me that Gareth couldn't have children. He'd been trying with Lisa for ages apparently. They went to the doctors and a specialist; Sue and Jim were devastated as they hoped so desperately to have grandchildren. Awful, isn't it.'

'But I thought he had a son with her, I saw him at the funeral.'

'No, no, she already had him when they met. That boy isn't Gareth's, although he took him on as if he was. His real father has never even seen him.'

'Well, if Gareth didn't get Hayley pregnant, who did?'

'Your guess is as good as mine, love,' Mum said, wiping down the surfaces.

34

The office was cold on Monday and I layered my shirt with a jumper and a jacket. The board covering the gap was good at keeping most of the elements out, but the chilly breeze still managed to whistle through. The glaziers would be coming on Tuesday as the pane was a bespoke size and had our logo running across the top like a watermark. Still, it was an impressive turn-around by the glaziers and the insurers, so I couldn't complain. I whacked the heating up as high as it would go. Everyone gawped at the damage as they came in and we had a quick team meeting once the tea was made so I could update them.

I assumed it would be busy as we were closed on Saturday and I wasn't wrong. Before I got on with work, I emailed over the footage gathered from the camera to Detective Wren. The camera was triggered by motion, so recorded snippets whenever there was any activity outside. There were over forty small files and I added a note about the voice recording down the phone, which I now believed was Gareth. Once that was done, I began my usual Monday-morning calls to all the homeowners to deliver their weekly update. Minutes after finishing my last call as I was about to get up and make tea, Mrs Davidson popped in.

'I've been trying to get hold of you,' I said, presenting my best smile and inviting Mrs Davidson into my office as Hope rounded the desk.

'Oh no, what's happened?' Mrs Davidson's mouth gaped, awaiting bad news.

'Nothing, you'll have a missed call from me that's all. Everything is going fine. The survey came back with no major structural concerns. The buyers are happy, so it's ticking along. I like to make sure all our homeowners are up to date on a weekly basis. There's nothing worse than being out of the loop.'

Mrs Davidson lowered herself onto the chair. I sat too so I wouldn't be towering over her.

'Wonderful news. I wanted to come in and tell you we're going on a little break. We've decided to move in with my sister until the house is sold. She's in Cornwall, so it'll be like a holiday for us. I've arranged the movers to come in on Friday to pack everything and they're going to put it in storage. The house will be empty, but you have a set of keys if you need access. I'll only be at the end of the phone.' She smiled and clapped her hands together, excited by the prospect of leaving 32 Park Lane.

'That will be perfect. And don't worry, between Whites and Howells solicitors we'll see the sale through.' I promised. It wasn't something I normally did as you could never tell what would happen with a chain. Sometimes buyers would pull out at short notice because of the tiniest detail. Or people changed their minds for whatever reason and decided not to sell after all. However, I was determined to see the sale of that house through to the end. I wanted it to be someone else's problem.

'It's the end of an era. I've been in that house since 1997.'

I shivered, so the Davidsons had bought the house through

my dad all those years ago. It was their house we sneaked in to for the evening. I felt my cheeks flush, embarrassed at my wanton behaviour back then. I didn't even think about whose property it was, only that I had access to the keys. 'That's a long time,' I eventually acknowledged.

Mrs Davidson was keen to hear all about the window incident, so I gave her the same story I told Dad. The same story I told the staff later that morning. Only Frank knew more, and I darted him a warning look to keep quiet. He didn't bat an eyelid, more concerned with how my foot was. I'd put on smart trousers, but I had to wear my soft boots over the bandage. It wasn't exactly chic, but at least I was there.

I didn't ring Robyn until the evening, once everyone had gone home for the day and I'd eaten beans on toast to fill the hole. I couldn't be bothered to cook anything. That was the beauty of living alone; I could do what I wanted, whenever I wanted. Robyn answered on the fifth ring.

'Hiya.' She sounded gloomy.

'Hi, how's things?'

'Shit. That bitch fired me after I got arrested at work. She was looking for an excuse anyway.'

'God I'm sorry, Robyn, that sucks.'

'Yep, but I'll find something soon enough. I've applied to be a blood courier, think I'd enjoy that, whizzing around on my motorbike.' Now that did sound like the perfect job for Robyn.

'I wanted to ask you a bit of a personal question, Robyn.' My palms hot.

'Shoot.'

'When you "did it" with James, did it all go to plan?'

Robyn snorted. 'It was hideous, he struggled to get it up. I kept giggling because I was nervous, which probably didn't help. It was cringeworthy and even now I struggle to look the guy squarely in the eye. Finally, we managed to get going, it was like building flatpack furniture.'

I laughed out loud, trying to match James back then to the James of today. Thankfully he'd moved on since then. 'Was he with you all the time we were in the house?'

'Yeah, don't you remember? We all stood outside didn't we, waiting to leave, then we realised Gareth and Hayley weren't there. Why do you ask, Soph?'

'I'm not sure, it's a theory I'm working on, but I don't want to say anything until I've got more information.'

'Fair enough,' Robyn said flatly and that was the best thing about her. If it was Becca, she'd be pleading with me to tell her more, as would I with someone else. Robyn didn't give a shit about that stuff. She hadn't changed a bit.

She explained that the police had dropped the charges once her alibi with Chloe and another friend had been confirmed. Which made it all the more frustrating that she'd lost her job. I wished her well and I said I'd be in touch when I had more news and I hoped to meet them both soon.

So, if James had been with Robyn all the time, he couldn't have snuck down to have sex with Hayley. Although, there was nothing to say Hayley got pregnant that night. It could have been before, or after.

* * *

The rest of the week whizzed by. The glaziers fitted the new pane and the office looked as good as new. James had kept his distance, giving me the time, I'd asked for. Detective Wren called to say the footage didn't really show anything useful, as we'd expected, but he had been in touch with Hertfordshire police and they were now searching CCTV in the area on the night of Gareth's accident for whom he had spent his last few hours with. Wren had also written up the cards, rat and calls as harassment and linked the report with the one filed for criminal damage.

His next step was to speak to Becca to hopefully clarify the connection with the arson attack on her car. There was still no sign of Hayley, but he said he'd made inroads there. I was relieved it was being taken seriously.

Work was busy and I'd been stuck in the office resting my foot whilst the others were out on viewings and new instructions. I'd had four people list their properties because of recommendations from Mrs Davidson and the leaflets brought in another two. The team pulled together, and we worked long hours all week. By the time Friday came, Gary had two sales and Lucy and Hope had one each. I had nothing in the fridge for dinner so suggested a trip to the local Indian restaurant to save me having to go to the shops. I was pleasantly surprised when everyone agreed to join to me at short notice.

Beth came along for a starter as her boyfriend was taking her to the cinema, mainly because Gary ribbed her about being under the thumb.

'Oh, piss off, he's had tickets for the Halloween remake booked all week and I can't be bothered with the row it'll cause,' she hissed in her defence as she got up to leave.

'Bloody hell, what number remake are they on now?' I asked.

'No idea! I'm just going for an easy life.' Beth laughed.

'Ignore Gary, it's fine, thanks for coming, Beth. Have a great weekend and I'll see you Monday,' I said, patting her arm.

The five of us continued drinking until the early evening, our tablecloth stained with wine, beer, curry and the vivid orange mango chutney. Gary and Frank had a heated debate on Brexit, with Gary a fierce Remainer, who was going to London the following day to march in protest. Supporting the campaign for a 'people's vote'. I zoned out, instead listening to Lucy and Hope talk about how gorgeous Princess Eugenie's wedding dress was last week.

Frank was the first to leave and stumbled out of the door, after a few too many Cobras, into the cool night air to zigzag his way home.

'I need the loo,' Hope announced to the table.

Lucy rolled her eyes and took her by the arm to the ladies. Hope had consumed a bottle of wine to herself. Every time we went out, she seemed to drink more and more.

Gary moved around the table and wedged me in to the corner, slurring his words. 'I worry about you, living above the office. All by yourself.' The smell of hops emanated from his lips. My stomach churned in response and I leant back, shoulders against the partition separating us from the next table.

'You don't need to worry, Gary, I'm perfectly safe,' I said, eyeing the door to the ladies' toilet.

Gary put his forearm across the table as I shuffled further into the corner, telling myself I had no reason to be intimidated. It was just Gary and he'd had too much to drink. 'But I do worry. I'd look after you better than that James,' he said, placing his hands flat on the table as though laying his soul bare.

My insides squirmed and I smiled tightly. His words took me by surprise. Had I missed some signals over the past few weeks? 'Thanks, Gary, but I really don't need looking after, by anyone.' At six years younger than me, I should be flattered he found me attractive, but this kind of attention was the last thing I needed on top of everything else.

Thankfully Hope and Lucy were almost at the table, back from the toilets.

'I'm going to head out.' Gary said, grabbing his coat and stalking out of the restaurant.

'What the hell was that about?' Lucy asked, downing the last of her wine.

'Can we have the bill please,' I said to the waiter clearing our table. He nodded and walked away. Hope sat with her head in her hands, eyes rolling. 'Nothing. He's pissed that's all,' I replied.

Lucy shrugged. 'Thanks for the meal.'

'You're most welcome. Congrats on the sale!' I said, now wanting to get home.

I stayed in the restaurant with Lucy and Hope until their taxi arrived and headed into the night.

The restaurant was only round the corner, but alone, outside in the dark, I felt vulnerable. My foot had almost healed, but not so much I'd be able to run without tearing open the wound. I was still limping. It was past eleven and the roads were dead, no one was around, and the tapping of my low heels echoed on the pavement. Announcing my return. What if someone was waiting for me?

35

OCTOBER 2018

I didn't like the front entrance to the flat. The back of the office was dark with virtually no street lighting and lots of bins and places to hide. It was even quieter than the front. I never saw anyone. Most of the time, it was my imagination that scared me the most, one too many horror films as a teenager. When I moved out of my parents' and lived alone, I no long watched them.

It wasn't even late, barely nine o'clock, but the sun had set two hours ago. I held my keys as I walked, listening out for noises but only managing to freak myself out. Could whoever had been targeting us be waiting for me to stroll by, ready to jump out?

As I neared my front door a cat darted from behind the industrial bins, shrouded in darkness, and I swore loudly. My heart thundered in my chest and my hands shook so much I struggled to get the key in the door, fearing someone was coming up behind me, but when I turned, no one was hiding in the shadows.

Gary had gone home, maybe somewhat embarrassed at what he had said. Work and pleasure should never be mixed, it always ended in tears. Luckily it wasn't an issue as the only thing I found attractive about Gary was his work ethic. I still felt a little unsettled about what had gone on at the restaurant but that might have been down to the cards I found in his desk.

There had been an absence of messages, cards or texts since last weekend. Was the whole thing over? Would Hayley stop now? I hadn't heard from James, which was strange. I'd asked him for space, but I thought he'd have been in touch by now. I switched my phone off to stop myself from texting him. Never text drunk was one rule I always stuck to. I climbed into bed. Gary would be mortified in the morning for sure, knowing he'd have to face me. To say it would be awkward was an understatement.

* * *

As it happened, the conversation was over fast. Like pulling a plaster off. Gary came and found me making tea early in the morning soon after we opened. He stood in the doorway, his large frame filling the space.

'I'm sorry about last night.' His cheeks were a muddy red and he gave a slight shake of the head.

I chuckled awkwardly, instantly relieved. 'Don't worry about it. We were all pretty drunk and, anyway, I don't allow any of my employees to dip their pen in the company ink. It's not good for business and nine times out of ten, it ends badly. That goes for me too.' I gave him a tight smile, hoping I'd given the message loud and clear that I wasn't interested.

'Understood. Again, I'm sorry for the way I behaved.' Gary left the kitchen, his apology delivered.

Hope arrived half an hour late and looked dishevelled and green around the gills. She was very apologetic and did call ahead to say she'd slept through her alarm. When she did arrive, I considered sending her home but decided against it, what signal did that give to my team? That it was okay to show up late because of a hangover? I did however make her a strong coffee and had a lunch delivered from the bakers. I wasn't completely heartless.

'I feel awful. I'm never drinking again,' she wailed, pulling her hair out of her ponytail and letting it cascade around her shoulders. It was so dark, almost black. It couldn't be natural, although it suited her.

The office was empty, it was almost one and I was getting ready to shut for the day.

'Hair of the dog?' suggested Gary, winking at me.

Hope hung her head. 'No thanks!'

'Perhaps try to pace yourself next time, and you need to eat more, you're like a whippet,' I said, remembering Hope pushing her curry around her plate last night while the rest of us shovelled it in.

'Maybe. Anyway, how's that bloke you're seeing?' she asked, changing the subject. Gary started packing his desk, head bowed like he wasn't listening.

'I don't know, I haven't seen him all week.'

'Ah, he seemed nice. You should ring him.' Hope gingerly put her coat on, it was like watching her in slow motion.

I wished everyone a good weekend and locked up the office, checking all the machines were off and the alarm was set.

I composed a text to James, a simple 'hi, how are you?' but four hours later I sat alone in front of the television still with no response. It seemed odd. To distract me, I watched a movie I'd had on my Netflix list for ages, but I couldn't concentrate on it long enough to absorb the plot. Instead looking at my phone every couple of minutes to see if James had responded.

'This is ridiculous.' I grabbed the phone and dialled his number. It rang and rang, eventually going to voicemail. Had I been dumped? Irritation niggled at me even though I was the one that said I needed space. The poor guy couldn't win.

I tried again and this time a woman answered. My heart sank and I considered hanging up.

'Hello?'

'Hi, can I speak to James please?' I said after a pause.

'He's sleeping right now. Can I ask who this is?'

I could hear a familiar beeping in the background, but I couldn't put my finger on what it was. The woman sounded more like his mother than the lover I'd been picturing laying naked next to him in bed.

'It's Sophie, his, ummm, friend,' I stuttered.

'I'll let him know you called. Shall I tell him you'll be visiting tomorrow?' Her whisper was kind, but her words left me with a sense of foreboding.

'Visiting where?'

'Oh, my goodness, I'm sorry, dear, I assumed you knew. James is in East Surrey Hospital, on Ockley Ward.'

My stomach plummeted to the floor like a broken elevator. 'What happened? Is he okay?'

'Yes, he's out of the woods. He had a nasty wound to his side, but we've patched him up.'

The nurse told me the visiting hours began at two o'clock tomorrow and I asked her to let him know I would be coming.

I slumped back onto the sofa, questions flying around my head. When did it happen? Is that why he hadn't been in touch? Had someone tried to hurt him? Was he going to be okay? I felt sick at the thought of anything happening to James. Regardless of my trust issues, I still cared. If he was attacked it had to be related, it was too much of a coincidence not to be. Plus, it was virtual proof that him being attacked meant he wasn't behind any of it.

* * *

Visiting hours could not come round quick enough. I popped to my parents on the way, and Mum made me a quick sandwich. I'd already told them I wouldn't be staying for dinner this week. They were fine and happy to see I was on the mend, now walking without my crutches. Mum showed me a cottage she'd just booked for Christmas in Ashurst Forest. It looked picturesque and I was happy to witness her excitement about the trip away with friends, although I was sure they would be quite sombre festivities with Sue and Jim. I couldn't even think about Christmas yet, Halloween was only next week, but I knew how much Mum got out of the planning of these adventures.

When I reached East Surrey, I used the opportunity to hand the crutches back to reception before asking for directions to Ockley ward. It was on the fourth floor and I made my way up the stairs instead of using the lifts. I hated being trapped in there when a patient's bed was wheeled in. It all seemed so undignified, amongst strangers, wearing bedclothes. At their most vulnerable, although it couldn't be helped. How else were they supposed to move about the building?

As I reached the ward, I steeled myself for what I was about to see, my palms sweating. Would James be covered in bruises, tubes sticking out of him and monitors bleeping?

When I got to his bedside, he was sitting, propped up on pillows, sipping some water from a plastic cup and reading the paper. His face pale but bruise-free. I let out a loaded sigh and pulled across a chair. Pleased to see his lips curve upwards as soon as he saw me.

'What happened?' I asked, reaching over to take his hand in mine.

James lowered the sheet and raised his gown to reveal a large white bandage across his left side. 'I was jumped, stabbed.'

'You were stabbed?' I repeated and James's eyes shot around the ward.

'Sssshhhh.'

A few seconds passed, but the silence was broken by a loud snore coming from the next bed. I got up and pulled the curtain right around us before resuming my seat.

'I didn't see who it was, someone in black, wearing a motorcycle helmet. Didn't feel it at first, thought I'd been punched. They were long gone by the time I saw the blood and collapsed.' He sniffed.

'Jesus, are you okay? Is it serious?'

'Not life-threatening, not now anyway.'

'Where were you? Did they take anything?'

'No, nothing at all. I'd just left the flat, popping to the shop to get some cigarettes.'

'When did it happen?'

'Sunday afternoon?'

'James you've been in here a week! Why didn't you ring me?' I leant forward, squeezing his hand a little too hard.

'You did say you wanted some space,' he said, lips curled into a half-smile as he looked at me through his lashes.

I sighed and shook my head.

'What did the doctor say?'

'There were some complications, the knife went between the ribs, thankfully missing all the vital organs, but it did cause some internal bleeding. I was pretty groggy for a few days. I'm hoping I can go home today or tomorrow. Once my dressing has been changed.'

I sat back in the chair, staring at James's white face and the dark circles underneath his eyes. What next? I grabbed the chart at the end of the bed, but it was all numbers, BP, pulse, fluid, it meant nothing to me.

'Did you see the knife?' I wrung my hands together, this was all getting real, much too real.

'No, it all happened so quickly, but it was small apparently, the doctor said, from the shape of the wound.'

'Have you told the police?'

'Yeah, they were called, but there wasn't much to tell.' I glared at him. 'But yes, I've filed a report, they've been in to see me. They are going to look at surrounding CCTV.'

I already knew nothing would come of it. Whoever it was, they were too clever for that. I had to warn Becca, Mark and Robyn. She or he was out to hurt us now. It wasn't a game any more. No more cards or balloons, that was the warmup.

James passed me his phone, the line in his hand poking out, ready for medication to be administered. It made my throat constrict. I didn't like veins, or needles. Thankfully the bandaging hid most of it, but James hadn't failed to notice my fingers trembling.

'Look at the text messages.'

I opened the message icon, there was one from me, someone called Rob and a number with no contact attached. The same number that I'd given the police.

'Top one,' he instructed.

I swiped at the screen:

TWO DOWN, FIVE TO GO

I dropped the phone onto James's bed as though it burnt my skin. Tears spilled onto my cheeks as the stress of the last couple of months leaked out like a broken tap.

'Hey, hey. It's okay,' James said, leaning over to comfort me.

'It's not okay. It must be Hayley, she's alive and she's trying to kill us. She almost killed you and it's practically an admission that she killed Gareth,' I gestured at the text, still open on the display. 'We have to do something.' I wiped my eyes on my scarf, feeling like my head was going to cave in from the weight of it.

'We'll talk to the police. If it's Hayley, we'll find her,' James said, his voice soothing.

'I just want to know why James. What did we do?'

'Maybe it's what we didn't do.'

36

James was due to be discharged on Monday afternoon and I was going to the hospital to pick him up. I would leave Frank to run the agency, which I seemed to be doing more of lately. When I came down in the morning, I found him checking all of the locks and testing the alarm before we opened. He brushed it off, but I could tell from his hard stare and how deeply furrowed his eyebrows were that he was worried.

I shut myself away in my office and left a message for Detective Wren to tell him about James's attack. Then I phoned Becca and Robyn in turn to tell them the latest. They were both horrified to hear of James's stabbing, how this had escalated further into a physical attack. I could hear the trepidation in Becca's voice, she feared for the safety of her children. She was right. Any of us could be next.

'Do you think we should pack up and leave?'

'I'd consider it. If I didn't have Whites to run, I probably would. Leave it to the police. Detective Wren is going to get in touch with you to ask about the car fire. He's connecting the reports.'

'Are we seriously still thinking that this is Hayley? It's crazy!'

'I don't know,' I replied.

Before I ended the call, Becca's voice broke, her fear almost palpable down the line. 'I don't understand why this is happening.' Neither did I.

Robyn took the news more calmly, but I heard Chloe in the background, so maybe she was playing it down in front of her girlfriend.

Frank knocked on the door once I was off the phone to let me know Hope had called in sick.

'She can't have a three-day hangover surely?' I rolled my eyes, happy to change the subject from my drama. I knew it was playing on his mind and I wished I could turn back time to when he didn't know anything about Hayley. It was only because he was there when I explained it to the policewoman, otherwise I wouldn't have told him. Since then I always felt his eyes on me and Frank hovering all the time made me nervous. I knew he was only concerned for my safety and it was for my own good, but it substantiated my fear that I was in danger. I couldn't bury it under the carpet and pretend it was nothing if Frank was worrying on my behalf too. It was like a constant reminder Hayley, or someone, was out there, wreaking havoc, inching ever closer.

When Frank left, I rang the homeowners as usual and confirmed with Mrs Davidson that we were getting closer to exchange, and in a week or two the sale would be complete. She sounded pleased and much more relaxed now she was in Cornwall.

When I picked James up, we had to wait for ages at the hospital pharmacy for his prescription to be filled. We shuffled away with a bag of antibiotics and painkillers. By the time we got back to his place, it was late afternoon and I tucked James onto the sofa before popping out to purchase some provisions for him for the week. Twenty minutes later, I was back preparing an early dinner.

His kitchen was basic, obvious he was a single man, living alone. There weren't many plates or enough cutlery to hold much of a dinner party and the most extensive piece of kit, other than the microwave, was a pasta machine still in its dusty box. Perhaps the mysterious Helen had never lived here? He did say they were together in college and I doubted he'd lived in the flat for long.

I purchased microwave meals, prepared oven dinners, and a small amount of fresh food. Much like a shopping basket of my own, filled with food for one. Perhaps one day, I would be shopping for the both of us, together, under one roof? The idea made me feel light-headed. I'd never lived with anyone other than my parents. I'd come close, once or twice but something always got in the way, either that or it didn't feel right. Even though our relationship so far had been full of obstacles and I wasn't even sure if we were together in the normal sense, the connection I felt with James was strong. I cared for him and now I knew he wasn't targeting me over something that happened twenty years ago, I'd be able to open up and perhaps let him in.

I did have to confront him about the secrets he was keeping. I felt confident he was not the father of Hayley's unborn child; Robyn said so herself, she was with James the whole time that night. But why had he been searching for her? Why had Gareth asked him to? We'd have to talk about it soon. There were too many unanswered questions.

'Here, something to eat. Keep your strength up.' I handed James a bowl full of tomato and basil pasta.

'I could get used to this.'

'Do you want me to stay, for tonight, to, you know, look after you?' I asked as I headed back to the kitchen, hiding my rosy cheeks.

'I'd like that,' he called after me.

I headed back home to collect some things, calling Frank on the way to ask if he could open the office tomorrow if I wasn't there for nine. Was I relying on him too much? I realised earlier when I was in the shop that I hadn't bought Frank anything to thank him for helping out when the agency front window was smashed. I picked up a bottle of Glen Moray whisky and made sure to leave it on his desk when I popped home.

When I returned, James's spare key hot in my hand, he'd fallen asleep. I'd brought my laptop with me, so I sat in the armchair, listening to him snore gently beside me. Hoping the light from the screen or the tapping of the keys wouldn't wake him. I googled Hayley Keeble, but there were still no hits. Staring at the list of irrelevant links, it occurred to me that she might not even be Hayley any more. We'd considered the possibility of her being married with a new surname, but she didn't need to get married to change her name. She could have changed her name to anything. Become anyone. Isn't that what people do when they want to disappear? It's what I'd do. Change my name, change my appearance. She might not be a redhead any more, but the one thing she couldn't change was her age. We were both thirty-six, but aside from her freckles, I couldn't remember any distinguishing features, other than her Roman nose. She had no moles or scars that I could recall.

I searched how easy it was to change your name via deed poll. The process was a simple form and one-off payment of around £30. You didn't even need a birth certificate.

I moved on to Facebook, saw that Robyn had tagged us all, including Elliot, in one of the group selfies from our night out in Brighton. All of us beaming at the camera with bloodshot eyes.

From there, I clicked onto Gareth's memorial wall. Anonymous Amy had left another comment – this time a single word on his condolence page:

RAPIST

I shook my head, disgusted that Gareth's fiancé Lisa would have to see it. She didn't deserve the pain it would cause, to have Gareth's memory muddied with such an accusation.

I turned off the laptop, the search leaving a sour taste in my mouth. James began to stir and I got up to make us a cup of tea.

'Ah thanks,' he said when I placed it on the coffee table. He reached his arms up to stretch and then winced clutching his side.

'You okay?'

'Yep, forgot for a second that I'm the walking wounded.' He blew out a long breath.

'Listen, can you tell me why you really visited Hayley's parents? It's been playing on my mind. I have to know if it's all connected.'

James's eyes darkened for a second, but he nodded. 'Gareth asked me to go. His brother Craig said some stupid stuff, when we were all drunk one night. He said he'd slept with Hayley, trying to wind Gareth up, but we didn't believe him. That same night, after we left, Craig picked a fight with the wrong crowd and was pretty much beaten to death in the pub car park.'

I gasped, realising the story was vaguely familiar, Mum had told me when it had happened, a couple of years ago.

'Gareth looked up to his brother; I have no idea why; he was a real waste of space. Craig was the one that got him into steroids when we were in our twenties. For a while, they were juicing every day and hitting the gym hard. When Craig was killed, Gareth was devastated. He wanted to find out if what he'd said was true. That's why we went looking for Hayley. We found her parents and went to see them, only Gareth couldn't bring himself to go in, so I went instead.'

'So, Craig could have been the father of Hayley's baby?' I stiffened, my muscles rigid. Every fibre tensing as I tried to picture what I was suggesting.

'Maybe. But we never found Hayley and Gareth didn't want anyone to know that his precious brother might have knocked up a schoolgirl. He swore me to secrecy, to protect Craig's memory, for his parents. I promised I would, and now their sons are both gone.' James stared out of the window for a second before clearing his throat and taking a slurp of his tea.

'I wish you'd told me,' I said, feeling my chest loosen and nudging his arm with mine.

'I was trying to be a good mate.' James replied with a sigh.

* * *

The following morning, I left James sleeping and hurried home for a shower. He'd said his mum would be round and I didn't want to meet her and it look like I was sneaking out the door, the morning after the night before. Also, I'd been nervous leaving the flat, and office, unattended overnight, but nothing was amiss when I returned. Everything was where I left it, no cards or presents in sight. I had an extra spring in my step and concluded it was down to a good night's sleep, being away from home and with James who, despite the circumstances, did wonders for my mood. It felt fantastic to get everything out into the open; I could relax now there were no secrets between us.

When Frank arrived, we had a tea together, but I hadn't

missed much. I sent James a text to ask if he was missing me, not expecting a reply as he'd still be asleep, and got to work.

The morning whizzed by with customers dropping in and the phones seemed to be constantly ringing. Everyone was in, and at their desks, the air buzzing. Business was good and if it carried on, I would have to take on another salesperson, part-time maybe.

I sat behind my desk, eating a sandwich I'd nipped upstairs to make. When my mobile rang, it was Robyn and she was sobbing so hard I couldn't make out her words.

'Robyn, what's happened?

'There's been an accident,' she shrieked.

My heart stopped, like a clock that had abruptly ceased to tick. Whatever Robyn was about to say, I knew it wasn't good or an accident.

'Mark's in intensive care.'

37

OCTOBER 2018

I couldn't speak at first, my voice caught in my throat, instead a faint gasp left my lips. First Gareth, nearly James and now Mark. My whole body tensed until muscles began to twitch in my arms and legs. I wasn't aware at first how tight my jaw was clenched until I released it to speak.

'What happened?'

'Mark was hit by a bus, waiting at traffic lights outside Victoria station,' her voice shook.

I took a sharp intake of breath, my chest feeling like it was going to burst. 'Jesus! Will he be okay?'

'I don't know, Becca said he's critical, so it doesn't sound good.'

'Where is Becca?' I asked in a calm voice which sounded like it came from someone else.

'She's at the hospital, the girls have gone to her mum's, in Portsmouth.'

'Good,' I said, my brain whirring.

'What do you mean good? Did you not hear what I fucking said?' Robyn's voice was shrill and loud, the panic evident in her voice. I had to keep as calm as possible although deep down I wanted to scream too.

'You need to go somewhere, Robyn, go and stay with your parents or something, take a trip. Look this wasn't an accident. First Gareth, then James, now Mark. Hayley's back and she's after all of us.'

Robyn didn't speak for a few seconds as she absorbed my warning. Then, 'Okay, I'll go pack.'

'I'm going to ring the police right now,' I said, ending the call without another word. I sat, staring at my computer but not focusing on anything. The screen a blur as I tried to work out what to do. I had to find Hayley, to stop her. I didn't need proof to know that Mark's accident wasn't a coincidence.

I called Detective Wren, who said he would come by the agency in an hour or so; he was just tying up some loose ends.

I couldn't sit still and wait, instead I unlocked the tin of property keys inside my desk and grabbed 32 Park Lane; it seemed like the best place to start. The key burned like it was an evil talisman in my hand, and I squeezed my fingers around it. I left the office, mouthing to Gary I wouldn't be long as Frank had a customer, and hurried down the street, my head in turmoil.

Poor Mark was seriously hurt, and Becca would be devasted. I truly hoped he'd be okay. Those poor children had their father's life hanging in the balance and for what?

I pulled my phone from my coat pocket and dialled James.

'James, it's me.'

'Hiya, you okay?'

'Mark's had a bad accident, hit by a bus outside Victoria station.'

'Oh my god.' I could hear James's breathing quicken down the line.

'I know. I can't believe it. He's in intensive care at the moment.

I'm going to ring Becca, but I just wanted to let you know. Listen, don't open the door to anyone okay?'

'Sure. Where are you? You sound like you're outside.' James's voice was panicked.

'I'm fine, I'm heading back to the agency,' I lied.

'Okay, call me once you've spoken to Becca.'

I agreed and ended the call before dialling Becca, unsurprised when it went to voicemail. She would be by Mark's bedside I knew, but I left a message offering support and well wishes. It was all I could do.

The breeze whipped around my face and neck and I clutched the collar of my blazer tightly. It was cold enough for a coat, but I'd left mine behind. I marched with purpose, head down, striding along the road, nearing my destination with every step but my apprehension growing. Halloween pumpkins littered doorsteps and the wind blew up the yellowing leaves around my feet as I walked, whisking them into the frenzy I felt.

I didn't want to go back inside that house, a strange blend of good and bad memories now attached. *It's only bricks and mortar* the voice in my head comforted, *it can't hurt you.* But what if it could?

I went in through the back garden, the gate squeaking and dragging on the concrete slab, the old hinges loosened and dropped over time. I knew as soon as I unlocked the back door that something wasn't right. The air was musty, and a slight odour of greasy food lingered in the air. Now empty, Mrs Davidson's furniture and trinkets packed and gone, 32 Park Lane was the shell it had been back when we'd used it that night. Somewhere safe to go, private, where we could lose our virginities, and no one would ever know. How had it all gone so wrong?

I was fifteen again, stepping over the threshold, tiptoeing across the linoleum floor, trying not to make any noise. The ghost of Gareth leaning against the counter, face forlorn, the feeling of his gentle kiss still on my lips. It was bizarre reliving moments from twenty years earlier like they had been preserved perfectly in time.

The house looked just the same, left untouched, like I'd been transported back through time. Clean and tidy but aged. I opened a cupboard, but everything had gone. The kitchen was empty, nothing left to show anyone had been there, the lounge too with its brick-built fire as centrepiece. Wind whistled down the flue and echoed around the walls, my limbs trembled in reply. Marks of previously hung paintings, as though they had been drawn around, remained on the wallpaper.

My skin tingled, hair standing to attention and I felt like I was being watched. Perhaps I wasn't alone?

The smell intensified as I moved towards the den, remembering the atmosphere that hung heavy the last time I was there. When Mr Davidson had sat in his recliner watching television. It was the room where Hayley had been.

I edged around the corner, expecting to see her sitting on the floor, her long red hair hiding her face, knees tucked to her chest. The room was empty, but someone had been there. Cans of Coke and crisp packets littered the floor, the cause of the smell was a paper bag displaying the logo of the local Chinese takeaway, China Garden. Left by squatters? How? Mrs Davidson hadn't even been gone a week. Copthorne hardly had a squatter problem. Or was Hayley sleeping rough? And if so, how did she get in?

I searched around, checking all the ground floor doors and windows before moving upstairs. The main bedroom, which had been my room that night, looked just the same. The imprint of a bed, the rectangular dent in the carpet. The corner where Elliot and I had done the deed. Tiny water droplets remained on the shower screen and bath. Someone had been inside.

Had someone taken my keys? I felt for them inside my pocket, unsure what to do next. I had to get back to the office and wait for the police. Thankfully, there had been no damage to the property, therefore there was no need to contact Mrs Davidson. I didn't clear up the mess, I wanted Detective Wren to see someone had been inside. It was evidence.

Once outside, I reached for a cigarette from the emergency packet in the pocket of my blazer. They'd been there for a couple of weeks, untouched, normally only brought out in times of stress or after a few drinks. I looked around the garden, transported back to that night. How we'd hurried out onto the street, away from the house and lit cigarettes for our walk home. Hayley and Gareth nowhere to be found.

My phone rang, it was James. I answered straight away, concern growing.

'Are you okay?' I asked.

'Yeah fine. Where are you?'

'I just went to 32 Park Lane.'

'Jesus. Sophie, why?'

'To see if she was there.'

'Fuck's sake. I'm coming over.' I heard him groan as he got to his feet.

'No, don't. It's fine. I'm on my way back to the agency. Detective Wren is coming by and when he's gone, I'll come over. Is your mum still there?'

'No, she left a little while ago.'

'Okay, stay safe and remember don't answer the door.' It sounded ridiculous, but I had to make sure Hayley couldn't get to him.

Locking the door of number 32 Park Lane, I hurried back to the office, the heads of Hope and Gary snapping up as I entered.

'Where have you been?' Gary asked, his voice jovial.

'Out,' I snapped, not willing to entertain his cocky manner. I saw them shoot a look at each other, but I ignored it and returned to my desk. I'd missed a call from my mum and called her back for a distraction. It was nice to talk about something else other than the panic I felt. She was still pushing the cabin at Christmas on me. I could tell she felt guilty about potentially leaving me alone for the festivities. I had to remind her that, at thirty-six, I was a big girl.

'I know, but you mustn't be on your own at Christmas. I'd rather cancel the whole thing.'

'I'll probably stay with James, so please don't worry, Mum.' The idea that our relationship would involve planning for the future sent a thrill running through me. I hadn't realised how much I'd missed being part of a couple. I changed the subject to Dad, and Mum told me was toying with taking up golf. Apparently, Jim played and had taken him to the driving range twice now.

An hour later, when everyone was out on viewings and I was alone with Beth, the bell above the door tinkled and Detective Wren entered. I jumped up to invite him in and he pushed his glasses up his nose, smiling tightly. I offered him a drink, but he gratefully declined.

'Beth, can you hold the fort until one of the others gets back please.'

Beth nodded and moved to Hope's desk by the door to continue stapling the property particulars together.

In my office, I explained to Detective Wren: 'I've been to the house, 32 Park Lane, someone has been there. It could be Hayley.'

'Okay, let me have the keys and I'll head down there once we're finished here.'

I rummaged in my pocket and passed the keys over. 'I'm not sure whether you will have heard about James Miller's stabbing last week and Mark Emmerson had an "accident" yesterday too,' I said.

'Yes, I knew about Mr Miller's attack. We have a good shot on CCTV in close proximity to where it happened. However, the person in question was wearing a bike helmet and dressed in black unidentifiable clothing. But I'm certain the perpetrator is female, by her stature.'

A chill drifted across my shoulders, and I shuddered. So, it was Hayley.

'What kind of accident did Mr Emmerson have?' Wren rubbed his forehead, never breaking eye contact.

'He was hit by a bus outside Victoria station. But don't you see, it can't be a coincidence. You said it yourself, you don't believe in them.'

'Yes, that's true, however we also need proof. What hospital is Mr Emmerson at?'

'St. Thomas's, I believe, but I don't think he's conscious yet,' I admitted, realising I hadn't heard back from Becca.

'I'll head up there after I've been to Park Lane. If anyone will be able to tell us what happened, it will be him. The local police on the scene would have taken some witness statements.'

'Okay, thank you,' I said, running my hand through my hair and gripping it tightly at the base of my head. The pressure was comforting, my nerve endings firing, letting me know I was still alive.

'I strongly suggest, Ms White, that you move out of the flat for a while, stay somewhere anonymous. We're closing in, but in the meantime, it appears this is gathering momentum.'

There was no doubt that was the case and the reason was obvious; Hayley wanted payback.

38

'Sophie, have you been sent the fixtures and fittings list for Church Road?' Gary poked his head around my door.

I was staring blankly at my screen, unable to focus on anything after Detective Wren left. I hadn't even noticed the rest of my team return from their viewings.

'Mr Barnes said he emailed it to you yesterday?' Gary continued, his tone apologetic.

'Sorry, Gary, I'll check now and send it over,' I replied, shaking the fog from my mind. I had to get my head back in the game.

As soon as Gary left, Frank came in, the same concerned look on his face.

'Everything's fine, Frank,' I said, exasperated. I sighed and turned my attention to Gary, who had slipped in behind Frank to hand me an envelope.

'Sorry to interrupt, this was on the doormat,' he said before disappearing out of the door.

I lifted the envelope, ripping open the flap, my eyes on Frank, who I could tell was working out how best to handle my deteriorating mood.

I lowered my eyes to the card, the next second jumping from my seat and flying past Frank and out of the front door to see who was in the street, the bell jangling in my wake. Straining my eyes, I searched up and down the road, but no one was there except for an elderly couple in the distance returning from the Co-Op.

I staggered back inside, my legs shaking. The bell tinkled again behind me and a customer entered, unaware of the bomb that had been dropped in the middle of the office. I could see everyone looking at each other, wondering what on earth was going on.

Lucy was the first to jump from her chair to assist the customer and Frank's strong arm wrapped around my shoulders, practically carrying me out to the kitchen and up the stairs to the flat. Tears began to roll down my cheeks, I couldn't hold it together any longer. I was scared, terrified I'd be next.

Frank didn't speak until I was sat at the kitchen table, a hot steaming mug of tea in my hands. He prised the card out of my hand, fingers still tightly wrapped around it. The cherries shining in the reflection of the ceiling light.

> I DO HOPE JAMES IS RECOVERING WELL,
> CAN'T WAIT TO SEE HIM AGAIN

I covered my face with my hands and sobbed.

Frank's palm rested lightly on my shoulder. 'Sophie, what's going on?' He pulled a chair up and sat closely to me, leaning forward, his forearms resting on his knees. His grey eyes searching my face for answers. I told him about James and Mark and how this nightmare was never-ending.

'Are the police investigating?'

I nodded and rubbed at my eyes, mascara left behind on my knuckles. I was starting to unravel.

'I'm worried about you. This is making you ill! Come and stay with me and Diane? You wouldn't have to tell your dad.' Frank's grey eyes were damp. My chest seared. Frank loved me like I was his own.

'I'll think about it,' I lied, raising a smile. At least I'd stopped crying. I grabbed my phone to text James, just to check he was okay. A minute later I got a response, he was fine, and waiting for me to join him. 'I think I'm losing the plot.'

'Go and take a few days off, go away with that fella of yours. Everything will be all right here.' For a few seconds I considered it, but what good would it do to run? Hayley would find us or be waiting when we got back. I had to put my trust in Detective Wren, that he would come through and be the one to find her

'I'm going to go to James's, I'll spend the night there and see you in the morning.'

Frank made to go back downstairs. 'Okay, love, I'll close up. Take it easy. Ring me if you change your mind and want to come to us.'

I smiled as best I could as Frank ducked down the stairs leading back to the office.

I whipped my head back to the fridge, to what had caught my attention a second before. A fresh red cross had been drawn over Mark's face in the photo. This time I didn't make the sink before I threw up my lunch.

* * *

Hours later, curled in James's arms on the sofa, I was still unable to relax. Someone had been in the flat again. How had they got in? I'd had the door changed, a different set of keys. It didn't make sense. My stomach churned with it and I felt like a massive ball of nervous energy, permanently on red alert.

James and I hadn't talked much, neither of us in the mood for conversation. A massive cloud hung overhead, our minds working double time, anxious at what was to come. I told him about the card and warned him to be careful, although he joked that he was hardly out and about much at the moment. I had no idea what the true impact James's stabbing had on him. He seemed fine, but he looked drawn and his pallor had a greyish tinge, like he hadn't seen sunlight in a long time. Surely there had to be post-traumatic stress after such a serious incident. We were both looking over our shoulders all the time.

'Frank suggested we should go away somewhere,' I said, laying my head on his arm.

'Where?'

'I don't know: Paris, Rome, Skegness?' I laughed, trying to make James smile but failing miserably.

'Maybe we should go and see Hayley's parents, together; see if we can find out anything else?'

'I don't think that will help; her mother was adamant she hadn't seen her for years.'

James didn't respond, instead rubbing his eyes and stifling a yawn. The painkillers were so strong, they made him woozy. 'I'm so tired.'

'Come on, let's go to bed.'

'I need to change my dressing first,' James said, easing himself to his feet.

* * *

I slept badly, tossing and turning. James was mumbling in his sleep, although I couldn't make out the words. I gave in and got up at six, accidentally waking James in the process.

'Go back to sleep, I'm going to head home. I'll ring you later,' I whispered, brushing my lips across his forehead. Outside, it was still dark and the road quiet, but I'd parked right outside the flat, underneath a street lamp. It didn't stop me rushing to my car like it was a covert mission and locking the doors once inside at lightning speed.

Back at the agency, I checked inside the office first instead of heading straight upstairs. The heating was yet to come on and it felt cold. There was nothing waiting for me – no surprises on the mat or anywhere else. Detective Wren must have returned the keys to Park Lane as they were back in the key drawer.

I was about to turn the lights out when a sheet of paper left on the printer caught my eye. I grabbed it to put in the recycling box and noticed one line on the bottom edge, a printout from a web address. The other pages collected but this one left behind, accidently or on purpose I wasn't sure: http://www.dealchecker.co.uk/Australia/ Flights.

Who had been looking at flights to Australia? Gary? Hope? Beth and her boyfriend? It couldn't be Frank, he hated flying and there was no way he'd get on a plane for twenty-four hours.

I folded the page in half and put it in the box with the other recycling. As I locked the door and climbed the stairs to my flat, I pictured the beautiful beaches of Australia, of barbeques and surfing. How envious I was of whoever was going. Then my mind turned to Elliot. Shit, Elliot lived in Australia.

This whole nightmare had taught me there was no such thing as coincidences.

I had a long shower, the water as hot as I could stand it, before getting ready for work. Bags were beginning to appear under my eyes and no amount of concealer was going to hide them. I brought a flask of extra strong black coffee downstairs with me that I hoped would see me through the morning.

I left another message with both Robyn and Becca, looking for news on Mark. I could ring the hospital, but I knew they wouldn't tell me anything. I sent my love to all in the voicemails, telling Becca how sorry I was, and that, if she needed anything, I would be there. We weren't friends any more, acquaintances really. In fact, after what happened to Mark, she must be wishing I'd never got back in touch. All I'd brought with me was pain and suffering. It was me who'd led Hayley to Becca, Mark, Robyn and James.

How stupid was I? Hayley always seemed to be one step ahead and the memory of a shy, introverted girl who wouldn't harm a fly was being replaced by a vindictive, malicious and bitter woman. A woman I didn't know or didn't understand; one that still hadn't made her motive clear. None of us knew what this revenge trip was about. We didn't know who had hurt Hayley. It was a riddle and I'd exhausted myself trying to work out what it meant.

Diane called in sick for Frank. She was curt with me; no doubt cross I was working him so hard when he was supposed to be slowing down. I asked her to wish him well and not to hurry back. Inwardly, I felt trapped. Without Frank in the office, I was tied to my desk. But it was for the best, I had to leave the investigating to the police. I had caused nothing but problems playing Nancy Drew and was no closer to finding Hayley.

Beth had covered the front window in black bat and pumpkin decals, and we had a bowl full of sweets at the desk closest to the door. Halloween had arrived, but I didn't have a disco to go to this year. The memory of the night still fresh in my mind. It was the last time we were all together. I didn't feel excited about the date, if anything I was creeped out. I called Gary in after nine for a chat. I was dreading Frank retiring, but I had to face it and it was time to prepare Gary to take more on.

'How are you doing?' I asked.

'Yeah, great, it's such a different energy working here, no one is trying to swipe your sales out from under you. I feel much more relaxed and not on my guard.'

'I'm really pleased. You're doing a fantastic job and I value your contribution to the team. As I mentioned when you came on board, Frank is due to retire soon. We haven't set a date yet, but I want him to start slowing down and handing over the ropes to you. I'm going to talk to Frank about setting a date to work towards, for both of you. How does that sound?'

Gary leant back in his chair and grinned. 'Brilliant, I'm keen to move up when Frank's ready.'

'Excellent.'

'Is everything all right with you?' Gary said gingerly.

I was going to brush it off, tell him I was fine but on second thought, someone else keeping their eyes peeled wasn't a bad thing. I had to learn to let my guard down and accept help.

'I think me, and my friends are being stalked, well, harassed. The police are involved, but if you see anything weird at work, let me know.'

Gary's mouth dropped open.

'Actually, one of the cards I'd received, I found a blank one in your drawer when I was searching for the Brampton file.'

'And you think it's me?' Gary said, raising his palms towards me.

'No, no I don't.'

Gary frowned. His expression was one of surprise and it didn't look faked. 'Really? Listen, if it was there, then someone else put it there. I'm not involved in any of it. The only thing I'm guilty of is being messy!'

'Of course, and I'm sorry I may have been a bit erratic. It's down to the police now, so they'll catch them soon I'm sure.' My eyes searched Gary's, to detect the slightest flicker of panic in his face, but there was none. It wasn't him; I'd known deep down it wasn't. He was being played as much as I was. The bottom line was Hayley had been coming and going as she pleased, in the office and into my home. The new front door hadn't made a blind bit of difference it seemed as I recalled the bright red cross over Mark's face on our group photo. She was picking us off, one by one. Who knew what traces she had left behind to incriminate my staff and throw me off her scent?

Gary left to check his drawer, returning a minute later with a grimace and a shake of the head. The card had gone.

The day passed without a hitch, I called James at lunchtime, but he sounded groggy as though I'd just woken him up. I had a feeling he needed to go back to the doctors and get some more antibiotics. He wasn't healing as fast as I'd thought he would.

I offered to take the team to the pub after work, to get back to normality and although I was disappointed Detective Wren hadn't been in touch, I reasoned that no news was good news. It wasn't until we were all sat around the table at The Boar later, which had been decorated with cobwebs, I had a text from Mum.

Can you come over tonight? Dad wants to see you.

It made my stomach lurch, which was ridiculous. I was thirty-six but still felt like that child whose mum said 'wait 'til your father gets home'. The sense of dread made me abandon my wine ten minutes later to get whatever grilling that was coming over and done with. I bought Gary, Hope, Lucy and Beth another round before I went. They were deep in conversation discussing the latest Netflix American drama the girls were binge-watching, *Haunting of Hill House*. I didn't even have satellite TV; I was practically living in the dark ages, according to Beth. No doubt, being in her late teens, she thought I was a relic.

'Hi Mum,' I called as I came through the door. I always announced myself, so I didn't sneak up on them. Dad's hearing was slowly fading, I could tell by the volume the television had risen to. They were both in the kitchen, sat at the table looking grave.

'I've been trying to call you.'

'My phones died, what's happened?' I asked, panic rising as I dumped my bag and shook off my coat.

'You and that phone! Sit down. We've had a call from Diane.'

I rolled my eyes, knowing where this was going.

'I know he's supposed to be slowing down, it's just that we've been really busy.' I sank into the chair like a petulant teenager and Mum tutted.

'That's not what this is about. Not exactly,' Dad continued, clenching his jaw.

'Frank's had a heart attack.'

My mouth dropped open.

'Oh no! Will he be okay?' I whispered, frightened to tempt fate with my words. I managed to hold back the tears that were threatening to spill.

'Yes, they got to him quickly, Diane knew when he started clutching his arm, he had shooting pains, so she called the ambulance and gave him an aspirin to chew.'

'Thank God,' I sighed, reaching for a tissue to blow my nose, a tear slipping down my cheek.

'So that's it now, no more work. He's officially retired,' Mum said firmly.

'Well, Diane says anyway,' Dad countered.

'Yes, and Sophie will make sure of it, won't you, Soph?'

I nodded. Did my Dad think I wouldn't manage without Frank? It stung like a slap in the face but doubt crept in. Could I cope without Frank? I would have to.

Mum told me that Frank was in hospital but would likely be home in a day or two with medication and prescribed rest.

I stayed for a late dinner after texting James to say I wouldn't be round. Mum rustled up some leftover chicken kebabs and noodles, but the mood was sombre. We all adored Frank and Diane, they were part of the family. The seriousness of his condition hung in the air and my appetite evaporated. I was devastated that Frank wouldn't be back, but I couldn't put my own selfish needs above his health.

'He's going to be sixty next month,' Mum said to no one in particular. My parents were both already in their sixties and I saw them glance at each other. Were they questioning their own mortality, the circle of life?

'I'm sure he'll be fine. He's as strong as an ox,' I said, as brightly as I could manage, scraping the uneaten food from my plate into the bin. Trying to lift the atmosphere but to no avail. It wasn't long after that I made my excuses and left. I could sit around and question my own existence at home, preferably with a glass of wine in my hand. I hugged both my parents that extra bit tighter before leaving, hoping they hadn't noticed.

Once outside my thoughts turned to Mark and I rang Becca again. This time she answered, sounding like a whirlwind.

'Hi, Sophie, I'm just on the way back to the ward. Sorry I haven't texted back. Mark's awake, he's going to be okay. They don't think there's any brain damage, just some swelling which they need to watch. Oh, and a broken collarbone.' Becca sounded exhausted but happy.

'That's great news. I'll let you go. Give him my love, okay, James's too. We're all thinking of him.'

'Thanks, I hope you're all okay too.'

The knot in my stomach loosened slightly, thank goodness Mark was going to be okay. I had so many questions, but now wasn't the time.

On the way home, I drove past 32 Park Lane, stopping outside to watch for movement. Detective Wren hadn't been in touch after his visit to the property and I craned my neck to see it through my windscreen, but the house was dark and there was nothing to see. Could Hayley be waiting, watching from the shadows? I put my foot on the accelerator, visions of her jumping in the back of my car gave me the jitters. I'd never been a scaredy-cat before, but it was funny how quick that changed when you were being stalked by a murderer. It was like the plot of a movie and here I was in the starring role, unable to connect the dots. I imagined there'd be thousands of people shouting at the screen at my stupidity. I couldn't sleuth my way out of a paper bag.

My stomach fizzed as I approached home, as it always did now. Driving past hordes of trick-or-treaters dressed in their ghoulish costumes. It gave me the shivers. The flat hadn't been my place of sanctuary for some time. But, again, there was nothing waiting for me. Not this time. It wasn't enough to let my guard down and I wouldn't be opening my door to anyone seeking sweets or otherwise tonight. Something was coming, someone. It was only a case of where and when.

40

We had a team meeting the following day, where I broke the news about Frank. Beth got a bit teary, which almost started me off, she was midway through taking down the decorations. November already, it wouldn't be long before she'd be putting up the tinsel as I used to for Dad years ago.

'I can't believe it,' Beth's voice wavered.

Frank was the heart of Whites Estate Agents and had been for over thirty years. Everyone was sad to hear of his heart attack and looking forward to visiting him when he was home. I ordered an obscenely large fruit basket and bunch of flowers to be delivered to him and Diane the following day, from all of us. I let Gary know it was unlikely Frank would return to work and I would change his role to Office Manager at the end of the month. I could tell he was pleased, but he was restrained, respectful of the circumstances that had preceded his promotion.

Business continued as normal; Gary left the office to take on a new instruction –a townhouse near the train station which would be lucrative on commission and an easy sell. Minutes after he left,

I heard someone come in and Hope escorted Detective Wren through to my office.

'Miss White,' he said, extending his hand, which allowed his mac to part and a flash of red braces over his shirt caught my eye. I stifled a smile.

'Detective Wren, please take a seat. Can I get you a tea?'

'No thank you. I was passing, so I just thought I'd pop in. Give you an update.'

I raised my eyebrows and waited for him to continue. He took his time to sit down, shuffling in the chair that was slightly too small for him, until he was comfortable.

'We've searched for Miss Keeble but haven't found any trace of her after the hostel her mother told us she was at in 1997.'

'You've been to see her parents?'

'I've had a colleague visit her mother, yes. We also found no records of an abortion at the clinic she was taken to; no records of her at all.'

'That's strange. Her mum said she took her there. What about the house? Was there nothing at Park Lane?'

'No. There was no sign of forced entry, but we've dusted for prints and removed the takeaway cartons as evidence.'

'It's like she disappeared into thin air.' I sighed. We were back to square one.

'Yes, and it's extremely unusual to leave no trace of where you've been. I think we must assume some harm has befallen Miss Keeble.'

'She's the one doing harm, not the victim of it,' I spluttered.

Wren waved his hand to temper my impeding outrage before continuing. 'Also, I visited Mark. He'd not long woken up when I got there, but he has no recollection currently of being pushed in front of the bus.' He pursed his lips and gave a slight shake of the head.

'He wouldn't just jump in front of a moving bus,' I countered.

'Well, that as maybe, but with no evidence we cannot pursue it at the moment. In regard to Mr Miller, even after an extensive search, we haven't been able to recover the knife used in the stabbing.'

Do you think Hayley could have changed her name?'

'It's a possibility, but unfortunately there's no requirement to officially record a change of name in the United Kingdom. It's only recorded if you choose it to be enrolled. We have looked at that, but it's not turned up anything.'

I slumped back in my seat.

Detective Wren frowned and ran his thumb underneath his red brace, stretching the elastic. The brass connector hidden by the overhang of his belly. 'All is not lost. We've looked again at Mr Dixon's fatal accident and there were reports of him spending most of the evening drinking with a young lady, one that none of the regulars recognised. It's not widely known, but we recovered DNA from the accident that isn't a match for Mr Dixon. If we can find a match, then it proves your theory and we are looking at all angles.' My eyes widened.

'She found him,' I whispered.

'Well, we don't know that for certain, but we're trying to establish a link between these incidents.'

'What about the calls and texts, anything from the number? Also, I forgot to say, an "Anonymous Amy" posted on Gareth's wall that he was a rapist. Surely that has to be connected to this?'

'I'll take a look at the Facebook page, we should be able to track that. Regarding the mobile, it's an unregistered pay-as-you-go SIM card, so it's unable to be traced as to who is using it. Triangulation gives us this area but nothing much to narrow it further. I've got someone looking at the mobile phone shops to see if we can see where it was bought.'

Detective Wren got up to leave, his update delivered, as I remained in my chair, reeling from the new developments. Had Hayley found Gareth? It sounded like she had. Maybe she pretended they'd bumped into each other, a coincidental meeting of two old friends. She could have encouraged him to get drunk or even spiked his drink before he got behind the wheel. It was anyone's guess, but at least the police were taking my claims seriously. I was under no illusion my story sounded crazy.

I tried to focus back on work, but it was hard. I resumed trawling through my emails, collating documents I needed when Beth came in with the post, placing it on my desk. I almost winced, jumping on it immediately but stopped myself, leaving it where it was.

'Can you ask Hope to email over the land registry search for 11 Highland Grove please, Beth?'

'She's gone out, had a viewing apparently. Think she forgot about it.' Beth rolled her eyes and good-naturedly turned on her heels. 'Tea?' she called back over her shoulder.

'Please.' A niggling sensation prompted me to check the online office calendar as there was a viewing schedule that Beth had inputted. She kept the diary for the office and always knew the whereabouts of everyone. More so than I did, but I didn't need to micromanage. It was why I was so insistent on only employing staff I could trust, which was why I was surprised to see the calendar empty for Hope on Thursday 1 November.

My mobile rang, skittering across the table, distracting me. It was James.

'Hiya, how are you feeling?' I asked.

'Rubbish, I'm going to the doctors today. It's healing but very slowly, the skin feels weird and tight. I'm worried I'm going to roll over in bed and tear my stitches.' James laughed half-heartedly. 'But otherwise I'm okay. I've had your detective come and see me.'

'Detective Wren? He's been here too; they are going to look at connecting everything to one person. They've got DNA, they just need to find a match.'

The line went dead. Had James hung up?

'James you still there?'

'Yep, yep, still here. Dropped the phone. Reflexes aren't what they used to be.'

'It can only be a good thing, right?' I pushed.

'Sure. When can I see you?'

'I was thinking, why don't you move in here, just until all this is over. I can look after you and you know, safety in numbers.' I felt my cheeks flush.

The pause was drawn out and I was sure I'd just made a fool of myself.

'Okay, if you don't think I'll get under your feet? Mum's going to run me to the doctor later and I'll get her to drop me over after, shall I?'

'Sure,' I replied, beaming. My palms beginning to sweat. Was this the beginning of us moving in together? Or would it be temporary? All I knew is that I felt safer with James around.

Later that afternoon, around six, the others had left for the day when James arrived with a bulging holdall. I briefly met his mum who dropped him off and invited her up for a cup of tea, but she said she had to get back.

We spent the evening on the sofa before I convinced James, with a few kisses, that we should have an early night. He was still pretty sore; his doctor had given him another batch of antibiotics and I'd been warned to be gentle with him.

* * *

I was thankful when Friday arrived, it had been one hell of a week. All of the paperwork was now through for Park Lane, gearing up for exchange of contracts. I'd be glad when that property was sold. It felt like a bad omen, forever tainted. Everything was connected to it. The sale was due to go through and complete next week; I could hand the keys to a new owner and perhaps the history would erase itself.

Frank had been kept in hospital longer than planned as there had been an issue with his blood sugar levels. It seemed like all the lunches from the bakers were contributing to an early diagnosis of type two diabetes. Diane was not happy, and he was being sent home today with a strict diet to follow in the hope it could be reversed. I couldn't wait to see him but wanted to give him a couple of days at home to get settled first. Plus, I was dreading facing the wrath of Diane.

I dragged myself out of bed after another lousy night's sleep. James was still snoring beside me, the noise a comfort, although I was sure that would change. My phone pinged as soon as I switched it on, a tirade of messages from the WhatsApp group. Another photo of us all from Brighton, one from Elliot buried up to his neck in the sand. Becca had said Mark's diagnosis was good and they were hoping to release him in a few days. The swelling on his brain had almost gone, and he was recovering well. Robyn was staying with Chloe's parents and she was safe. I was pleased to read that she'd got the job as the blood courier. I composed a message to say James was healing and I was looking after him at the flat, which got an instant smiley face and heart emoji from Robyn. Hayley was doing her best to ruin us all, but we were pushing on, living as best we could in the circumstances.

Mum text in the morning to say she'd received something through the door pertaining to me, but she wouldn't say what it was. Alarm bells rang in my head. Whenever Mum was upset, her voice would go shrill and it was a dead giveaway as to why she didn't call. I knew how long it took her to compose a text. I said I'd be over later, fighting the urge to rush there now and see what had been sent. Whatever it was, it would be bad. I hoped it didn't mean I'd have to spill the beans about everything. What did my parents have to do with Hayley? Why was she getting them involved?

I showered and dressed in little enthusiasm for the day ahead. I was tired of the fight. I just wanted the nightmare to end. What had we done that was so wrong?

I came down at quarter to nine to find the office already full. Gary had made tea for everyone, including me. I knew straight away something wasn't right, the atmosphere was tense, and Lucy was frantic, swearing at her machine with frustration.

'What's happened?'

Gary answered, frowning at me, his hands on his hips. 'The system has gone down, looks like everything on the server has been wiped.'

'We've lost everything. All our property details, every document, every contact. It looks like a deliberate attack.'

'For fuck's sake,' I swore, storming into my office to find a business card I knew was in my top drawer. I tapped the number into my phone, and it rang once before being answered.

'Hi, this is Dave,' a droll voice said. Dave Harper was our contracted IT help. A stand-alone guy with his own business that looked after the servers, printers, hardware and any software we had installed, and could be called upon for any ad-hoc issues. I explained we had an emergency and he said he'd be right over.

'Okay, business as usual – for now. Beth, do you remember if we had any viewings planned today?'

'Only Nymans Drive, that was Lucy's. Ten a.m., I think. Mr and Mrs Daniels.'

'Great, thanks Beth. Lucy, you deal with that. Gary, I've got our IT guy on his way in. Hope, can you look after any walk-ins – take details by hand and show them anything we've got printed out.'

'We're up to date with the paper copies,' Beth interjected. She was an amazing organiser, practically running the office from behind the scenes.

'Brilliant. Hopefully this will be a blip and in a couple of hours everything will be recovered,' I said, sounding more confident than I felt. I didn't believe this was an accident.

When Dave Harper arrived twenty minutes later, I introduced him to Gary and he got started at his desk, finding the problem almost straight away. He ran some tests and entered some code to show the latest sequences actioned. It appeared that a virus had been uploaded last night.

'From this office?' I whispered, not wanting to be overheard.

'Not necessarily. It could have been done remotely. I can't tell. It doesn't look like a professional job, but it's definitely deliberate. We just need to put everything back on the server and download it from the cloud. Once you're back up and running, I'll write a stronger encryption and install malware software. Tougher than you had before.'

I stretched my neck from side to side, listening to it crack. My muscles were tight from hunching my shoulders. At least it was fixable, but it didn't change the fact we'd been targeted. Or rather, I'd been targeted. I dreaded to think what Dave would invoice me.

'All okay?' Gary asked.

'Yep, should be back within the hour,' Dave replied, tapping on his keyboard so fast his fingers were a blur.

I slumped lower in my seat, willing the rest of the day, and the weekend, to be drama-free. I still had to navigate to my parents and see what they'd received. I hadn't told them anything about Hayley and I wasn't about to. I hoped I could pull the wool over their eyes, if nothing but for their own safety.

Dave still wasn't finished at lunchtime, it appeared everything had been slow to reinstall due to an unrelated broadband service failure, so we closed the office for an hour and left him to work. Deciding to head to the café for lunch. It was busy, but we squeezed five of us on a table meant for four and dug into a selection of jacket potatoes and baguettes.

'What do we have closing next week? Is anything likely to be impacted by today?' I asked.

'No, I doubt it. Two potential completions, if all goes to plan. Park Lane and Mason Close,' Gary said, wiping his mouth with a napkin to remove a dollop of brown sauce, leaked from his bacon baguette.

Hope coughed, spluttering on her tea, liquid dripping from her nose. She covered her face with her hand and Gary handed her a clean napkin.

'Wrong hole,' she squeaked, her eyes streaming.

Gary gave her a gentle pat on the back, but I didn't miss her miniscule flinch at his touch. Had something happened between them? Gary, on the other hand, was oblivious and carried on tearing at his baguette like it was his first meal this year. I wrinkled my nose. Lucy giggled and nudged my knee under the table. There wasn't enough room to swing a cat, it was claustrophobic.

'I'm going to nip out for a ciggie.' I stood up too fast, the blood rushing from my head, and wobbled for a second.

'I'll join you.' Hope stood and we made for the door, the cold breeze smacking us in the face as soon as we opened it.

'I felt like I couldn't breathe in there,' I admitted, trying to light my cigarette with little success.

'Here.' Hope opened her coat and shielded us to get the lighter to work. 'He's so gross, I can't bear to watch him eat.' Her nostrils flared, inhaling deeply.

'Hmmmm,' I agreed, although I didn't want to start bad-mouthing Gary. It didn't look good coming from the boss.

'You smoking full-time now?' Hope asked, sucking hard on the filter.

'Trying not to go back to that, just every now and then. So, you got yourself a new car yet?' I said, changing the subject.

Hope narrowed her eyes at me.

'You said you and your mum went to look at them?'

Then the penny dropped. 'No, not yet. She likes Fords, I like VWs but can't afford one. Anyway, how's things with you and that fella of yours, what's his name?'

'James,' I said without hesitation before adding, 'he's moved in, for the time being anyway.'

'Ahh, he seemed like a nice guy when he came in. Most of them end up being lying, vindictive bastards,' Hope spat.

My eyes widened at her choice of words. 'Not all of them.'

'Nah they're all the same,' Hope said, flicking her cigarette high into the road before turning on her heels and slipping through the café door. Leaving me staring after her.

Back at the office, the servers were up and running and the installation of a new protective and more secure firewall had been completed. I thanked Dave and asked him to send me his invoice so I could pay him as soon as possible. He was handy to have on speed dial and over the past few years had been the saviour of numerous crisis. I didn't want to think about how much personal data had been floating in the ether.

I popped upstairs to the flat, but James wasn't there, he'd left me a note to say he'd been called to see his editor about a potential magazine feature and would be back later.

'Can you to lock up when you leave?' I said to Gary when I returned to the office, fearing I couldn't put off Mum and Dad any longer. I lay the bunch of keys on Gary's desk, noticing his ears tinge pink at the significance of being left with the responsibility. He scooped them into his pocket. 'Let me show you how to set the alarm.' Before leaving, I ran through the keys, locks and alarm, how to set and reset it with the code, which Gary absorbed with the concentration of a surgeon mid-operation.

The atmosphere when I arrived at my parents could be cut with a knife. Mum's eyes were red-rimmed and Dad sat in the front room, so engrossed in the crossword he didn't respond when I said hello.

'What's up?' I gestured at Mum's eyes.

'Oh nothing, onions,' she replied, and I could tell she was lying. Mum was about as good at it as I was. She stood at the stove, stirring a risotto continuously which smelt delicious. 'It's over there.' She signalled towards a pile on the table, newspapers and catalogues and a leaflet with my photo on. A professional one taken from the Whites website. SLUT stamped across the top in big black letters.

'Nice,' I muttered sarcastically, sliding into a chair.

'Read it,' Mum bit back.

I did as I was told.

This is Sophie White.
Sophie White is a SLUT!
When Sophie was fifteen, she organised an orgy at an empty property being marketed by her parents' estate agency. The one she now runs.
She and her friends all had sex with one another at Sophie's request.
Sophie is a SLUT!
Don't be like Sophie.

It was so ridiculous I almost laughed, but one look at Mum's thunderous face stopped me.

'Tell me it's not true.' Dad's voice came as a surprise, I looked up to see him filling the doorway. His face lined and wispy grey chest hair poking out from beneath the neck of his polo shirt. He looked like he'd aged another ten years.

My stomach clenched. 'Of course, it's not true, Dad. What do you take me for?'

'Is it all lies? Tell me that isn't how Hayley got pregnant? At some orgy you organised?' I'd never heard my mum speak to me in such a venomous tone and I was taken aback. She didn't break eye contact with me, we were at a stand-off, all the time her arm kept stirring as though she was possessed.

'Answer your mother,' my dad snapped. I stood to leave. I'd had enough.

'Sit down.' Dad's fist thumped the table.

I recoiled, tears pricked my eyes and I balled my hands into fists. 'It's partly true. We had a *gathering*. We lost our virginity. We didn't all have sex with each other, we each had sex with one person,' I clarified matter-of-factly.

'Jesus Christ,' my mum hissed, and Dad shook his head, unwilling to look at me.

I was soiled and mad at being made to feel that way.

'And what about the property? Did you steal the keys to one I was selling?'

I lowered my eyes; it was the only thing I was ashamed about. 'Yes.'

'How dare you. How could you have done that?'

'Dad, I was fifteen, a teenager. Teenagers do stupid shit like that.' I couldn't stop the tears from falling, which enraged me further. I hadn't cried in front of my parents for years.

Dad walked out of the room, the conversation over. I looked at Mum, but she'd turned her back on me, still stirring.

'You do realise I'm thirty-six and this was over twenty years ago?' I raised my voice. No one replied.

I grabbed my coat and marched from the house. Fury running through my veins like lava, shooting my adrenaline sky-high. A volcano spilling over and destroying all below it. I screamed into my steering wheel as I started the car.

42

I entered The Boar half an hour later and sat at the bar. I'd parked my car outside the office and walked straight to the pub without bothering to go home first.

'Jack Daniels please, a double. Make that two actually.'

Phil was behind the bar and didn't bat an eyelid. He lined the drinks in front of me and I paid. Necking one and starting on the second.

When I was on my sixth and starting to relax, Gary tapped me on the shoulder.

'Do you want to join us?' he asked, pointing to the table, where Colin and the other Osbornes staff were sitting.

'No, I'm all right, thanks though.'

'No worries,' he replied unfazed, returning to his table. Anger fizzed at the tips of my fingers. So powerful I felt like I could shoot laser beams from them. The need to hit something, to run, to expend energy was only quelled by the trickling of alcohol into my bloodstream and its numbing qualities. What right did my parents have to make me feel like that? Were they never young and foolish? What I did with my body was up to me. It was my decision to make, mine to live with. I hadn't regretted anything until recently. Now, I wish that stupid party had never happened, but I couldn't turn back time. I was so livid, I never wanted to speak to my parents again.

Phil ringing the bell at the end of the bar to call time jogged me from the pit I was wallowing in. A graveyard of empty half-pint glasses littered the bar. Telling the story of my evening.

'Come on, I'll walk you home,' Gary said, appearing from nowhere and slipping on his jacket.

We stumbled down the road, fireworks cracking overhead. I hadn't even realised the display was on. Gary talked about a new restaurant opening around the corner that we should visit, but I wasn't listening. James was standing at the door, frowning. I'd texted him earlier to say I'd be home late, although he probably thought it would be earlier than chucking-out time at the pub.

'I'll take her from here,' he said, guiding me inside. 'Thanks for bringing her home.'

'No problem.' Gary said goodnight and turned to leave as I pulled myself up the stairs and headed straight for bed.

* * *

Bright sunlight streaming through open curtains woke me in the morning, my head spinning. I vacated the bed; the stench of alcohol permeated the air. I threw open the window and called out to James, but there was no answer. It was past ten on Saturday morning and I should have been in the office. My phone had registered two missed calls and a text from James last night. He'd probably gone back home, pissed off at me for ignoring him. I gritted my teeth, remembering being too drunk to respond to him.

I threw on some clothes and brushed my hair, wiping the

mascara smudges from under my eyes and spraying a mist of perfume in the air above my head. I'd fucked up at work, with James and my parents too.

In the office, Gary took one look at me and tried to stifle a laugh.

'Are you all right?'

'No,' I admitted, rubbing my forehead.

'Your top's on back to front.'

'Fuck! Sorry, Gary, sorry to leave you in the lurch this morning.'

'It's fine, go back to bed. I've got it covered. Hope's in too. I'm office manager now remember, so let me manage.' He smiled conspiratorially.

'Thank you, and thanks for getting me home last night,' I said, my stomach rolling over as I headed back upstairs.

I sat in the bath for a long time, until the water grew cold and forced me out. I usually enjoyed soaking with a good book, but I couldn't focus on anything other than dwelling on how my life had turned into a shitshow. As though it was a penance, I spent the rest of the day cleaning, scrubbing every inch of the flat with bleach until my fingers stung. Waiting to hear back from James after I text through an apology this morning.

I half expected my mum to call, to apologise and try and smooth things over, but she didn't. A heavy weight sat on my chest now the anger had dissipated. I'd never fallen out with my parents as an adult. Half of me had the mindset of, sod it, they'll need me more than I need them soon. But I was being an arse and licking my wounds. Which were still fresh the day after.

Who knew how long my parents would be around for? Look what happened to Frank. I didn't want to fight over something that happened twenty years ago. I could hear my dad's voice in my ear 'But it's the principle' and winced. Yesterday, in their kitchen, I was that teenager again, getting scolded for a detention at school or talking back to my mother. It was demeaning.

James came back, knocking on the door around six that evening, it reminded me that I had to get him a key cut. I'd had two with the new front door but had given the spare to my parents. He'd been out to Ikea with his sister Marie, who had recently bought her first house, and carried in a bag of tea lights and a cushion with a sloth on it, he'd bought for me. He was a little frosty, more so because a man he didn't know, or recognise, had walked me home. Once I'd told him who Gary was and that he'd got me home safe as I was so wasted, he softened. James was outraged by the flyers and understood my reaction to the dressing-down I'd received from my parents.

Feeling low, I ordered a pizza takeaway with ice cream, it was what Saturday nights were for. I moped over reruns of *The Office* which never normally failed to make me laugh while James tried his best to cheer me up. I abstained from wine, knowing it would make me sink further into the pit I was wallowing in. Which in turn meant that when it was time for bed my brain switched on and began reliving the events of the past week. When would it end?

* * *

On Sunday morning, I called Diane, hoping to visit Frank. I wasn't going to my parents', that was for sure. Not until we'd all cooled off. Diane was polite but still a bit standoffish and it was awkward over the phone. It was arranged I would come round in the afternoon, so I filled my morning with washing, ironing and responding to emails. With two sales due to complete next week and one being Park Lane I was eager to get that off my desk and out of my life. James wasn't feeling so great and moved from the bed to the sofa and then back again. I was sure his wound needed looking at, but he wouldn't let me take him to the walk-in centre.

When I got to Frank's laden with a large bag of vegetables and my Nutribullet, still in its box, unopened since I'd bought it, Diane welcomed me in and was warmer than she had been on the phone.

'You just missed our Tommy.'

'Ah that's a shame. I haven't seen him for years.'

'All grown up now,' Diane said, sadness hinting behind her smile.

'I bought this round. I thought you could juice him up double portions of his daily veg in there,' I said, handing Diane the box.

'I might have to hold his nose.' She laughed, before tapping me on the arm and leaning in to whisper. 'Listen, I don't want you to be alarmed, he doesn't look particularly well today.'

I gulped, worried that Frank's appearance might be the final straw for me this week.

The lounge was a mix of cream and duck egg blue with a heavy piled carpet. A large bay window immersed the room in sunlight. I tiptoed in, wanting to see Frank before he saw me, so I could make sure my face gave nothing away. He sat in a high-backed armchair, reclined with his feet raised. A pair of checked slippers adorned his feet and he wore navy blue jogging bottoms and a sweatshirt. Diane was right, his pallor was grey and he seemed to have aged since I last saw him. The stress on his body having taken its toll.

'Hello, Frank.' I mustered the largest smile I could.

He gazed upwards and the dark circles under his eyes made my chin wobble.

'Poppet,' he exclaimed, opening his arm to pull me in for a hug.

'How are you feeling?'

'Like I've been in the ring with Mike Tyson,' he said, stifling a cough. 'Although you don't look much better. You're wasting away!' he said, giving me a knowing stare.

'Thanks!' I nudged him playfully, I didn't want to talk about my problems.

'Well, you need rest, and plenty of it, lots of healthy food too. I've bought you a juicer, so Diane can keep you topped up with all your vitamins. No more bacon butties for you.'

He winced and it struck me how fragile he looked. This ginormous man, shrivelled to what seemed like half his size, in the chair.

'Don't you start.' He rolled his eyes.

I sat beside him, resting my hand on his arm.

'It's so good to see you. I was worried, we all were.' My voice broke and I blinked back tears, moving aside when Diane entered carrying tea and biscuits on a tray. Thankful for the interruption.

'You're only allowed one.' Handing Frank a lone digestive and a mug of builders'-coloured tea.

He tutted in response and nibbled on it.

'You have to do something, she's starving me,' he said in mock complaint.

It was Diane's turn to tut them. She sat on the opposite sofa, Frank in the middle of us in his chair.

'How's work?' Frank asked.

I was about to speak but Diane interrupted. 'You don't have to worry about that now dear.' Her voice curt.

'That's right, you don't, Frank. Everything is fine, you need to concentrate on getting better,' I replied and Diane smiled at me. I'd suspected it was what she wanted me to say and I avoided the topic thereafter.

'I'm so bored.' Frank shifted in his chair, narrowly avoiding spilling his tea.

'I'll buy you a jigsaw, 1000 pieces.'

He rolled his eyes to that suggestion. We made polite conversation for a while. Frank didn't ask me anything about Hayley in front of Diane and I was grateful. I was also sure they hadn't heard anything from my parents about the argument yesterday.

I stayed for an hour, trying to keep Frank upbeat about all the things he could spend his time doing now he was going to retire. When I left, my face ached from all the smiling I had been doing. Wearing it like a mask, pretending everything was fine. I'd got rather good at that. It pulled at my heartstrings and I let the tears fall, clouding my vision as I drove home. Retirement would be the end of Frank, not the heart attack. I just knew it. But I had no place to tell Diane. He wasn't my father after all.

43

I woke with a start on Monday morning, having had a nightmare that the leaflet brandishing me as a slut had been pasted all over the office windows. My own giant billboard, covering the glass front entirely. I was scraping it off as passers-by looked on and laughed when the beeping of my alarm clock sounded. I could only hope the leaflet at Mum's wasn't one of many that had been distributed around the village. It would be the easiest way to try and ruin my reputation. I had a brick in the pit of my stomach that wouldn't shift. James and I felt like we were living under a constant cloud.

I got to the office early to work on the completions and make my usual calls to the homeowners. Mrs Davidson was thrilled it was all going through smoothly and was on target to complete this week. She was having a great time in Cornwall; it was a different pace of life and she was contemplating purchasing a property there with the proceeds of the sale of Park Lane. I didn't tell her my suspicion that someone was living there illegally. I'd wait until there was confirmation from Detective Wren on his findings. I didn't want to worry Mrs Davidson unnecessarily.

I hadn't heard from either Robyn or Becca and sent a message out to the group chat to check everyone was all okay. It was easier to keep in touch that way. Becca, no doubt, was tied up with Mark's recovery and she had her children to look after too. I envied the life she had; one I may never know. The gift of a child was unlike any other. *There's still time*, the voice in the back of my head piped up. There was time; although the idea of becoming a parent terrified me.

'Sophie, we have a complication with Park Lane.' Gary poked his head around the door.

Even the road name made me shudder. I closed my eyes for a second – that property was a nightmare.

'What is it?'

'The buyers are having issues with the transference of funds, it seems their mortgage offer has expired and it's going to take a few days to sort another.'

'Jesus.' I shook my head and picked up the phone to dial the solicitors. Perhaps I could delay completion until Friday. Covering the mouthpiece with my hand, I called out to Gary who'd disappeared. 'Tell the Barons to pull their finger out and get another offer in place asap otherwise the whole chain could collapse.' I knew the Martins further down the chain had lost their buyers twice and threatened to pull out altogether if it didn't go through this week. I had to make sure it would. Park Lane was one property I wanted off the books. With everything else falling apart, I had to keep the business going. I was clinging on to it like a raft in choppy waters, it was the only thing keeping me afloat.

The rest of the day was tied up with Park Lane, emphasising the importance of the chain collapsing to all the solicitors involved if we didn't get everything ready to go as soon as the new mortgage offer was in place.

Robyn called to say she was fine and asked whether there had been any updates on the police investigation. I told her I was expecting a call from Detective Wren, but Hayley was proving increasingly difficult to find.

Becca messaged back with a photo of Mark smiling with his thumb up, his right arm in a sling. It looked as though he'd been allowed home.

By six o'clock, I'd had enough for the day and logged off. I was taking my cup out to the kitchen when I noticed the post on Beth's desk still sitting there – it hadn't been distributed, which was unusual.

Gary was out taking on another new instruction and Lucy and Beth had already left.

'I don't think she felt too well today,' Hope said, noticing my disapproving look. They were buddies enough already that she was covering for her?

I was too tired to disagree and shuffled back to my desk to sort through it. When I got to the white handwritten envelope, an icy finger caressed its way down my back. My shoulders tensed, inching upwards at the familiar sight. I chewed my lip as I tore open the flap and saw the blood-red cherries on the inside. The cute picture I'd become accustomed to, one that made my stomach sink. What was written inside? What more could she do to us? But this time it wasn't an attack, it was an invitation.

Free to see an old friend?

I left the card on my desk and grabbed my keys and coat without pause.

'Can you lock up if Gary's not back?' I said to Hope, chucking her the spare set I'd retrieved from my desk, without waiting for an answer.

'Sure. You okay? Where are you going?'

'Park Lane,' I called over my shoulder as the door swung shut. There was no doubt in my mind where my 'old friend' would be, only one place it could be. The house where it all began.

I lit a cigarette as I walked, my hands shaking, full of trepidation. What if the meeting was this morning? Should I have had that card at nine o'clock? There wasn't a stamp on the envelope, so it didn't come with the regular mail. Either way, in a few minutes I would see Hayley. I'd have the opportunity to try and talk some sense into her. Find out what the hell she was playing at.

As I was about to call Detective Wren, my phone rang. It was James, I declined the call, but another came through in seconds. I was trying to dial out when it did, and I accidentally cut off whoever it was. Cursing, I fumbled with the phone, my sweaty palm causing it to slip from my grip and fall to the pavement. Tiny shards of glass littered the ground, the phones screen smashed in the corner, the display fading.

'Fuck's sake,' I cursed.

Everything was going to shit. The chain for Park Lane was collapsing, my parents weren't speaking to me; Frank had left, and James and I were living in fear. My chin wobbled involuntarily. *Keep your shit together*, the voice in my head demanded, but my mind whirled despite the warning. I wanted to see Hayley. I couldn't decide what I wanted more, to hug her or kill her for everything she'd put us through.

I carried on, towards the house. Like it was drawing me in, about to swallow me whole. I wanted answers, I needed answers.

My phone beeped with a voicemail message, coming back to life, the screen flickering.

'Miss White, it's Detective Wren, I'm on my way to you now, we've had some results back. The DNA recovered from Mr

Dixon's accident is a match to the DNA from the cards you received,' I gasped.

Hayley had killed Gareth after all, Detective Wren had just confirmed it. I missed the rest of the message, there was a lot of traffic noise, he must have been on the road somewhere and replayed it from the start, to pick up what I'd not heard.

'Now, neither samples taken match the DNA lifted from Hayley's hairbrush that we got from Mrs Keeble, however it's—' The phone cut out again, the screen flickering and not responding. What had I missed? What was he going to say? However what?

So, Hayley wasn't behind it? I shook my head, trying to clear the fog. Realising I'd stopped in the middle of the pavement, my surroundings hazy. Who on earth was behind it, if it wasn't Hayley?

I resumed walking at speed, trying to make up time. I had to see who had sent me the invitation to meet, if it wasn't Hayley, then who was it? Park Lane was where it all started and where it had to end.

Grey clouds gathered ominously overhead. My pace slowing automatically as the back of the house came into view. Shit, I'd forgotten the keys. It was a sign and I shuddered, my body in the grip of an icy wave. I wanted to turn back. My feet were heavy, legs dragging. Drawn like a magnet, unable to stop. What was I heading into?

I stood out of view from the windows, lighting a cigarette. Whoever was inside could be watching. The flame from my lighter amplified the fading light. Dusk was like a cloak, slowly being drawn over the sky. Shutting out the light and cutting me off from everyone. The road was quiet, no passers-by. I should have told James where I was going? What if I never came out of that house?

I saw no movement through the patterned glass of the door when I moved around to the front. I rang the bell, which echoed too loud inside the empty shell, making me wince. My teeth chattered expectantly, nerves on edge, but no one came to answer. Was I too late? What did I expect, someone to throw open the door and welcome me in?

I retraced my steps around the side and opened the gate into the garden, its groan announcing me. It was rush hour, but there seemed to be little traffic. As if everyone had been told to give Park Lane a wide berth. Everything was quiet except the wind, which had ramped up, whipping around my legs.

My heart skipped when I saw the back door was ajar. I stood, rooted to the spot, afraid to take another step. Someone was inside, but they wanted me to come round the back. I could hear the thudding of my heart in my ears now, louder and faster. A relentless beat that was so loud I couldn't think. I faltered, could I turn back? No. I had to find out who was waiting for me. Sweat pooled under my arms, the moisture soaking into my blouse. Forcing myself forward, I slowly pushed the door, its hinges screeched as it opened, and I recoiled. Pressing my lips together tightly to quiet any noise my jabbering teeth were making. First the gate, now the door. There was no chance I hadn't been heard.

'Hello?' I called into the gloomy kitchen. My voice tremoring, the word sticking in my throat. There was no reply. I crept over the threshold, trying to reason with my imagination, which had taken the opportunity to run wild. I visualised a masked intruder jumping out from behind every shadowed corner. I'd given away the element of surprise, so switched on the kitchen light and moved forward to peek around the archway into the living room.

'Sophie?' A voice came from behind me and I squealed, spinning around. A pale-looking James stood in the doorway, the breeze from outside gushing past him into the house uninvited. A few autumnal leaves flew in and scattered around our feet.

'James. What are you doing here?' My hand jumped to my chest.

'I just missed you at the office. Hope told me you were here, so I jumped in the car. What are you doing?'

Without answering I resumed peering round the corner, but

no one was waiting for me in the living room. Steeling myself, I moved round into the den. But that too was empty.

Behind me, I heard the back door close and James shuffled in to the room.

'God, you look awful.' Now that he was closer, I saw his skin was ghostly white with beads of sweat on his top lip; his hands trembled as he fumbled inside his coat.

'I think I've got an infection,' he said, lifting his shirt gingerly to show a fresh bandage over the wound at his side.

'You look like you should be in bed,' I scolded, gently kissing his lips. I couldn't pretend I wasn't glad to see him. The house signified something terrible and I was relieved not to be alone.

James's eyes darted around, squinting. Something about his expression put me on edge. He was afraid.

I turned to make my way upstairs. 'I've had enough.'

'We've got to finish this,' he called behind me as I climbed. James's voice was flat and lifeless. My shoulders shook, the shiver running down the backs of my legs, skin prickling in its wake.

I heard James cough and a stair creaked behind me. I reached the landing, considering where to go: three bedrooms and a bathroom. My 'old friend' had to be up here if they weren't downstairs. The box room was empty. I crossed the hallway, glancing back down the stairs, seeing the top of James's head as he pulled himself up. Levering his body against the bannister. He looked so weak, I was worried he'd fall.

'James, go back down. I'm fine,' I whispered, trying the second bedroom.

James was still coming, I could hear his footfalls.

Both bedrooms were empty, no furniture for anyone to hide behind. Exactly how it was back then, twenty years ago. The sun outside had set, the darkness crept in, swallowing 32 Park Lane whole.

James hadn't made it up the stairs and I couldn't see him from the hallway. I flew down, two at a time.

'James, I think we need to get you home or even to the hospital. You must have a temperature?' I found him rinsing his face in the kitchen sink, leaning heavily on the counter by the back door. Splashing water everywhere. 'You're not well. Let me get you home. What on earth did you come out for?' I stepped towards him; my arm outstretched to hold him steady.

'Detective Wren called,' he croaked.

'Well, what do we have here? Two for the price of one?' A voice sounded from behind me, interrupting James.

I jumped at the intrusion and spun around. Hope appeared out of the darkness from the archway, like a bear emerging from a cave. She spun the keys around her fingers, the familiar brown tag looping. Gary's handwriting blurred. What was she doing here?

'You?' James uttered, collapsing in a pool of sweat, his face drenched, skin clammy.

I knelt to unbutton his collar, feeling the panic rocket.

'Hope, what are you doing here?' I gasped over my shoulder, my fingers fumbling with the buttons of James's shirt. His breath coming in rasps.

Hope didn't reply. I pulled my phone out of my pocket, stabbing my fingers at the cracked screen but it wouldn't respond.

'We need to call an ambulance. Give me your phone.' I stretched out my hand to Hope, fingers twitching, but she remained in the archway, staring at me blankly. It was as if I hadn't spoken. I bit my lip, tears springing to my eyes feeling helpless. 'Fuck's sake, Hope! James, honey, stay with me. Keep looking at me. Where's your phone?' I scowled, thrusting my hands in the pockets of his jeans. They were empty. Had he left it in the car?

I stood to open the back door, but it was locked. Why was it locked? What was happening? Why wasn't Hope helping?

'What the fuck is going on? Help me!' I begged, spinning round to confront Hope.

James looked so pale he was translucent.

'Don't worry, he'll pass out in a minute. Come on, I want to show you something.' Hope turned around, melting into the gloom.

45

The sky outside was a Saturn grey, but indoors the shadows loomed large. I chewed my lip, tasting the metallic bitterness. Torn between wanting to follow Hope to find out what the hell was going on and staying with James. He looked like he was fading; his eyelids were beginning to flutter, and his forehead smouldered. If only I'd brought my bag. I would have had some paracetamol to lower his temperature. I looked around, for something, anything. Pulling open drawers and cupboards but all were empty. Park Lane was useless. All I could do was lay a soggy tissue across his forehead in a desperate attempt to ease his pain.

'I'll be back in a minute,' I whispered, crouching to squeeze his hand.

He mumbled something incoherent in response.

I walked into the living room, swallowing hard, my mouth filling up. All the time pushing the power button on my phone as it sat useless in my pocket. Praying it would vibrate and jolt back to life. Hope wasn't there; instead I found her in the den, gazing out of the window onto the street. Her hair was wild, as though she'd run all the way here. Her usually perfect exterior slipped, the cracks beginning to show. I didn't understand. Why was she here? Why wouldn't she help?

'What's going on?' My voice trailed off.

'This was where it happened, you know.'

'Where what happened?'

'Where I was conceived.' Hope turned to face me, her lip curled back into a snarl. 'Where my mother was raped.'

'Hayley?' I whispered.

'You were here, you were all part of it. I know all about the *party*. You're all accountable for what happened. He ruined her life, you know.'

'Gareth?'

'Yes Gareth, he raped her here on the floor. His hand over her mouth as she wriggled underneath him. Too frightened to fight back.' Tears rolled down Hope's cheeks.

I gasped, shaking my head vehemently, unable to comprehend her words.

'Yes, your precious Gareth. He became quite loose-lipped after I bought him a few whiskies. Sat alone at the bar. We got chatting. I flirted a bit, you know, we drank a lot and I got him talking about the night he popped his cherry. He admitted it was you he wanted, not my mother. He confirmed everything once the alcohol hit, before I helped him off the road.' Hope's eyes glinted and a smile played on her lips.

'He can't be your father, Hope,' I stammered, still shaking my jumbled head.

'He is, or should I say was,' Hope snapped, her chin jutting forward. There was no point in arguing with her, she was determined she knew the truth.

'Where's Hayley now?'

'At home, and here too.' She patted the locket that hung from her neck, I flinched at the movement. 'I always have a piece of her with me.'

I felt sick, I needed air, unable to take it all in.

'I'm going to check on James,' I announced, my limbs quaking as I turned to leave, my hand on the wall.

'I wouldn't do that if I were you.' Hope drew a large kitchen knife from behind her back and waved it at me.

I stood frozen to the spot, my eyes mesmerised by the silver point. The urge to open my bladder overwhelming as I desperately tried to connect the dots. Hayley was raped? Hayley was raped by Gareth? She got pregnant but never had the abortion? My head swam, Hope's voice bringing me back to the present.

'So, once I'm done here, I'm taking a holiday. Australia seems like a good place. There's someone there I've always wanted to meet.' Her eyes sparkled, and she grinned; she looked maniacal, mascara stained her cheeks, eyes wide, mouth twisted. 'I can't say it's gone completely to plan, I hoped to ruin your business with that virus. But I figure I've caused enough damage with Robyn and Becca. Robyn got sacked, and notched up another criminal conviction, so she'll find it hard to get a job. Maybe if I'm lucky, she'll turn to drugs or prostitution. With Mark's injuries, Becca will struggle. It'll be like raising children alone. She'll know how hard it was for my mother. That leaves you and James here. Until I get to Elliot anyway.'

I gaped at Hope, who spoke as though she was reciting her shopping list. She didn't know the truth, that Mark was recovering, and Robyn's charges had been dropped.

'How could you do this? You killed Gareth.'

'Don't look so shocked. You would too if you knew what my mother had been through. I read her diaries after she died, they were worse than any Stephen King novel. The things she had to do, the dicks she had to suck. All to make sure her child was warm, fed and safe every night. It disgusts me and it's all your fault. Slut Sophie with her virginity party. You ruined her fucking life, Sophie; you all did. You ruined mine too.' Hope shouted, her voice echoing around the empty room, face an angry red mess of tears and snot. Eyes crazed, she began waving the knife animatedly.

I shrank back, pressed against the wall, barely able to breathe.

'You sit in your fucking ivory tower. Successful business, lots of money, parents that still want you. We could have had that, given the chance. My grandparents disowned her, they wanted me sucked out and thrown away. That's where it started; she wrote in her diary what she had to do to get the nurse to say she'd gone through with the abortion. What you can get when you trade sex for favours. She learnt to be a whore from a young age. I bet you're thinking it was heroin that killed her, aren't you? But she was clean, always, she never dabbled in any of that stuff. She brought me up the best she could. We were a team. She was my best friend.'

'I'm so, so sorry, Hope.' My heart aching as the anger and bitterness spilled out of her. The release of years clinging on, living on the breadline and the loss of the person that meant the most in the world.

'Last year she found a lump. It turned out to be breast cancer and within two months she was gone. Just like that. She'd hidden all this stuff from me, I never knew any of it. We had nothing, but we were happy. She worked two jobs, anything she could to keep a roof over our head. It wasn't until I was going through her things, I found her diaries. Years of misery, all to keep me.'

I edged along the wall, towards the door, in two minds whether to make a run for it, but as I moved, Hope shadowed me, step for step. Her eyes never leaving mine.

'I have all of this rage, Sophie, it burns inside me, and I can't control it. He had to pay. Gareth fucking Dixon had to pay.'

'Gareth's not your father.' James's voice a low rumble from the doorway. He leant heavily against it, the only thing keeping him upright.

Hope cackled and pointed her knife at him, pleased he'd joined the party. 'I have his DNA, dickhead. That night in the pub, I took a hair off his shirt and got it tested along with mine. One of those home kits. We matched.'

'Not a full match though was it?' he asked.

Hope appeared momentarily unsure what to say and rolled back onto her heels.

James cleared his throat and edged himself up the side of the door frame trying to stand to his full height. 'Gareth couldn't have children, he'd been trying for years with Lisa, so that Ben could have a brother and they could have a child of their own.'

'She wrote D in her diary, for Dixon.' Hope stammered, her eyes glazing over, recalling what she'd read.

James wheezed, clutching his side, his face a mask of pain.

'It was him, you're fucking with me. It must have been him.' Her voice trembled, unsure, the knife hanging limply at her side.

'It was a Dixon, but not Gareth. His older brother Craig is your father.'

I stared at James, eyes bulging. He wiped the sweat from his forehead with the cuff of his shirt and took a slow, deep breath.

'Around two years ago, Gareth and I were in the pub, his local. I'd come up to visit. Craig came in later, he was drunk, and started a fight with Gareth, like he always did. He was a user, first steroids, weed, then drink, another of life's wasters. No fixed job, continuously bouncing from sofa to sofa. He followed his brother up to St. Albans to sponge off him when he couldn't get anything else out of their parents. Gareth idolised his older brother, I couldn't understand for the life of me, why. But Craig hated him, he was jealous. Whatever Gareth did, Craig would always try to knock him down. I remember that night as I had to physically split them up.' James coughed and my legs shook beneath me, I feared they may collapse.

Hope looked on, lips parted, eating up James's every word.

'Gareth had enough, told Craig what a loser he was. It made him mad, of course, and then, in retaliation, Craig said he'd had sex with Gareth's first girlfriend because he was "too much of a pussy to do it himself". He said Gareth rang him, that night, for a lift, gave him this address, but when he arrived Gareth had already gone.'

The silence that followed was immense as I began to see the true horror of what had happened to Hayley. What had I done?

46

I imagined Hayley's terrified face, when Craig walked in to find her alone and vulnerable. Likely in tears after being dumped on what should have been the best night of her life. We were all upstairs getting on with it. She was there alone, helpless. I squeezed my eyes shut to try and stop the influx of tears. My throat constricted. Why hadn't she told us? Why hadn't she called for help? Anger struck me like a red-hot poker.

'You said there was a chance Craig may have got her pregnant, James, not that he raped her! Did you know? Did you know it happened that night?' I spat.

Hope seemed stunned, speechless, unable to comprehend his bombshell.

James slid down the wall, weak and exhausted, his body fighting against the infection. 'We didn't know if Craig was bull-shitting or not. He was a liar, he'd say anything to wind Gareth up.' James turned to Hope. 'It was only when we tried to track your mum down, when I saw your grandparents and they said she'd had an abortion that I connected the dots.' James panted. The conversation sapping the energy from him.

'Why didn't you tell me?' I hissed, my guilt turning to anger.

James had the good grace to look ashamed. He couldn't meet my eyes. With all Hope was doing to us, the threats, the attacks, he kept what he knew to himself? Why? Out of some misguided loyalty to Gareth's or, worse, Craig's memory?

'He made me promise to drop it. Hayley was gone, Craig too. We didn't know it had happened for sure. We didn't know Hayley had a baby. Gareth was worried about his parents, what they'd say.'

Hope interrupted, 'She changed our names, as soon as she was eighteen. She became Hannah Smith and I was Hope. The most common surname she could think of. No one was ever going to find us, including her wanker of a father or her spineless mother.'

Hope looked past us, out into the darkness the house was now cloaked in. I should have taken the opportunity to run, but I knew I'd never get James out too. I couldn't leave him behind. Even though he'd acted like an idiot. I had to keep her talking. Figure out how to get the keys.

'It was you all along? The phone calls, the rat, the cards. You were the one coming into my home?'

Hope smirked at my wide eyes. 'It was easy, I recorded Gareth that night on my phone, he was so drunk, he didn't have a clue. I thought you might like to hear his voice, a trip down memory lane.' Hope sneered, reaching into her pocket and jingling a set of keys in front of her. They weren't the ones for Park Lane, with the brown handwritten tag. 'I copied yours, you didn't even notice them go missing, I had them back in half an hour. Even when you changed your front door, I still managed to get in through the back of the office. Silly Sophie. And the calls? You gave me your number on my first day, remember? I got James's from your phone. You led me to all of them. All I had to do was follow you. I needed this place though, and when I saw Mrs Davidson had it up for sale with Osbornes, I only needed to give her a nudge to swap estate agents. It had to end here, where it began. Where my mother's life was ruined by you.'

'You killed Gareth. He was innocent,' I said, trying my best to keep my voice level. My heart raced and perspiration collected at the small of my back. My body entering fight or flight mode. How much longer could I keep her talking? How were we going to get out of this?

'None of you are fucking innocent, you sanctimonious bitch. I read the diaries; she was raped and forever broken because of it. What it set in motion, the life she had. It's all down to you,' Hope spat, and I winced, trying to stop myself from cowering. She shuffled closer, the knife held out between us, head tilted to one side.

'It won't bring her back,' James whispered, he was practically laying on his side, skin ghostly.

I had to get help; I didn't know how much longer he would stay conscious. I had no choice.

'Where is Craig now?' Hope demanded.

'Craig died that night. He got so drunk after we left, he got into a bar fight with some bikers. He was kicked to death outside in the gravel car park after closing. Maybe it was what he deserved?' James lifted his shirt to look at his bandage, which was blooming a sour yellow, the sickly-sweet odour drifting towards me. He needed a hospital and antibiotics urgently.

'You're lying! How can I trust anything either of you say?' Hope shouted, her chance of payback whipped away.

'Look it up yourself, you'll see we're telling the truth.' James's voice was becoming weaker and weaker.

'I had no idea what happened that night, or why she left Copthorne so suddenly. Do you think I would stand by and let someone rape my friend? She never told us, never asked for help.'

Tears rolled down my cheeks, they weren't just words, me begging for our lives, I meant them. I would have to live with the knowledge of what I'd caused. 'Hope, we can all walk out of here. You can disappear, carry on and live your life. They won't find you. We won't tell,' I pleaded.

Hope wasn't moved, her eyes darted around the room, she looked possessed. 'Now, why would I do that? I'm off to Australia tomorrow, taking a sabbatical. I'm sure my employer won't mind, will you, Sophie? Elliot will be the icing on the cake. Disappearing there will be much easier, I mean, do you have any idea how big that country is?' Hope waved the knife as she spoke as if it was a cigarette wafting between her fingers.

I spun around and hopped over James, running for the back door, but I didn't even make it out of the lounge. The knife sliced into my shoulder, swishing past my ear a millisecond before cracking the bone. I cried out and turned to wrestle the knife from Hope's hands, blood sprayed from the wound as my arms flailed. Her eyes bulged; face warped with rage. I was no match for her, she was petite, smaller than me, but her anger gave her strength which far exceeded mine. We grappled and I wrapped my fingers in her hair, yanking it downwards. Her nails clawed my face, trying to gouge my eye. I felt my strength waver, my arm weak and fingers turning numb. It was over.

Hope raised the knife, high above her head, ready to plunge. I closed my eyes waiting for the fatal blow which didn't come. I looked just in time to see her arms flap and she fell, her face a wash with panic as she began her descent to the floor. The knife had disappeared. James lay stretched out, gripping onto the heel of her boot and refusing to let go. He'd tripped her over. Hope hit the ground with a thud, her nose slamming into the carpet. A muffled crunching sound rose up.

I pressed my hand on my shoulder, down onto the wound.

Watching my fingers become gloved in the crimson liquid. Nausea made my head swim, but I saw Hope kicking out at James, her foot connecting with his jaw. A flash of silver, a howl and the carpet at my feet blossomed into a ruby red flower. James had stabbed Hope in the thigh. She whimpered on the ground, clutching her leg, eyes rolling.

'Come on. Get up,' I ordered, heaving James to his feet, my hands slippery with blood. The room around us a macabre crime scene photo in waiting, forever frozen in all its ghoulish glory.

James and I held on to each other as we stumbled to the back door, before realising it was still locked and changing direction, limping on to the front door. I dropped to the tiles and kicked at the pane of glass at the bottom with both feet. It shattered on the second try. I pushed James through, thrusting with what little strength I had left. All the time watching behind me, expecting Hope to fly around the corner, through the archway, wielding the knife. The villain left for dead numerous times but always coming back for more. But it was eerily quiet. I climbed through, catching my cheek on a shard of glass and wincing. My body a mass of slices, cuts, blood and pain. My shoulder was numb, my arm useless.

The next-door neighbour wasn't in or, if they were, they didn't respond to us hammering on the door and screaming through the letter box. Their neighbour, one along, came out to see what all the racket was about and called the police immediately. She helped us into her kitchen and wrapped our wounds in clean tea towels. James succumbed and passed out, causing us to panic we were losing him. The ambulance and police arrived together in a haze of flashing lights and yellow tape. Detective Wren pulled up as James was being loaded into the ambulance, him on the stretcher, me sat beside him, holding his hand.

'Where is she? Where's Hope?' I asked when Wren climbed into the ambulance.

'We don't know, they're searching the property now.'

I laid my head back on the grey leatherette chair, one paramedic was bandaging my shoulder as I stared at James, hooked up to monitors. His face almost translucent underneath the oxygen mask.

'Will he be all right?' I asked the other paramedic, who was busy redressing his wound. The dirty bandages placed in a cardboard sick bowl, yellow and sticky.

'His body has gone into shock because of the untreated infection. I've given him some medicine to lower his temperature and once we get some antibiotics in him, he should respond well.'

She shined her torch into his eyes, but there was no response.

As soon as I'd had my shoulder stitched and all my other scratches and cuts cleaned and dressed, I was discharged. I didn't leave the hospital, instead I curled up in the armchair beside a comatose James and fell asleep. Exhausted from the trauma and adrenaline which had now evacuated my system.

'Sophie?' Detective Wren patted my hand and I jumped in the chair, almost kicking him as my legs unfurled. Someone had placed a blanket over me, and it was warm and cosy beneath. 'Sorry, I didn't mean to frighten you.'

'What time is it?' I mumbled, wiping dribble from my cheek. I knew I looked a mess, but I didn't care.

'Half past ten. You've been asleep for a couple of hours. I need to take a statement from you. Do you feel up to telling me what happened?'

'Did you get her?'

'Hope? The lady at number 28 told us you were distressed, shouting that Hope was trying to kill you. She wasn't there when we got to the property. It was empty.'

I closed my eyes and felt my chest tighten. It wasn't over. I wasn't free.

Detective Wren handed me a polystyrene cup of water, which tasted amazing, the cold liquid soothed my throat. He pulled his chair closer and I eased my body more upright in the chair. Glancing at James who was still snoring, his drip delivering the antibiotics he so desperately needed.

'She's Hayley's daughter,' I explained.

'Let's start at the beginning,' Wren said, flipping his notebook over to a new page and poising his pen.

* * *

I spent that night in the hospital, too afraid to go home and not wanting to put my parents in any danger. Who knew where Hope would go? I asked Detective Wren to make sure Hayley's parents were safe. Hope's venomous words ringing in my ears. They would be shocked to know they had a grandchild. That Hayley had kept her baby all those years ago.

I sat by James's bedside watching his chest rise and fall. Would we be able to move past what had happened? He'd been stupid, a misguided loyalty to Gareth. Then I guessed he'd kept what he knew to himself, to protect Sue and Jim. They'd lost both of their sons. To know one of them was a rapist would be torturous.

I told Detective Wren everything that had happened, including Hope's admission of killing Gareth and being responsible for everything that had happened to us. He didn't speak whilst I recalled what had taken place at the house, only pausing from his writing when I fell quiet, unable to believe it myself.

I couldn't stop thinking about Hayley, about that night, the night that was supposed to be the best of our young lives. I couldn't stop thinking about how Craig had just wandered in looking for Gareth and taken advantage of the situation. How he'd finished the job Gareth wasn't able to start. It sickened me. Hayley's life, what had happened after the party, it has all started with me and my stupid idea. I'd be forever haunted by it. Just as Hope was.

* * *

They arrested Hope the next day. She'd tried to fix her leg and changed her Australia flight to one earlier in the day. I assumed she thought she might evade the police by switching flights. There was a quick swoop at the gate, and they led Hope limping away to receive proper medical attention on her thigh. She'd lost almost a pint of blood by all accounts and they believed, had she managed to board, she wouldn't have survived the flight.

When I arrived home from the hospital, a lone cardboard box had been left on the doorstep, the flaps open, moving with the wind. I cringed, bending to look inside. Unwilling to take anything left by Hope into my home. But inside were Hayley's diaries, four books tied in a yellow ribbon dating all the way back to 1997.

They were a hard read. Not in the beginning, it made me smile to read about our gang, her crush on Gareth and how Becca was driving everyone around the bend about Mark. The later ones were darker, of someone much changed by time and circumstances. I imagined the horror of Hope finding these after Hayley's passing, realising everything she'd gone through because of how much love she had for her child. The child of a rapist.

Hope was right, no one should ever have had to go through what Hayley did. Especially not as a child. I wrote to Becca and

Mark, Robyn and Elliot too, identical letters, so they knew what had happened, who Hope was and what she'd done. I wrote again to Hayley's Mum, Jackie, so she could finally find out what happened to her daughter and grieve for her. I also broke the news that she had a granddaughter.

The newspapers had a field day, of course, and for a while photographers loitered outside the estate agents. Our reputation wasn't damaged, weirdly sales increased. Villagers came in wanting to find out what had happened. I never spoke of it, of course, but the community reached out to us and that was comforting. I reconciled with Mum and Dad, they were relieved I was okay, although initially furious I hadn't sought their help. Dad said he'd step back and let me run Whites as I saw fit. So, I changed the logo.

Frank pops in every now and then. Him and Dad have taken up golf, schooled by Jim, the walking doing him good.

Hope was charged with one count of murder, two counts of actual bodily harm, harassment and threats to kill. Thankfully she pleaded guilty, so there was to be no trial. James and I wouldn't have to testify against her. There was a sentencing hearing, but I didn't go. I still carried the guilt and I guessed I always would.

Detective Wren allowed me to visit the bedsit where Hope lived, which, to my surprise, was across the road from the office. She'd been able to watch my comings and goings, out of her bedroom window, depending on what entrance I used. Photos of all of us were stuck to the wall. Drawing pins through each of our eyes. It made me shudder, but even that couldn't allay my conscience.

Hope had done some terrible things, but it was obvious the passing of her mother, and subsequent finding of Hayley's diaries had devastated her. All her childhood memories tainted by what she now knew. She'd been brought into the world as a result of a horrific crime on a fifteen-year-old girl. I could understand the need for justice, for the mother she loved and missed dearly. The weight of it hung heavily on me; I'd been the catalyst for a chain of events that had ruined Hayley's life.

I collected a box of things – there wasn't much: a few books, papers and of course Hayley's ashes in a beautiful oak box. I considered returning them to Hayley's parents, Jackie and Alan, but it didn't seem fair to Hope. She was her mum. I paid for a long-term storage locker and sent Hope the details in a letter written to HMP Downview. All she would need to access the locker was her passport and I knew she'd had that with her when she was arrested. I had no idea when she would get out, it would likely be around twenty years according to Detective Wren. I heard that Jackie had been to visit her in an attempt to build a relationship and I truly hoped it would help heal them both.

James and I managed to put everything behind us. A clean slate, no keeping secrets. It was going well; he's still living with me at the flat and has been hinting about making it official. I'd love to settle down. Maybe one day I'll get to be a parent; then I'll fully understand what a mother will do to protect her child.

ACKNOWLEDGMENTS

Thank you firstly, to my amazing partner in crime Dean, without you running things at home I'd never be able to do this. I'm incredibly lucky to have you by my side.

Thanks to my lovely reader and colleague Denise Miller who is always front of the queue to look at my very rough first draft and be the sounding board for ideas.

To my Mum and the rest of my family and friends whom I've bored stiff about the book over the past few months, I'm sorry. I promise I will talk about other things now!

Thank you to my amazing editor Caroline Ridding, who champions my work and pushes me to make it the best it can be. I'm learning so much from you. Boldwood Books, I cannot thank you enough for this journey! Jade Craddock, your eagle eyes are second to none, thank you for reading and please can you forever look after my books!

Thanks again to Mark Zivilik for being on hand for all my police procedural questions. I'm so very grateful. You rock!

Lastly but by no means least, thank you to the Savvy Writers'

Snug, a group full of the most talented, friendly and helpful authors you could ever wish to meet.

A NOTE FROM GEMMA ROGERS

Thank you so much for reading *Payback*, I do hope you enjoyed it. I've had this story rattling around in my head for a while now, so I'm thrilled to have finally got it down on paper.

Please leave a review or recommend it to a friend if you enjoyed it. *Payback* is also available as an ebook, digital audio download and audiobook CD.

If this is the first book of mine that you've read, please consider taking a look at *Stalker*, my debut novel.

If you'd like to keep up to date on my news, competitions and updates on future books, please sign up to my mailing list:

http://bit.ly/GemmaRogersNewsletter

ABOUT THE AUTHOR

Gemma Rogers was inspired to write gritty thrillers by a traumatic event in her own life nearly twenty years ago. *Stalker* was her debut novel and marked the beginning of a new writing career. Gemma lives in West Sussex with her husband, two daughters and bulldog Buster.

Visit Gemma's website: www.gemmarogersauthor.co.uk

Follow Gemma on social media:

facebook.com/GemmaRogersAuthor

twitter.com/GemmaRogers79

instagram.com/gemmarogersauthor

bookbub.com/authors/gemma-rogers

ABOUT BOLDWOOD BOOKS

Boldwood Books is a fiction publishing company seeking out the best stories from around the world.

Find out more at www.boldwoodbooks.com

Sign up to the Book and Tonic newsletter for news, offers and competitions from Boldwood Books!

http://www.bit.ly/bookandtonic

We'd love to hear from you, follow us on social media:

facebook.com/BookandTonic

twitter.com/BoldwoodBooks

instagram.com/BookandTonic